STANTON'S SINS

A BAD BOY BILLIONAIRE BIKER ROMANCE

MONIQUE MOREAU

STANTON'S SINS

A BAD BOY BILLIONAIRE BIKER ROMANCE

Cover Design by Cover Couture
www.bookcovercouture.com

MEET MONIQUE!

Join Monique's Newsletter (and receive goodies and release information)
https://www.subscribepage.com/moniquemoreau
Like her Facebook Page
facebook.com/monique.moreau.books
Follow her on TikTok
https://bit.ly/MoniqueTikTok
Follow her on Instagram
https://bit.ly/MoniqueMoreauIG
Follow her on Book Bub
http://bit.ly/MoniqueBookBub
Learn all about Monique's books
moniquemoreau.com

1

STANTON

Stanton stood inside the double doors of the entrance to the rehab center, tugging at the collar of his button-down shirt and adjusting his tie.

Normally he'd have worn something more casual, but his mother was arriving any moment. Since he hadn't exactly been in a position to drive himself to Tully Drug Rehab a month ago, she insisted on driving up to retrieve him. Or, rather, being driven there. In the family limo, that is.

One of the reasons he'd chosen this place was that it had a name among professionals and law enforcement, of which he was both. A close second was its reputation for privacy and seclusion. If he was going to do this thing, he needed to be as far from Poughkeepsie and his father as possible. Not that his father would have visited. The very thought of him and his accompanying barrage of recriminations would've been distracting, to say the least.

But there was no getting around the fact that he was an addict. Not some guy with a little cocaine problem. Not a guy who partied too much or had a bit of a control issue. Nah. He was a fucking addict, through and through. Stanton twisted the family signet ring on his finger as he peered through the frosted glass pane of the front door.

He drew his cashmere coat collar up to cover his neck from a brisk draft coming from the entranceway. An addict who wouldn't snuff white powder up his nose again is who he was now. After four weeks in this place, and the hard work he'd put in, he had no intention of backpedaling and ending right back where he started. Not. Fucking. Happening. If for no other reason than that he didn't have it in him to take a month off work again. Being a high-powered, respected prosecutor did not allow for that kind of lapse of time. He shuddered to think of the state of his files when he got back to the office tomorrow.

Besides work, the thing he missed the most was the lack of fucking. Thank Christ he was back at court tomorrow. Hopefully, he wouldn't have too much trouble finding a soft woman he could sink his cock into real soon. His sponsor, who was about as much of an asshole as Stanton, did make one stipulation. Find a new woman. Cut off the old ones because they were potential triggers. Which meant no speed-dial party girls. Gregory made him delete every last female contact on his speed-dial list. Brutal.

Unfortunately, that didn't include Melanie, the one he most wanted off his phone. He'd taken her off the cheat list during his miserable attempt at monogamy. He sighed inwardly. What a clusterfuck that had been. Old family friend turned other woman turned jilted fiancée. He'd have to make amends to her at some point in the future. It was a one-day-at-a-time program, so he didn't need to dwell on that hellhole right this moment. Or so Gregory told him when his thoughts tumbled down the rabbit hole. His sponsor was a man who'd been through exactly what he had been through and was willing to waste his time with Stanton to bolster his own recovery. Go figure.

He never thought that was how shit would go down. For Stanton, sacrifice was sacrifice, without expectation of anything coming his way. Not approval. Certainly not an ounce of relief.

A limo rolled up to the curved driveway. He checked his Piaget watch. Just on time. Waving goodbye to the receptionist, he stepped out the door, towing his Rimowa rolling baggage.

Anthony hurried out of the limo, rubbing his gloved hands together as he walked around to open the back door of the limo for him. "Welcome home, Mr. Prescott," he greeted as he stood at attention in the frigid air of January in Upstate New York.

Nodding to the older man, he replied, "Thank you, Anthony. It's good to be out." *That's the truth, the whole truth, and nothing but the truth.*

Handing Anthony his baggage, Stanton slid into the seat beside his mother and placed a kiss on her right cheek. She squeezed his hand, giving him a quick but thorough once-over. "How are you doing, darling? You look well."

"Much improved from the last time you saw me, I'm sure," he said, squeezing her hand back.

"Now, now. Don't be so hard on yourself."

"Oh, Mother, only you would say that. You found me plastered in my own vomit, shielding Amy from getting a good look at me while calling nine-one-one. I think we're past suggesting that I was anything but a fucking mess."

"I see they didn't get you to stop cursing," she reproved mildly.

His mother. Always working to better others. She was tenacious that way. Never gave up. Certainly didn't give up on his father after Jax's death, and God knows he wouldn't have given the bastard a second chance. Then again, cast in his father's image, Stanton shouldn't be one to talk.

"You know your father can't handle anything *irregular*. It is the only reason he didn't come with me today," his mother said. *Yeah, right. Excuses, excuses.*

"For an alcoholic—"

"Former alcoholic," his mother interjected.

"There's no such thing, Mother. One of the many things I learned back there." He jutted a thumb in the direction of Tully.

His mother turned her face and gazed out the tinted window as the car started. "He stopped drinking quite a long time ago. That's past history."

If only past history stayed in the past. "He never stopped raging," Stanton threw back. "Or controlling everything." He expelled a weary breath. This was an old argument and he should know better than to go down this dog-eared, worn-out path. But dammit, he'd spent the past four weeks dredging up family ghosts. Outside of detoxing, which was *the* ultimate kick in the balls, he was done with burying shit or circumventing issues.

His mom turned back from the window, and her startling cornflower blue eyes locked on him. "In any case, I'm glad you're better and that you're home. I'll do whatever's necessary for you to remain clean. Anything," she vowed. He grasped her hand again and she weaved her fingers tightly between his. If nothing else, Marie Bethany Prescott, née Astor, was a good woman who'd go to any lengths to keep her family together.

Convincing his mother that he was better off going home and preparing himself for court tomorrow instead of swinging by his familial birthplace to see his father hadn't been as difficult as Stanton had expected. Marie had probably been too afraid to push, but he'd be damned if he wasted tonight on his father.

He dropped the perfunctory kiss on his mother's cheek and exited the limousine. There was next Sunday brunch to serve as catch-up on his session of torture. Waiting for the elevator, he heard a *ping* and checked his cell phone.

AMY: What's up? Sorry I wasn't there to pick you up with Mom.

Yeah, right, like I'd put her through that for my ass.

STANTON: Stop apologizing. I specifically told you not to come. I wouldn't subject you to 4 hours in a car with Mom. 2 hours is one thing. 4 hours is to be avoided.

AMY: [Laughing crying emoji] You're my hero. [Winking kissing emoji]

STANTON: Always got your back, little sis.

AMY: How'd it go?

STANTON: Manageable. It wasn't bad.

AMY: I'll be there for Sunday brunch to act as buffer.

STANTON: I don't need you to do shit for me. I protect you, remember?

AMY: I like to help.

STANTON: Don't need you here. Take care of your life in the City.

AMY: You big brother. Grunt. Pound chest. Me little sister. [Winking emoji]

STANTON: Now you got it.

Stanton walked out of the elevator and down the hallway. He'd put in the effort to develop a different relationship with his sister, but the *you scratch my back, I scratch yours* way of life was ingrained in them so young, he routinely had to remind her of the difference in their roles.

AMY: You're so protective! The best big brother a girl could have. You're going to make a great father one day. [Winking kissing emoji]

STANTON: Yeah, not going to happen. Ever. Hope you find someone soon to fill Mom's need for grandchildren.

AMY: Ugh. Whatever. I miss you, asshole.

STANTON: Can't wait to see you either.

2

———

STANTON

S tanton twisted the key to the lock of the door of his luxury apartment and paused in the quiet hallway.

It was too quiet. Back at Tully, there was always some kind of noise. Employees or residents walking by his door, the muted sound of people talking in the courtyard out back during the evening, where people smoked in the freezing weather.

Shoving the door open, he halted. Huh. The lights were still on. *Whoosh.* The leather swivel armchair by his desk rotated.

Cornell.

A grin broke over his face.

Cornell was seated, forearms draped on the armrests, sporting a bright, wide smile. "Welcome home, brother," he said as he stood up. Crossing the living room, he grabbed Stanton's shoulder, clasped his hand, and gave him a man hug.

Stanton returned the embrace with relief. "Glad to see you. What are you doing here?"

"You didn't think I'd let you come home and mope around

alone, did you?" Cornell drawled. "What kind of friend would that make me?"

"A sane one," he retorted.

"Didn't want you coming back to an empty apartment, and while I love Marie, I wasn't about to spend four hours traveling back and forth to pick you up. Especially since I'm certain the last half hour was an all-out attempt to convince you to stop to see your father."

"You know her too well."

"It's been a decade."

"True that," Stanton replied, with a smirk. Cornell was his first-year roommate at Yale, and they'd been inseparable through college and law school. Although visits to Cornell's family in the suburbs of New Jersey were far more enjoyable, Cornell had visited him during many summer vacations. A head poked out from the white leather couch of his loft. Seconds later, a little body hurled into Stanton's legs, causing him to take a step back and clutch onto the little boy's shoulders.

Cornell crossed the living area toward the kitchen. Over his shoulder, he said, "Wesley couldn't let his favorite person in the whole wide world come home alone. Hungry?"

Stanton sniffed the air and recognized the aroma of Cornell's famous pasta recipe. His stomach rumbled. "I could eat."

"My famous carbonara sauce," Cornell confirmed. "How about I make my tagliatelle? I brought the white truffles that just came in from Umbria through special delivery to make a quick sauce."

"It's my favorite," replied Wesley from below. Casting a glance down, his heart melted when the boy said, "Uncle Stanton, I missed you."

Stanton broke into the first smile of the day. "I missed you too, buddy," he replied and gave his tousled hair a ruffle. "Your dad's recipe is my favorite as well. You know nothing is as good as his cooking. Even your grandma's."

"Hush, don't talk nonsense," Cornell laughed. "Go on and change." Flicking his finger in Stanton's direction, he noted, "I know you wore that for your mother. Wesley, let go of

Stanton. He needs to freshen up."

Wesley's eyes lit up. "Yay! I got *three* new killer Pokémon cards since you left. I'll lay them out on the table, and I'll teach you all about them."

Shaking his head, he said, "Sounds good," and rolled his luggage into his bedroom. After emptying it, he took a quick shower and donned a pair of sweats and a soft, worn Legal Aid T-shirt. Ambling back into the main living area, he followed the scent of garlic, butter, and white wine simmering in his kitchen.

Cornell glanced up from the stove. "I'd offer you wine, but I don't think that's in your purview right now."

"Nah, I'm not touching any mood-altering substances for the next ninety days. To start with. But, go ahead and drink. It doesn't faze me. You know, alcohol wasn't my weakness." And Cornell also knew why. Once upon a time, it had been his father's great weakness.

Nodding, Cornell went to the fridge and opened a bottle of white pinot grigio. Reaching for a wine glass, he poured a little, swirled it around, and tasted before pouring himself a full serving. Turning back to the cutting board, he asked, "So. What's your next move now that you're out? By the way, I'm proud of you, man. You did right by yourself."

"You don't need to say that. I know it was pretty ugly in the end," his voice dipped low so that Wesley couldn't hear.

"Which is why it makes what you did all the braver. It's not like I'm not familiar with the ravages of addiction in my own family."

"You saved my life, Cornell," he returned soberly.

"Please, don't go making me sound like a hero. You did the hard work and it's nowhere near over."

"You saw the signs before anyone else and confronted me enough times that I was willing to listen once my mother and sister found me." Stanton swallowed.

"Shut up, man. I didn't do anything special. If you want to do me a solid, then don't fall back into that hole. You're like a brother to me, and I'm not feeling another funeral. Anyway, I bet you suffered long and hard from being away from court for a month. I bet you're in no hurry to miss any more work."

Stanton gave a fake shudder. "Christ, that's an understatement. Day in and day out, talking about how I messed up my life, talking about my father. And Jax. If that wasn't repentance, then I don't know what is. Oh, that reminds me, I have to text Gregory, my sponsor." He went over to his bedroom for his cell phone. Back on the high stool of the bar that separated the kitchen and living room, his fingers flew over his phone and he hit send.

"Is he cute? Your sponsor?"

Laughing, Stanton rolled his eyes. "You're already married."

"I like to check out the competition to gloat about how hot my man is. So sue me."

"If only you had taken me up on my offer that one night," Stanton joked in a wistful tone.

"First off, you were drunk and not at all serious."

"So you keep reminding me. Again and again and again..."

Cornell leaned over and whispered, "You like the taste of pussy too much to give it up. Even for me." He winked. "I see you, Stanton. Be an ally all you want, but you're as straight as the edge of this knife." He held up the paring knife he was using on the white truffles. "Every time you're unhappy, you wanna be my bitch, but you forget your love affair with pussy. How'd it work for you last time you denied yourself, *hmm*?"

He winced. Truer words were never spoken. He was a pussy man. Loved licking pussy. Might sound crude, but he didn't give two fucks. He loved every aspect of fucking, but, speaking for himself, going down on a woman was the most intimate of acts.

Each time he did it for a woman he felt something for, it was a step into his heart. He hadn't been able to do that with Sage. He'd already been halfway in love with her at the time, and he had to stop it from going any further.

Sure, he'd had one-night stands when high on blow, but he liked relationships. Relationships were his comfort zone.

He just didn't like marriage.

Marriage led to children and that, he could never allow. His father had expected him to marry Sage. She didn't come from money, but she was a defense attorney, which his father felt would help him get liberal votes. Resentful, Stanton refused to relinquish what little control he had by falling for Sage. If he'd been insane enough to go through with their wedding, they would've been fucked for life.

Stanton shuddered internally. Christ, what he'd suffered to refrain from going down on her. He had no choice but to lie and claim that going down on a woman was disgusting and unmanly. If he'd licked her pussy, he would've been a dead man walking. But there was a cost, because every damn night he'd lain beside her in bed, bright-eyed and fists clenched, imagining how wet he could make her. It was a living hell. Worse still, his sacrifice didn't do the trick. Each time he felt himself slipping into love, he panicked and cheated on her with another woman.

It was no wonder she'd fallen for a man who was the exact opposite of him in every way. The president of a biker gang. He snorted. *Jesus. He'd* pushed her into that. Stanton had caught a lucky break with Melanie, his second fiancée. It was no hardship going down on her because she was always more of a friend.

"Alright, point taken," he muttered. "Speaking of pussy, my sponsor said I can at least go back to that."

Cornell guffawed. "He must not know how addicted you are."

Stanton's voice resumed its normal volume. "Okay, okay, settle down. No need to be crude."

Tossing the egg pasta into a pot of boiling water, Cornell's only response was an unimpressed "Mm-hmm."

"You know what they tell addicts?" he asked Cornell.

"Which part? Gone to enough meetings for family and friends of alcoholics that I can probably guess, but give me a clue."

"Don't take on too much. Put your effort into battling one demon at a time. That's why you see so many addicts smoking outside Alcoholics Anonymous meetings. This is my version of smoking, because the one thing I can*not* do is fail and pick up hard drugs again." Turning to face Cornell, he declared solemnly, "I can't go back there and do that shit again. Wasn't just the physical withdrawal. I went all in. Did everything that was asked of me. Did all their damn *suggestions,*" Stanton made air quotes around the last word.

Cornell clapped his hand on Stanton's shoulder. "I believe in you, brah."

Stanton nodded tightly and swallowed around the lump in his throat.

Nodding toward the living room, Cornell said in a voice

loud enough to reach Wesley, "Go put on the TV. The Yankees are playing tonight."

"Yankees! Whoo-hoo!" shouted Wesley as he rushed to grab the remote control. "I can show you my Shadow Lugia card. It's the strongest card I have. We can play a game and I'll beat you just like the Yankees is gonna beat the Cardinals."

Stanton groaned. He and Cornell had a notorious rivalry between the Yankees and the Mets. "He'd be the perfect child, the son I will never have, except for this one glaring delusion about the Yankees. Did I do something to you when I was high that I don't remember? Is this torture some form of payback?"

"No, this is called a lesson in baseball. Maybe now that you're not in a drug fog, you can pay attention and learn how the game is really played. By the best of the best."

"The best," Stanton scoffed, as he flicked through the channels. "In your dreams, bro." He loved himself an underdog. Little had he known, he'd end up being one. But, in terms of recovery, he'd do a Daryl Strawberry. Each day he didn't pick up was a home run.

3

SAMMI

Grr. That idiot just had to get himself arrested, didn't he?

Sammi's red Corvette coupe went up the curb as she parked across the street from the clubhouse. Letting out a string of low curses, she winced and backed up carefully until the front wheel rolled off the curb, causing the car to bounce. Her coupe was her baby, and she usually treated it better than this, but this was Puck's fault not hers.

Puck.

She squeezed the steering wheel tightly. The coupe was a gift from Puck when she got her driver's license at sixteen. One advantage of growing up with a club full of bikers was that a dozen pairs of hands could work on any bike or car her little heart desired. Although she looked kick-ass in her Squad leather jacket and a pair of chaps, she herself didn't ride. She loved riding on the back of a bike, but all those oil stains. *Ugh.* So not for her.

She may have a few quirks for a biker bitch, but these were her people and she was theirs. She was the mascot baby of the Squad and she had zero issues with it. She loved being coddled.

She whipped off her seat belt and screeched when the stretch of nylon caught a few of her long, dark curly tresses as it retracted.

"Goddamn," she yelled as she disentangled her hair. Seriously, she was a hot mess. Throwing the car door open, Sammi grabbed her handbag and lifted herself out.

Growing up, the brothers and bitches lovingly teased her about the stacks of *Vogue* and *Elle* magazines she'd go through in one afternoon, sitting up by the bar. She was unabashed in her love for all things fashion. Drooling over Carrie's outfits on the reruns of *Sex and the City* made her realize that she wanted to be a personal stylist. Although, her take on styling had a certain twist.

Didn't make her any less of a biker bitch, and she'd kick anyone's ass who suggested otherwise. Her gaze flicked down to her black patent leather Jimmy Choos. Or, she'd simply get Puck to kick their ass. His shoe choices were more appropriate for ass kicking. She ground down on her back molars. He'd do it if he wasn't currently in *jail*.

Sammi tore through the clubhouse door, as much as a girl wearing four-inch heels could, scanning the open space of the main room. Her gaze passed over the bar, with its club banner sporting the Squad logo in bold Germanic lettering hanging over it. Crossing over the area used as a dance floor during parties, her gaze bounced off the wall of windows at the back, near the pool table. Then it swept back up to the lounge area where she finally spotted Sage.

She was sitting on one of the beat-up black leather couches, leaning back against Kingdom's chest. Sammi's heart melted when he reached around and rubbed Sage's protruding belly. She whispered a sigh of relief as she hurried across the unswept floor (*those prospects are falling down on the job, yo*), waving to brothers at the bar.

"What the hell did the moron do this time?" Sammi grumbled, throwing her hands up.

Unbuttoning her dark plaid, fitted winter coat, she threw it over the back of the couch and plopped down beside her friend.

Sage turned to her, startled, and instantly brought her in for a tight embrace. "It's not his fault. It's mine, and I feel so guilty."

"I assure you," Sammi drawled with narrowed eyes, "it's not your fault. He's an idiot. It's *always* his fault. He invites trouble."

Shaking her head resolutely, Sage explained, "I didn't warn Puck ahead of time. I didn't think her ex-husband would show up, but I should've known better." Tears popped out from the corners of her eyes, and Kingdom's hand clasped Sage's knee.

Grabbing her shoulders, Sammi shook her gently. "No, Sage, Puck would never have tolerated a man laying hands on a woman in his presence. Regardless of what you did or didn't tell him, he would've gotten involved."

"Sometimes an abuser backs off when they get a restraining order, sometimes they come at the survivor harder. I was sure Kerri's ex was the back-off type."

"Kerri? Oh, hell no. Puck would've never put up with another man touching her. She's under Squad protection."

"It's true," Kingdom piped up.

"He should've called the police once that man showed up and threatened Kerri," insisted Sage.

"Wasn't going to happen. Not by a long shot. Kerri's ex is a biker from that weekend riding club right outside of town. There's no way in hell he'd call the police. He'd deal with it himself," Sammi insisted. "You can't blame yourself. Puck's a grown-ass man, and he did what he felt he had to do."

"Yeah, but did he have to *confess* to the policemen in the squad car?" Sage griped. "He should've known better."

"By that point, he might've been in a temper, and you know how he is when he gets mad," interjected Kingdom.

"His arraignment is tomorrow, but guess who's the judge? Judge Korman. And you know how he is. Puck pistol-whipped Kerri's ex, so there's going to be a felony weapons complaint on top of assault and battery. This is a guesstimate, but we're looking at bail set at fifty thousand cash or a bond of one hundred thousand dollars, at best. Worst case scenario, Puck won't get out on bail." Groaning, Sage pressed her fingertips to her forehead. "And Kerr's ex fled the scene, so we have a madman roaming free, preparing to do God knows what."

"Bail won't be an issue," intoned Kingdom.

"No, Korman will be our main problem throughout this ordeal. I've checked, and he's already in Central Booking at the courthouse. I'll see Puck tomorrow morning before the arraignment."

Central Booking. Arraignment. Bail. Court. *Prison.* So many scary words jumbled together. The last word, especially, was doing a loop-de-loop in her head. She'd never lived without Puck.

Sure, he'd gone on rides, or left for brief periods for jobs, but he *always* came back to her. She could take care of herself, but the idea of her big brother being in prison.... She shook off the horrific images crowding her brain. *He'll survive.* Puck could do anything he put his mind to, but the thought of him behind bars with dangerous, violent people day terrified her.

Sammi wiped her brow. "This is a mess."

Sage grabbed Sammi's hands in hers. "I'm so sorry, but I promise I'll do whatever I can to get him out."

Staring into Sage's clouded eyes, Sammi replied, "I trust

you, but I can't believe he bragged about what he'd done. Idiot."

"Yeah," Sage breathed out, chin sinking to her chest.

"We'll get through this," said Kingdom.

Sage raised her head and gave Sammi a pleading look. "When Puck called me, he insisted that he doesn't want you at court."

Charging to her feet, her fists slammed on her curvy hips. "What?!"

Fury and frustration boiled over inside her. As if it wasn't bad enough he'd gotten arrested, this overprotective nonsense was going too far.

Sage gazed down at her hands. "I'm sorry. He made me promise. He doesn't want you seeing him like this."

Sammi flung a curly, dark lock of hair out of her face and huffed out, "Oh, hell no, he can go fuck himself. I'm seeing him, Sage. He gets arrested and then he thinks he can shut me out. You can't keep me away so you better off not trying."

"I made a promise," she replied in a small voice.

"That's a promise you'll have to break because there's no way I'm sitting outside the courtroom while my big brother gets arraigned."

"It's not just you. He doesn't want any of the brothers there," Sage persisted. "It makes sense, since Judge Korman hates bikers so much."

"Look at me," Sammi swept her hands down her consignment-bought Fendi turtleneck sweater and the fitted pencil skirt that hugged her hips. She'd rushed to the clubhouse from a new client appointment, so she was dressed to impress.

Hooking her thumbs around the thin leather belt looped around her trim waist, she declared, "I don't dress like a typical biker. If anything, I look like his rich, fashionable cousin from his mother's side, once removed. There's no reason not to let me in there."

"I promised him." Sage lifted her pleading face up to Sammi.

"I'm going and I'll storm in there dressed for a *funeral*. Because it will be. It'll be his funeral once I'm done tearing into him."

Sage buried her face in her hands and groaned. "I don't need this drama."

Tugging Sage's hands off her face, Sammi said, "Okay, okay, no drama. I'll behave... I promise. I'll be dressed to perfection and behave, but you have to let me be there, Sage."

She had to see him. Imagine if they didn't get him out on bail. She didn't know how long it would be until the next opportunity came around. And he could very well refuse to see her, the stubborn fool. Her hands balled into fists. With his overprotective streak, Puck could be obscenely single-minded. No, it was her best chance to make sure he was okay and to show him she cared, even if it was partnered with a volley of curses and shouting. She sniffed. Once she looked into his big brown eyes, and confirmed that the idiot was safe, she'd get back to being tough as nails.

Kingdom chimed in, "Let her be there. I'll take the heat for it. Tell him I told Sammi to show up on behalf of the club."

Sage shook her head. "I'm not telling him anything before the arraignment. I need him focused on my what to expect at the proceedings. It's his only chance of understanding what's going to happen in there."

"He might go ballistic when he sees me, but he'll have to suck it up," Sammi mused.

"*Might* is an understatement, but at least I'll have his complete attention before court. I wonder who the prosecutor will be." Her brows gathered. "I haven't seen Stanton around, which is unusual. Hopefully, I won't have to deal with him and Korman."

"I'm sorry for the added stress, especially with the pregnancy, but you do understand, don't you? I have to see him. Not just to make sure he's okay, because I'm betting the other guy is worse off, but because I have to be there for him. Whether he wants me to or not. He's always been there for me," Sammi ended in a murmur.

Taking her hand, Sage replied solemnly, "I understand, Sammi, of course I understand. I feel obliged to follow my client's instructions, but being an attorney is about taking care of the family as well as the client. And you're not just Puck's family, you're part of my family, too."

Swallowing, Sammi allowed Sage to draw her into a hug. "Thank you, Sage. Same here."

Sage had become like an older sister to her. They'd grown closer, especially since Abby and Greta joined the Squad as old ladies of Loki and Cutter.

Sammi's hand slid over Sage's belly and rubbed it. Sage had trouble staying pregnant, and the whole clubhouse was ecstatic over the baby coming in a few months. A wave of excitement and warm, chocolatey gooiness melted in Sammi's chest.

Leaning her face close to Sage's belly, Sammi crooned, "Hey sweetie, how are you doing in there today?" She felt a small kick against her hand and yanked her hand off, a peal of laughter bursting from her. "Oh my God, Sage! Baby just talked back to me."

Leaning over again, she resumed her one-way conversation, "Are you talking to me, little one? I think you're a little guy with your kickboxing moves. You want to get out and get on a bike like your daddy, don't you?"

"Don't give him or her any ideas," Sage chided. "Although, I won't lie, I'm also beginning to think it's a boy."

Sage and Kingdom had decided they wanted to have a surprise in the delivery room.

"There's an easy way to find out," suggested Sammi slyly.

"Not going to happen," muttered Kingdom.

Sammi folded her arms over her chest. "This isn't just *your* baby, you know. It's going to be my little niece or nephew. Can't *we* find out and you guys stay ignorant till the end?"

Kingdom snorted. "With the way the brothers are? Hell no. They're worse than a pair of gossiping grandmas. After they use the information to taunt me about it, someone will break and spill their guts."

"So selfish," she mumbled half-heartedly.

Always the youngest in her family and in the Squad, Sammi was looking forward to the next generation. Until recently, Puck and the Squad satisfied her very real need for family. She didn't grow up with a father, and her mother died suddenly when she was thirteen years old. Puck joined the Squad soon after, but didn't bring her in until he'd patched in and felt it was safe for her. That left her with two very lonely years. So grateful for her new extended family, she didn't think she'd ever need more. She hadn't even had a real boyfriend yet. If she had an itch to scratch, she hooked up and moved on.

But seeing Sage, and now Abby, glowing with the happiness of upcoming motherhood had kicked up a new set of feelings. Sammi may have always been the youngest in the club, but she'd grown up fast. Hell, she certainly felt older than her twenty-one years.

4

STANTON

S tanton stood behind the long wooden desk that served as his pulpit, facing the Judge.

There was something about walking into a courtroom, with its odor of aged wood, that got Stanton's blood pumping. Seeing the circular golden Great Seal featuring the eagle with its raised wings behind the judge's chair, flanked by American and state flags, puffed his chest up with pride. The clock to his left had the same hands frozen in place since he started as a prosecutor five years ago. The high ceilings of the courtroom echoed Judge Korman when he shouted, and he always shouted.

The courtroom was mostly empty, which was typical of a routine arraignment like the one currently in process.

Which made it all the more surprising when a feminine voice rang out behind him.

"*Puck!* Don't fight them. I'll get you out."

His head whipped around in the direction of the sultry voice.

He blinked. Once. Twice.

A drop-dead gorgeous, raven-haired beauty was talking to

the biker on the stand. By their resemblance, she was undoubtedly his sister. Dressed in a black satin dress that hugged her curves in all the right places, a little black pincushion hat sat jauntily on her head at a provocative angle. He was surprised it managed to stay affixed to her head.

She sure didn't look anything like a biker.

Attached to the hat was a wisp of black lace that floated above a twin set of perfectly arched black brows. Which hovered over a pair of wide-spaced coffee-colored eyes and lush pink lips.

He was gripped by the sudden urge to wipe the shiny lip gloss off her full lips.

With his cock.

"Goddammit, Sammi," the biker bellowed at her. Stanton stiffened at the way he was talking to the beauty. "I told you not to come here. I said, *no one but Sage*."

"Mr. Brandywine, please stop this outburst immediately," intoned Judge Korman into his mic.

Talking over her brother and the judge, she called out, "I'm your sister. No one was going to keep me out."

Sage turned around, shushing her over the wooden banister dividing court personnel from the public. Talking low and fast, Sage said something that got her pressing her plump lips closed. Dropping down on what he guessed was a plum-shaped ass, she crossed her arms over her ample chest, and set a scowl on her face.

They resumed the hearing, although half his mind was focused on the rustling satin and huffs to the left and back of him where the feisty sister sat. Without a good reason to look back, he had to suffer through one of Judge Korman's interminable lectures, because the man obviously thought it was his mission in life to convert every biker back into civilian life.

Stanton side-eyed Sage, who was sitting stiffly, red flags on her cheeks. He had little pity for her. Hey, he'd never told her to dump him and get knocked up by a biker president, although a pang of guilt hit him in the chest when she rubbed her large belly.

Rising to his feet, he interrupted Korman's rambling discourse, "Your Honor, I have a high-profile first-degree homicide with Judge O'Connor in approximately ten minutes. I wouldn't want to be late for her hearing."

That should shut him up, since he was crushing on O'Connor like a first-class nerd on the head cheerleader. Sage let out a breath of relief, but it was the response of the sexy young sister that got his cock standing at attention.

He felt pricks on his nape like her eyes were on him. From a side-glance, he found her taking him in with one long, incisive head-to-toe look-over. A swoosh of heat rushed over him as her eyes coasted from the top of his close-cropped, groomed hair to the tips of his leather wingtip shoes. That was worth whatever grumbling complaints Korman was lobbing at him at the moment.

The gavel slammed down with a loud thud, and Brandywine was dragged away by two guards.

The sister shot to her feet, swaying over the wooden banister, calling out, "Puck, I love you. Puck, be good."

"You stay away, Sammi, you hear?" he hollered, from between two burly guards. "Stay away and don't visit me!"

The words echoed from the high ceilings as he was manhandled out the side door of the courtroom.

Sage stopped to talk to the sister, who nodded her head brusquely to whatever Sage was explaining to her. She bit down on that plump bottom lip of hers and batted her eyelashes quickly as if urging her tears to stay in place. Something tore at Stanton's chest, like vultures ripping a hole in his core. He didn't like seeing that girl struggle to remain calm.

No, he didn't like it one bit.

Sage patted her hand, pointed toward the exit, and then pivoted and walked toward him. He groaned inwardly as his fist clenched around the case file he was holding. He did not want to converse with his ex. Not now. Not ever. He'd rather run after the hot-to-trot chick who was sashaying her fine ass down the aisle toward the double doors at the back of the courtroom.

Chewing on his lip, his eyes narrowed on the curves of her undulating body. *That ass.* Christ, the way she swung those hips. Like a fucking siren calling for him to follow. *Don't worry little girl, I'm coming for you.*

Jamming files into his briefcase, he turned a fake smile on Sage as she stopped a couple of feet away from him. He'd just gotten back into the courtroom and now a sweet, sexy little bundle like that had dropped into his courtroom. What were the chances? He was finally, *finally* getting a dose of luck. He had to seize the moment, not let Sage, or the past she represented, trip him up.

"Thanks for intervening, Stanton. Korman likes to go on whenever I show up with a client who's a member of a motorcycle club."

"Not a problem. I hope you don't think I was anything but fair with your client."

"At times I do find you a tad zealous, but today you were perfectly within your rights." She sighed. "It didn't help that he confessed to the policeman."

"He did seem proud of his actions," Stanton noted.

Once upon a time, talking to Sage was fraught with tension. Four years later, guilt still weighed heavily for cheating on her with Melanie. But now that she'd moved on and was now pregnant and seemingly happy, their interactions had settled into professional decorum. Even though their breakup was his fault, it had initially grated on him that she'd gone with a hardened biker, of all people. She was a good person and he had no one to blame but himself. Soon, he'd approach her with true and sincere amends and would seal shut that chapter of his life for good.

"Stubborn idiot," she said under her breath.

His eyes caught the closing of the large wooden door at the far back of the courthouse. He didn't have much time if he was going to catch up and introduce himself to that chick.

"Well, if there's nothing else." He lifted his briefcase, along with another case stuffed with the rest of his files for the day. "Like I said, I have O'Connor in a few minutes." He fake-checked his watch for good measure.

Sage tipped her head to the side, a furrow between her brows. "I didn't hear about you having a high-profile case with O'Connor." *Of course*, Sage would catch on to that little lie.

"I don't have time to get into it right now. I have to find one of the witnesses before we go in. Don't mean to be rude, but I really have to go."

She took a step back from him, her brows still knitted. "Oh, sorry."

He flung open the wooden gate of the wooden banister, rushed down the aisle and out of the courtroom, hoping to find the intriguing sister before she got lost in the maze of the courthouse.

5

SAMMI

S ammi pushed open the door of the women's bathroom on the basement level of the courthouse and crossed the crowded waiting room of the Clerk's Office.

Clusters of people were sitting on benches. Doors opened and closed as pairings of lawyers and clients entered and exited rooms reserved for attorney-client conversations.

She was passing the last row of wooden benches toward the stairs leading back to the ground floor when a man stepped into her path.

Not bothering to glance up at him, she muttered, "Excuse me." He didn't move. She began to sidestep him when he followed her movement and stepped in front of her.

"Are you the sister of Mr. Brandywine, Samantha Brandy-wine?" came a low, deep rumble.

Sammi's eyes snapped up and her breath caught. It was the prosecutor of Puck's case.

She stumbled back a step and her butt hit the back of a long wooden bench.

"Yes, my name is Samantha, b-but people call me Sammi."

Oh, God, what does he want with me?

"Sammi," he repeated, rolling the syllables of her name over his tongue as if he were savoring the taste of them. Damn, his voice. The hairs on the back of her neck lifted off her skin. If a voice could be described as dripping with sex, then bingo.

She took a moment to look him over carefully a second time, since she'd already checked him out in the courtroom. Yup, just as she'd suspected. Up close, he was still fine as hell. His close-cropped dark-blond hair was styled a bit severely for her taste. Not a strand out of place. Only made her fingers itch to mess with it. What he must look like after sex.

She stifled a small sigh.

He sported the kind of chiseled jaw that could cut through a plank of wood. But it was his suit that really did her in. The navy pinstripe was tailored to perfection. To cover those broad shoulders of his, she was certain his light wool jacket had been tailored to his frame. This man was wealthy. He seemed so austere, but with a dark and dangerous edge. If a large and lean panther was put in a suit, this is what it would look like.

Every aspect of him called to her. Intelligent blue eyes scrutinized her carefully. Her body temperature was heating up to the point that she wanted to bust out a fan.

Although it was teeming with people, no one was paying attention to them as the prosecutor leaned in a touch closer to her and said something. Attention fixated on the slight smile curving the corners of his lips upward, she'd missed half of what he'd said to her.

"—to say that I'm sorry about what happened upstairs. My hands were tied."

Come again? He was a prosecutor; he knew what he was doing. Even though Sage had told her their choices were limited, with Puck's ridiculous confession and the judge's prejudice against bikers, she wasn't thrilled about being in the presence of the man who was prosecuting her brother.

"It would have helped if your brother hadn't boasted about his actions," he finished with a sigh, as if harassed.

"A-are you blaming him?" she sputtered, incredulity lacing her tone. Her *big brother* was going to jail, and she didn't need this asshole flaunting it in her face. She knew Puck was mule-headed, but this guy certainly didn't have the right to point it out. Sage was already at her wit's end with Puck, yanking at her hair on the car ride to the courthouse. All on top of being six months pregnant. Sammi was beside herself with worry.

"I don't need this shit," she seethed and made to move around him.

A hand shot out and touched her arm, setting off a shudder up her arm.

"Wait a moment, I'm not blaming him in the least," he assured her immediately.

This man had some gall touching her. Her eyes shot to his large fingers, warm against her skin.

She peered up at him and was stunned by his piercing blue eyes, staring at her intensely, as if seeking the answer to a question only she had the answer to. Her gaze skittered away from his deep stare. A turmoil of conflicting feelings wrangled in her chest.

His fingertips rested below her chin and gently turned her face toward him. The prickling along those couple of inches of contact had her heart beating against her ribcage like a jackhammer.

"I apologize," his voice rumbled.

Her eye twitched. She wanted to nab one of the lawyers scurrying past her and ask, *Excuse me, ma'am, do prosecutors usually approach the other side, give them their condolences, and apologize?*

Umm...she seriously doubted it. His eyes glanced over her figure, pausing on her chest for a good beat. When they returned to hers, they held a distinct flare of bright blue heat. The arousal she saw triggered a small tsunami in her own body. Suddenly, her clothing felt too tight and itchy. Her panties. Well, let's not go there.

Err...that's 'cause they're drenched.

He released her, stepped back, and offered her his hand. "Allow me to introduce myself. I'm Stanton Prescott."

Her eyes flew wide and her mouth dropped open. As in, jaws unhinged and flapping back and forth as wide open as a barnyard door. This was *Stanton*. Stanton, the bastard who'd cheated on Sage just before they were about to get married. It happened long before Sage met Kingdom, but she'd heard enough grumbling about Stanton while volunteering at Sage's law office, helping with the domestic violence clients. Not that she'd heard of Stanton impeding Sage's work in that regard. No, just general griping about what the lowlife cheater had done regarding her other cases as a defense attorney. Holy shit. Indignation warred with concern, which unfortunately also warred with lust.

The clerk called out a name from the Clerk's Office service window. Needing a moment, Sammi followed the movements of a lawyer and her client hurrying toward the clerk. Her gaze returned to him.

His head canted to the side slightly, a small pucker marring the skin between his brows. "Do you know of me? Or perhaps my father?"

She clamped her jaws together and shook his hand, which had a few calluses. Surprising for a man who was the furthest thing from blue-collar she'd ever laid eyes on.

"I know of you, yes," she replied. "Not your father. I know you from Sage. She's a *very* good friend of mine."

"Ahh." That was all he said.

This guy wasn't flustered a bit. No, *Oh, yes, I'm the sorry-ass loser who cheated on Sage during our engagement.* Or maybe an admission to the effect of, *Oh, yes, I'm the man-whoring asshole you've heard about.* Not that she had much to say on that last point, since Puck could give this guy a run for his money any day of the damn week.

Still, his only response was a murmured *ahh.* That took guts. Although, he was tugging on his collar, so he may be a tad uncomfortable.

Then he even stopped doing that. Really? No other signs of discomfort or embarrassment?

"Well, that was wreckage from the past. I'm not the man anymore," he declared firmly.

Her eyebrows hit her hairline. *Huh. Okay. I hadn't expected a confession-slash-explanation.* She hated him on principle, but everything this guy did threw her off balance. He was an older, wealthy prosecutor, who was also a total stranger any yet he was honest and seemed genuinely concerned about what she thought about him.

"You're not? So tell me, how does a man-whore change his ways? Enlighten me, I'm all ears."

She clapped her hand over her mouth. *Oh, God, shut up woman.*

A deep rumble emanated from him. The sound entered her body and reverberated down to the tips of her blush-colored toenails, which of course matched her lip gloss.

"Tell me how you really feel, why don't you," he replied in a husky tone that vibrated somewhere in the region of her lower belly. Rats, just her luck. The first guy her body reacted to after a lifetime of hibernation had to be the rich, man-slut ex of one of her favorite people.

"No reason you should believe me, but I'd love the opportunity to *prove* it to you."

Say what now?

"Are you, like, coming on to me?" she asked, because, while all signs pointed to yes, she felt like she'd fallen into a time-space wormhole and popped out in an alternate universe. A universe where men like him ran after women like her. He gave another one of those delicious chuckles that caused the warmth in her lower belly to go even lower, pooling more wetness in her panties. Swear to God, that sound had a direct connection to her clit, because it'd been jingling like a little bell since his first chuckle.

"Yes, I am. I'd like to take you out for a—" The clerk shouted out another name so loudly that it muffled his last word, but she could speculate on what he'd just proposed.

"A drink? Well, that's bold of you. You're the prosecutor on my brother's case. And Sage's ex. Hello?!"

"I do play a part in his case. Unfortunate that," he mused aloud, completely unruffled. *This guy.* She almost shook her head ruefully at his ballsiness. That kind of inherent, smooth confidence couldn't be faked.

"A *huge* part, I'd say."

"A significant part, I agree. Normally, I wouldn't approach a defendant's family. I tend to get passionate when I'm arguing a case, but this time, your brother was the maker of his own destiny. That, and the bad luck of having Judge Korman. Nothing I said would've changed Korman's mind, and I'm not overexaggerating when I say *nothing.*"

She bit down on her lip and stifled a cry. Her rear butted against the back of the wooden bench. Her chin trembled and dipped low to her chest. She shook her head so that her hair draped down and covered her face.

"Hey, hey there." His hand cupped her cheek. "It's going to be okay."

The compassion in his tone almost made her grab his broad shoulders and bawl into his chest, but she had to be strong. She was normally a badass, but this was her first time without Puck, and she was scared. God knows how long he could be put away for the crime he'd admitted to. She wasn't going to cry, dammit. Puck wouldn't want her crying on this man's shoulder. Especially this man.

Swatting his hand until he dropped it, Sammi straightened and threw her shoulders back. Not only would she not cry, but she had to figure out a way to help Puck. She owed him that much, at least.

Carefully eyeing Stanton, she debated how far she was willing to go with this.

All the way.

It wasn't much of a hardship.

Let's face it, I'm intrigued.

If it included hooking up, she would've gone there anyway. The fact that being involved with him in any form could influence Puck's case was like sprinkling crack juice on a regular incentive. In her experience, men were simple creatures. The chance of swaying him were in her favor. If, once it was all said and done, she got to kick his ass to the curb, then hey, that'd be giving him the "fuck you" he deserved for how he'd treated Sage.

Come to think of it, the possibilities were endless.

❋❋❋

THE BEAUTIFUL, brave girl standing in front of him sniffled as she worked to stifle her tears, and the sound nearly brought him to his knees. He'd drop down to the dirty linoleum floor, wrap his arms around her waist, and hold her close. If they'd had privacy, his next step would've been to pull up her skirt and tongue-fuck her little pussy. Anything to wipe away the sad, defeated look in her big whiskey-colored eyes.

"What is it that you do, little girl?" It was the first question that popped out of his mouth to distract her.

She sniffled a bit, but then her little chin lifted a fraction and she replied, "I'm twenty-one. I'm hardly a little girl." *Too fucking cute.* "As for what I do, not that it's any of your damn business, but I'm a personal stylist."

He enjoyed the way she put him in his place, but then answered his questions anyway, as if she couldn't help but follow his lead.

Inspecting her thoroughly, he let his gaze linger down her lush form. Hot. Damn. Although dressed in black from head to toe, nothing could hide the flare of those hips from her pinched waist. If he didn't know better, he'd think she wore a corset. That's how dramatic her curves were, from her heavy tits to the tuck of her waist and back out to her spectacular hips. She was like a 1940s pinup girl. His favorite type. Tilted at a cocky angle was that saucy pincushion hat with the tiny black veil. She looked like she was going to a funeral, which he supposed was the case in her mind.

A stylist.

Made total sense from the way she was dressed. He could respect that. His father hired one for him in the past, during one of his re-election campaigns where if a man forgot to wear a flag pin at a gala for veteran's affairs, he'd be trolled to death on social media. How would he happen to know that? Because it fucking happened to him, that's how. After that incident, his father was adamant about having a stylist make certain he was presentable before any public appearances. It was somewhat degrading since Stanton took pride in how he dressed, but familial duty required him to do what he was told. There was no room for mistakes, especially during a campaign.

His eyes rolled back up to the gap in her satiny wrap-around dress, which showcased her lush tits. Then right back down to the split down the side of her dress, showing off a nice, firm thigh. Was that a black satin garter belt? She flicked her skirt out. *Fuck me.* It was. She was wearing garters.

His tone was almost a growl when he demanded, "Are you flashing me on purpose, little girl?"

She batted her thick black eyelashes. "Who me?"

He groaned.

Cock-fucking-tease, that's what she was. And he reveled in it. She was the total sexy package, this one. If a man deserved a little R&R after a thirty-day stint in hell, that man would be him. And this tasty treat he could have. It wasn't a row of thin white lines. It wasn't a bottle of bourbon. Although she sure as hell looked as tasty as a tall, cold brew on a steamy, hot day. And for a parched man like him, she was the perfect combination of delicious, but not addictive. For better or worse, women never were. Usually, his problem was getting rid of them. He already sensed he wouldn't easily tire of her. Besides her killer body, all her little expressions and quirks fascinated him. *Yeah, this one will take a while.*

"Now, why would I do that?" she continued taunting him in her husky voice.

In a flash, he was in her space, crowding her against the back of a long wooden bench. Curling his fingers over the smooth wood, he leaned forward, forcing her to lean backward. It had the advantage of thrusting her perfect tits out.

The lapels of his jacket grazed her tits and he spotted the pointy ends of her nipples through the stretched satin and flimsy bra she was wearing. Christ, his cock went from hard to *rock* hard. He glanced down the front of her of dress, and nestled in a lacy black demi-cup bra he found what he was looking for. Two puckered raspberry colored nips. *Mother*fucker.

"You'd do it because you want me to fuck you."

She gasped and placed a hand between them. Her nails clawed the material of his crisp shirt for a brief second before she unclutched it and put a bit of pressure on his chest. The pulse at the base of her throat was going double-time.

Oh, I see you, baby girl. You can't hide from me.

"That's a big jump of conclusion. And an extremely arrogant one, at that," she snapped in a haughty tone.

He barked out a short laugh. "Doesn't make it any less true. I may be arrogant, but I've been with many women in my time. I know when one is aroused, and you, little girl, are *aroused*," he confided in her ear.

Her breasts rose and fell provocatively, but the pressure of her hand on his chest increased significantly.

Fine.

He stepped back, giving her the space she was after. Two lawyers paused close to them, arguing over a recent court case that had come down the Court of Appeals.

Taking her by the elbow, which he was pleased to see her allow, he moved them off to a quiet corner. Reluctantly, he dropped his hand.

Her eyes narrowed. "Didn't your mother teach you never to mention other women?"

Feisty. And possessive. He liked that. It wasn't the way he'd talked to her or touching her in public that annoyed her. No, it was talk of other women. *This is getting better and better.* He'd never been possessive himself, but he imagined that if he cared about a woman enough, he'd be a jealous motherfucker.

Oh, but his little girl wasn't done spitting at him like a wet cat.

"And didn't she ever teach you general manners, because that is not how you talk to a woman, you pig. Who do you think you are to talk about arousal when you barely know me?"

His gaze flicked up and down her body. "Aren't you with the bikers?"

"*So?*"

She gave him a once-over, cold and full of disgust.

"Assuming you even know how bikers talk to their women, which I can already tell you don't." Her chin lifted a fraction higher. "I may be a biker bitch, but you are no biker. Don't tell me you speak to women like this on the regular. You either speak to me with respect or you don't speak to me at all."

"This *is* how I speak to women."

That was the truth, at least.

She snorted. "On first meeting them? At the courthouse? Not a bar or a club? Unlikely."

He liked to see her riled up. Poking the bear, he teased, "Don't tell me you're a prude."

"No, I'm not a prude, but here's your first lesson, buddy. You've got to *work your way up* to talking dirty to me, and let me tell you, you haven't even *begun* to work hard enough for it." She gave him that sassy, disgusted look-over again. *Fucking cute and hot.*

He folded his arms over his chest, and she mimicked his posture, although hers had the benefit of shoving her tits up—creamy, and just plain *lickable*. Oh, he'd lick her, first chance he got. From end to fucking end. "Is that right? I'm going to be schooled by a little girl?"

"If the shoe fits," she sassed back. "And stop calling me little girl." Her hands flapped down her frame. "I'm a damn woman."

Back in her space, the back of his knuckles found the line

of her cheekbone. "Oh, no. The term 'little girl' stays." His tone dropped an octave, coming out almost hoarse. "I'll do whatever it takes, *work as hard as it takes*, to have the privilege of taking care of this tight body of yours. To do whatever I want with it, whenever I want. But calling you 'little girl' is nonnegotiable."

She shoved his hand off her. He let the dismissal go and stepped back again. "You don't look old enough to be a sugar daddy. How old are you, anyway?"

"I'm thirty-two, and a sugar daddy is in how a man treats a woman, not in their age. Have no fear, I plan on treating you very, *very* well," he ended in a growl.

Looking him up and down as if thoroughly unimpressed, she cocked her hip and harrumphed. "I'll think about it."

"You do that, *little girl*."

She clenched her teeth, but didn't contradict him. A warmth suffused his chest. Score one for Team Stanton. He was always good at playing games, he'd just never had so much fun with it before.

"So, where am I taking you tonight?"

She sputtered. "You want to take me *out* out?"

"Of course. Wherever you want to go. Where do you live? What's your number?"

She poked him with her index finger. "First off, I'm not letting you know where I live."

"I can find it in your brother's file," he replied, unimpressed by her push-back. "Little girl like you still lives with her big brother. I'd stake my life on it."

Her eyes cut away from him and she cursed under her breath. Her gaze returned to him. She crossed her arms over her chest and raised her chin. "Doesn't matter. I'll meet you somewhere in town."

"How can I guarantee you'll show up?" It was a legitimate

concern that she better answer correctly, because there was no fucking way he was going to be stood up and lose his one chance with her.

"Oh, I'll show up, don't you worry. We have to talk about my brother."

He smothered a laugh. "Is that right?"

"Of course. You didn't think I'd voluntarily spend quality time with you without there being something in it for me?"

Stanton pressed his lips together firmly to prevent from laughing. *She's too fucking precious.* "You haven't had my tongue inside you yet or you'd have no doubt there was something in it for you."

He was satisfied to see her cheeks turn red. For a girl who probably grew up around bikers, she was feisty, but had been protected enough to still have a strain of innocence.

As if reading his mind, she said, "One thing you should know about me right off the bat. I don't play around. I don't bullshit. Everything is up front and center."

He leaned in closer and dipped his head until he was nuzzling behind her ear, scenting her. Something about her was so familiar, so approachable.

He murmured, "Are you going seduce me, little girl?"

Fuck, his cock was so goddamn hard at that moment. But for her, he'd go hours without coming as long as he could watch her break under his tongue.

She stiffened, but her breathing got shorter and choppier. "Of course," she croaked.

Although it was a bustling room, he moved in, pressing her closer into the corner, covering her from any wandering eyes. Once he deemed that they were in semi-privacy, he caught a curl of her dark hair and twirled it around his index finger.

"We're going to have so much fun together." Pulling away,

he let the curl retract from his finger. "But, I must insist on having a car pick you up from your house and bring you to the Champagne Room. It's a bar—"

"I know what the Champagne Room is. It's the hottest spot in Poughkeepsie. I'll meet you there."

He let out a weary sigh. It was necessary to get one issue out of the way from the get-go.

"Little girl, the sooner you learn to take what I offer, the sooner we'll get along and you can get to the business of seducing me."

He leveled her a serious look, because he had to know how annoying this part was going to be for her. "Do you have an issue with a man calling a car for you, giving you gifts, taking care of you, that kind of thing?"

"You mean, treating me like a kept woman, sugar daddy?"

There was a teasing glint in her eyes. She wasn't upset in the least by his suggestions. Good sign.

"God no, not at all. You want to waste your money on me. Have at it."

His eyes turned hard. "You're gravely mistaken if you think it'd be a waste. On the contrary, it'd be a privilege and a pleasure."

Sammi gulped.

"Okay," she said, in a small voice, as if chastised. There was that innocence, popping up again despite her attitude. He could only imagine what that beguiling mix of innocence and sass would like as she took her pleasure on his cock. Raw. *Aww, fuck. Focus, man, focus.* He could never let on what her little girl voice did to him or his cock.

He put out his hand palm up and said, "Phone."

She unlocked her cell phone and plopped it on the flat of his hand. He poked around and inserted his number, than opened the texting app.

"What's your address?"

She rattled it off and he texted it to his phone.

"Good. A car will pick you up a little before seven. We'll have drinks. Then, we'll go from there."

He handed the phone back to her and felt her slim fingers slide over his. What would they feel like wrapped around his shaft? Feeling assured after getting her number, he picked up his briefcase.

Walking backward, he gave her a hard look and said, "Till seven."

6

STANTON

Stanton was sitting at the end of the bar, on the red velour stool closest to the entrance, which was still halfway across the large space.

It was the best location to spot his little biker girl when she stepped through the door on this crowded Friday night. The Champagne Room was the swankiest bar and lounge in the city, famous for the rows of upside-down champagne bottles used as muted lights hanging above the bar. Black walls enhanced the dramatic lighting on the shelves of liquor, the bar, and the islands of tables. The champagne bottles were the only hint of retro in a bar dominated by a sleek modern design.

Stanton rapped his fingertips on the metal bar top and took a gulp of his seltzer water. He cast an eye over the rows of liquor bottles reaching to the ceiling. In the past, those bottles would've called to him. Now it was down to a low, muted buzz that he could ignore without much effort.

The place was packed, the small clusters of tables and chairs overflowing with people. With her sense of style, he guessed Sammi would appreciate this place. The upstairs lounge was even better. The lighting was more intimate and there were islands of red-and-black leather couches and oversized chairs, not including the private booths. Hell, couples have been known to fuck in those booths.

The moment Sammi walked in the door, his cock jerked at attention. By the time his eyes finished looking her over, it was as stiff as a goddamn pike. She was wearing a cobalt blue shirt with a deep V to showcase the swells of her gorgeous tits. As she turned to talk to the hostess, he caught sight of her exposed back. Damn, backless shirt. He was screwed.

Scratch that. He'd be the one doing the screwing by the time the night was over.

His gaze coasted down her torso to a tight black leather miniskirt with a big zipper down the middle that hit right above her knees. That zipper tantalized him. It had an oversized tab for his fingers to latch onto and drag down until it fell off her.

Once the skirt was gone, being a gentleman, the first thing he'd do was take care of her and her pretty little pussy. *The better to eat you with, my dear.* Yeah, he could play the big bad wolf. To top it off, she wore a pair of black pumps with laces that ended in bows, just below the knees. Holy fuck. For a biker bitch, she was beyond classy.

The hostess motioned toward Stanton, and Sammi's head veered in his direction. He stood up and her eyes raked down his frame and back up before giving him a saucy wink. Jesus *Christ.* He almost preened at her expression, because she liked his tailored button-down collared shirt, *sans* tie, and fitted jacket. From the lust oozing from her eyes, apparently that was enough.

Snapping her luscious hips from side to side, she followed the hostess toward him. Stanton had to move his head this way and that to follow her trajectory as she weaved between tables and people. Did she take belly dancing classes on the side, because, fuck, the motion of her hips was mesmerizing as hell.

Suddenly, she was standing in front of him.

Focusing his blurry vision on her face, he smirked. "Glad to see you made it."

"Didn't you make sure of that?" she asked, a teasing lilt in her tone. She was referring to the car he ordered to her front door. Bending down to kiss her cheek, he was hit by her scent. A light perfume mingled with her own distinct fragrance, caramel with hints of vanilla.

She made as if to follow the hostess, but he possessively wrapped a hand around her slim arm and pulled her back against his front. Her ass cheeks cradled his dick perfectly.

Clamping down a moan, he whispered in her ear, "Let's go upstairs to the lounge. It's more private."

Abandoning his drink at the bar, he grabbed Sammi's hand, and towed her through the main floor and up the stairs to the lounge.

Maroon velvet curtains opened upon his arrival by Vincent, the bouncer.

Stepping aside, he unhooked the velvet rope to the VIP area. "Mr. Prescott, good to see you this evening."

"Thank you, Vincent."

A blind man would've noticed Vincent's appreciative look at Sammi, and he barely restrained himself from snapping at the man. There was a time when he'd shared women, but he'd never partied with Vincent, so the fucker better pull his eyes back into their sockets.

Stanton stilled. *What the fuck was this?* Since when was he possessive over a woman? Sammi's eyes were round, taking in the red velvet walls and the groupings of low couches and tables under quiet lighting coming from chandeliers. Whereas the downstairs was chic and elegant, the upstairs definitely took a turn away from modern toward something sultrier.

Another hostess came out of the woodwork and welcomed them. Leading them to the back, she jabbered away at him. What she said, he had no idea. All he could feel was Sammi's small hand wrapped in his.

Fucking finally, they arrived at a corner booth.

Intimate, hidden, dark.

Perfect.

He gestured for Sammi to go first because he was polite like that. Not so that he could see the shape of her perfect ass encased in black leather when she practically had to crawl onto the banquette. His eyes shot to the ceiling. His cock was in a stranglehold and he couldn't adjust it right there in public, but damn did he need to.

Scooting in behind Sammi, they settled in and ordered drinks.

"A Snakebite," she ordered.

His eyebrows shot up. Whiskey and lime juice in a shot glass? A man's drink. She gave him a sugary smile at his reaction, as if to say, *Bite me.* He wanted to reply, *Oh, baby, I will. You'll be begging for my mouth on you very, very soon.*

Sammi set her clutch on the low table and leaned back, taking in a deep breath. Her chest rose and fell, giving him a sneak peek at her matching blue lace bra.

He slid closer to her and they stared at each other, silently taking each other's measure. His gaze slid over her face and what bare skin she had showing, which showed how confident she was in her body. He touched the only tattoo he could see, a sexy, cock-teasing tattoo at that. It was a lace choker. He traced the tatted lace, going back and forth along the front of her throat.

She swallowed, and his finger rose and dipped with the

movement of her throat muscles. Was Sammi aware of her nature? She was be a biker, but she also had a distinct air of innocence about her. Either way, that choker was something else. She was practically begging to be collared. If that was her instinctual way of laying down a challenge, then he was ready for it.

He withdrew his hand before it wandered farther down on its own accord. The urge to touch her rode him hard, and that was saying something because these weren't lines of coke taunting him to lose control. Yet, sitting there beside him, all creamy skin, dark curls, and glittering eyes, she was a tempting as all hell.

"The only tattoo I see is this collar," he observed.

"From the way you touched it, I'm guessing you approve," she replied.

"Oh, you have no idea. I like collars." He leaned in closer. "They're one of my favorite accessories for little girls."

She bit her plump bottom lip and her eyes flared with interest. Was it the talk of collars?

Her reaction made him imagine what kind of collar he'd buy her first. He cocked his head to the side. White lace or black leather with studs? So far, she didn't seem to have an issue with him taking care of her. She'd ceded to the car without much of a fight. Which he was grateful for, because it had been tiresome arguing with past women over this issue. Sage had rejected his gifts, even though she needed it more than most.

Stanton usually dated women from families like his, so it made no sense to him when Sage fought him as hard as she had. He knew she was prideful, but what she'd never under-stood was how she'd deprived him of the privilege of taking care of her. It was part of the dynamic that got his cock up and ready to play.

You know what I'd really love? A woman who got *wet* when he lavished her with gifts. That would be a fucking high like no other. His gaze turned to Sammi. Imagine watching her squirm, knowing her pussy was dripping as he placed a necklace around her neck. A nice fat gem dangling in the little indentation at the base of her throat. Then, because she was happy, because she was *pleased*, she'd lift her little skirt, straddle him, and ride his cock hard. *Fuuuck.* He bit back a groan. And not as a reward. No, she'd ride him because it got her hot that he spoiled her like a Daddy should his little girl.

"Eyes up here." Sammi cut through his ruminations. A line appeared between her brows. "You look like you're in pain."

He barked out a short laugh. Understatement of the fucking year. Going for broke, he confessed, "I am. If I had my way, I'd take you right now."

She tilted a little to the side, away from him, and glanced at his tented slacks. Rolling her eyes, she said, "Yeah, I got that."

"Good, then we're on the same page."

"*Humph*, I wouldn't go that far. If you think I put out for any random man, then you'll be sadly disappointed."

"Oh, baby girl, I have zero issues with working to get under that tight skirt."

He loomed over her, letting her feel of how much larger he was. He'd worked out incessantly while on lockdown at rehab. His shoulders stretched against his shirt, the fit tighter than usual. "I'm a hard worker. Always have been. My father taught me that nothing worth getting comes free."

His eyes roved over her face, down to her lips, touching the tip of her button nose and then back to her eyes. "Make me work for it, little girl. I *dare* you."

Her fingernail hooked on the opening of his shirt, and she dragged him closer until her glossy lips almost touched his.

Her breaths feathered over his lips and he wanted to devour her. Just *devour* her. But he held back.

"Oh, have no fear," she whispered over his lips. "I'm a hard-ass when I want to be. I'll have you on your knees by the time the night is over."

She shoved his chest back until his spine hit the leather of the banquette. God, she got him hot. He couldn't wait for her to make good on her word.

7

———

SAMMI

They were having a staring contest and Sammi was way, way, *way* over her head.

The woodsy cedar fragrance coming off him was making her faintly delirious. Her main reason for shoving him away was that she was drowning in his luxurious scent. She was flushed from head to toe. Hell, she might as well have been in a sauna dripped in his sinful essence.

There was no doubt about it—she was out of her league. Sure, Sammi had wealthy clients. She knew how to interact with them, but she was a simple person beneath her second-hand designer clothes. She was just a girl brought up among tough bikers.

Although, truth be told, his rough talk and the aggressive edge to his behavior was not much different from what she was used to.

Whether he took liberties because she wasn't from his social strata or because he was an asshole was yet to be determined. Either way, there was a dangerous air to Stanton. Something distinctly wild about him. The trappings of his suit and coiffed hair barely contained the menace roiling just beneath the ultracivilized surface he'd curated with care. It came out in his domineering language and actions. But it went even deeper. If she'd been dropped in an isolation tank with no sensory input besides his scent, she'd pick him out in a hot second. He emitted an aura, a vibration, that outed him as borderline barbaric.

The waitress materialized out of the dusky lighting of their corner and placed their drinks on the table, making sure to dip low enough to flash Stanton her tits. Sammi didn't blame her one bit. What woman wouldn't want to entice a man that exuded power, danger, and sexual prowess like Stanton did.

"Thanks, sweetheart," Stanton said.

The low buzz of other patrons in the lounge drifted over them as the waitress nodded and flashed him a smile. Sammi wasn't jealous by nature. She respected women who showed off their assets. So why did the flirting put her teeth on edge?

She, herself, flirted with men and hooked up when needed. Yet, she'd never had a reaction like this before. The game was getting dangerous, but she had no choice but to play it, at least until Puck's hearing was over. Add a splash of revenge for Sage, mix, and stir.

Leaning back, he draped his arm over the top of the banquette and picked up the gauntlet she'd thrown down earlier.

"So. If I understand correctly, you want me on my knees?" he drawled. "Never been on my knees before. Other than to tongue-fuck a woman, that is."

Whiskey spewed from her lips. *Crap.* She grabbed napkins and dabbed her drenched top as he sat back and laughed.

"Sure you don't have a prudish bone in your body?"

"Forgive me if I didn't expect you to say the words *tongue-fuck* right now," she replied snappishly.

His eyes turned a darker shade of blue and dropped to her lips. "Damn, say the word fuck again, baby girl," he ordered.

She gave a soft snort and stirred her drink. "Not on your life. I don't respond to commands like a dog on a leash, thank you very much."

"Oh, little girl, is that a challenge?"

"Hardly. Can we move past the dirty sex talk? It's getting old. Or is that all you can do? Because if you think you can fuck me by talking filthy and buying me a drink, you're in for a rude awakening."

She wasn't going to be treated like a whore, dammit. If that's what he wanted, then it was best to make it clear and move the hell on.

She narrowed her eyes on him. "Either you start treating me like a lady or I'm leaving."

Stanton stilled; his glass halted midair. Instead of bringing it to his lips, he placed it carefully back on the black leatherette coaster and turned to face her head-on.

Taking her chin firmly, he said, "Let there be no misunderstanding. You're not a whore, a slut, or whatever disrespectful term you have bouncing around in that head of yours. I *do* like to talk dirty. It's a turn-on for me, and don't lie and tell me it isn't for you."

Releasing her, he raised his hands, palms out, as if he was laying out all his cards on the table.

"Yes, I want to fuck you. Any man who says otherwise is a damn liar, and that's not me. But I'm done with just plain old fucking. I'm turning a new leaf. Starting with being honest and intentional in my every action and interaction."

He raised his glass to his lips. "For example, I've stopped drinking alchol."

That tidbit of information piqued her curiosity.

"Why?" she blurted out before she could stop herself.

"Because I'm a drug addict. A recovering addict."

Her brows jumped up. She hadn't expected a clean-cut man like him to be a druggie, but then again, his inner wildness was blatant.

"What kind of drugs did you do?"

"A bit of everything, but coke was my drug of choice. You might be curious to know how I can be in a bar after a confession like mine. Alchol was never the huge draw. Coke is an altogether different story."

She nodded solemnly, absorbing the new information. "How long have you been sober?"

"Clean and sober for thirty-two days."

Damn, she had to give him props for blunt honesty. In the circles he ran, drug addiction was not something to be flaunted about.

"Not long," she noted.

"No, not long," he conceded. "That's why I'm doing everything in my power to live honestly. I was dishonest in my dealings with women. Cheated on my girlfriends. Two fiancées. I'd like to—no, I have *no* choice but to do things differently. If I step out of the strict boundaries I've placed around my behavior, I'll stumble, and I can't afford to stumble. Not after what I've put my mother and sister through."

Two fiancées. There'd been another one after Sage. Jeez, this guy was a wrecking ball of a mess.

Crossing one leg over the other, she leaned back and linked her fingers over her knee. "Is that so? You've basically admitted to being a player who violated the trust of not one but two women you loved enough to be willing to spend the rest of your life with. How can I trust you?"

"I wasn't in love with them." She gave him a perplexed look. "My fiancées. There was Sage, whom you know. Then, there was Melanie. I wasn't in love with either of them. You know about Sage already. Melanie was an old family friend. We practically grew up together. One thing led to another…" He shook his head as if shaking off a bad memory. "But I should've never let it get out of hand. The drugs had a part to play as I lost my grip on reality."

"I don't know if that makes it better or worse," she muttered.

"It doesn't make a difference. It was what it was. I'm not blaming them for trusting me. The blame is fully on my shoulders, but if they'd looked carefully, my actions were loud and clear. I'm not proud of the way I acted and I plan to make amends, but moving forward, I'm laying my cards on the table. You told me earlier today that you were a straight shooter."

That I did.

"I'd like to make you a proposal."

I bet you do.

"An arrangement, so to speak."

Yup, I knew it.

"I've never done this before."

He cleared his throat.

Nervous, are you?

"I'd like us to have a clear-cut, honest sexual relationship," he continued. "For that to happen, we need a set of ground rules."

She nodded, impressed that he was able to come out and stated his case in plain language.

Note to self: the man doesn't do anything in half measures.

She took a sip from her glass. Normally, she'd knock back a shot like a Snakebite, but she had zero intention of losing control around this man. Inspecting him carefully, she considered her options. She had no issues with his past drug habit. She didn't plan to build a life with him, so that was his battle to win or lose, not hers.

"What kind of rules did you have in mind?"

"Do you partake in drugs?"

"No. I drink, but I don't normally get drunk. I have a life to lead and a business to run. Partying hard is not a priority."

"I can handle that because let's just say that partying, sex, and drugs were a dangerous combination for me. The second rule is no fucking other men. I insist upon it. I'll be taking you without a condom and to do that we need to be exclusive. Have no fear," his eyes raked over her body to the point, "It's my mission to tire you out so much you won't look at, much less think about fucking another man."

A playboy on a clean kick. She'd humor him, although she had little trust in his ability to follow his word. She could count on three fingers the number of men in her life who took their commitments seriously. Kingdom, Cutter, and Loki.

She shrugged one shoulder. "Fine, but not right off the bat. One step at a time. I've never had unprotected sex. Show me it's worth fucking bare, and I'll consider it. Exclusivity is only important in terms of unprotected sex, so make sure you're fucking only me without a rubber."

He nodded his confirmation.

"I have no problem with your terms. If you can't satisfy me, we'll revisit that rule."

He huffed out a small laugh, and said in a low rumble, "Oh, baby, I won't just eat you, I'll fucking devour you. I won't just leave you satiated; I'll leave you fucking exhausted."

Aww, man. Panties. Soaked. Again. Shit, how does he keep doing that?

"Will there be a time limit?"

Her heart palpitations increased rapidly. She needed enough time to help Puck. His hearing date wasn't set, but it had to last as far as that. Or perhaps as far off as Puck's sentence hearing, which could take months.

Stanton plucked a curl slinking down her front and twirled it around his forefinger. He seemed to like doing that. Well, it was only the second time, but still. She'd never had a man play with her hair before.

"Nah. I was in a rehab for thirty days. Let's just say, I have a fuck-load of energy to expend. It's going to take a while."

Just thinking of him, sleeping alone on a bed while in rehab, only him and his hand, got her all hot and bothered. She bit down on her lip as she imagined the same fingers currently twirling her hair wrapped around a thick, hard shaft.

"Besides," he went on, "we're all about honesty, right? Which means we can bring up any issues and resolve them like civilized human beings."

"Works for me," she squeaked.

"There is one last thing." He paused. He tugged her curl and she leaned in slightly, curiosity zipping up and down her spine as to what would make a powerful man like him hesitate.

"You know when you spoke about me on my knees? Begging. That's kind of my thing. Except the other way around."

Her breath caught in her throat. *For real?* It's like he could see into the heart of her because it was one of her longest-running fantasies. No way was she turning this down. One thing she learned from her mother's sudden death was to grab on to the gifts life threw in her path. They didn't come around often enough, and anything could change on a dime. She'd hit the jackpot. *Yes, baby!*

But she had to play it cool.

Tugging the lock of hair from his grasp, she drawled, "Oh, really? I'm not sure that's *my* thing." *Liar, liar, LIAR.*

"Hmm," he said doubtfully, as if he didn't believe her. "Never tried it before?"

"Nope," she said and let her lips pop on the last syllable.

She'd never gotten into anything kinky, but it might explain her off-the-charts attraction to this guy. She leaned in until her shoulder rubbed against his, accidently inhaled a whiff of his scent, and had to stifle a moan.

Don't breathe, bitch, or you'll never pull this off.

Holding her breath, she brought her teeth close enough to scrape the curve of his ear.

"Again, I'm more titillated by the idea of you on your knees, begging *me*."

She flicked one side of his jacket open and palmed his chest, the heat and current coming off him almost blistering her hand. Man, was he built. She'd already guessed from the bulges of his biceps, tight against the fabric of his sleeves.

Biting down on her bottom lip, she shifted in her seat to put pressure on her clit, although it was doing absolutely nothing to cool her off. She was going to tease the hell out of him and see what he does about it.

8

STANTON

T his *girl.*

The way she talked.

The way she was wiggling her lush ass on the leather seat.

He was going to consume her, lick her tight little pussy till there was nothing left but the smear of her come slathered around his mouth. Her lips, so close to his ear, were rapidly incinerating his willpower. Razing it to the ground.

But he had to stay strong because he knew she was purposely messing with him. There was no way in hell, and he knew his way around hell, that this girl was dominant. He might let her play around a bit, let her frolic in the park like the fresh, new babe that she was. But when it came to the down-and-dirty deed, it would be *her*—hands, elbows, and knees—hitting the floor as he mounted her from behind.

Twisting around until his lips hovered above hers, he said, "Alright, little girl, I'll give you the reins, but you'll have to earn them. It'll be your turn to work, and work for it you will. By doing whatever I tell you to do. You think you can do that?"

Through the low lighting of the chandelier above them, he saw the glint in her deep whiskey-colored eyes.

"Yeah," she croaked out.

He pressed his lips against hers. Fucking finally. She opened for him right away, which he *loved*. Delving in, he sparred with her tongue as she parried and retreated.

Palming her nape, he kept her in place so that he could go deeper and rougher. Sammi melted against him, and he reveled in the way she grasped the lapels of his jacket. His hand slid down the V of her top, landing on the pillowy flesh of her full breast.

She made greedy little sounds that had him pushing her against the back of the bench, ramming his tongue inside her mouth, letting her suck it to the roof of her mouth. Breaking off their kiss, he pulled away to watch his fingers twisting her stiff nipple.

Abruptly, there was a bright flash above him.

Blinded by several blasts of light, he instinctively thrust Sammi into his chest to shield her.

Covering her, his head whipped over his shoulder.

"What the fuck?" he bellowed out.

A paparazzi was being bodily manhandled out of the way by Vincent.

Stanton cursed, but the damage had been done. His father was going to skin his ass if those photos of him mauling a woman in public made their way into the papers.

Turning back to her, he touched her face and torso. "Are you okay?"

Swatting his hand away, she straightened her top to hide her bared breast. One thin blue lace strap and demi-cup glared at him with reproach before she covered it. He'd mistreated her in public, exposing her to the heartless, cruel society that had bred him.

"Fucking hell." He wasn't even able to protect a female from getting caught up in the bullshit that was his life. "I'm sorry, baby. Fuck, they can't usually get in here."

The waitress hovered over them and the manager, Johnny, came running in through a hidden side-door. "Mr. Prescott, I apologize profusely for this breach in security."

"You should be sorry," he growled. "A fucking photographer. Not just a grainy cell phone pic. That's a high-resolution professional shot of me and my woman he got."

A hand slipped over his. "It's not a big deal, Stanton."

He twisted around, his tone half-savage as he growled, "No it's not a big deal, it's a massive fucking deal."

"Stanton—"

"Don't even," he snapped.

A flash of hurt crossed over her eyes.

He breathed out heavily. He didn't mean to bark at her, but he'd failed to protect her, and that pissed him off to no end.

Speaking to the manager, he ordered, "Go and find out how a breach like this could occur. We'll talk another time, Johnny."

"Right away, Mr. Prescott. Drinks are on the house. Anything you want. Denise, get them another round." Pressing a hand on Stanton's shoulder, Johnny said, "Vincent grabbed the photographer and I'll take care of whatever's in the camera. I will personally make sure everything's wiped clean. He's going to pay for this."

"Fine, Johnny," he grunted.

Once alone, he turned his full attention back on Sammi, who had distanced herself by sitting at the far end of the booth.

Fuck.

He calmed his heaving chest. Knowing his luck, the pap somehow managed to salvage a copy, and by the morning, the front pages would plastered with images of the senator's just-out-of-rehab son partying at a nightclub, his hand on a strange woman's breast.

But that wasn't his primary concern right now. He knew how conniving the pap could be and he hadn't safeguarded Sammi from them. Stanton barely knew her, and yet he was driven to protect her from any possible harm. He'd never felt this about anyone but Amy and his mother. Yet, there was something distinctly vulnerable about Sammi despite her hard exterior.

Taking a deep breath, he crooked his finger at her and said, "Come here."

He'd wait her out for as long as it took, because this was her first lesson. She had to learn to obey him. Not that he'd shown himself worthy of her obedience yet, but the first step had been shoved onto them. Everything was ass-backward, but here they were. She pressed her lips in a tight line, and folded her arms over her chest.

Closing herself off was not acceptable.

"Here. Now," he insisted.

With a huff, she scooted over, eliminating half the distance between them. The waitress deposited two more drinks on the table and slipped away silently.

"Good girl," he praised her. "Closer."

Giving him the stink eye, she edged closer until their arms brushed against each other. Wrapping his arm around her shoulder, he pulled her in close. "I feel personally responsible for what happened."

Settling into his chest, she glanced up at him. "It's not a big deal, Stanton. I didn't realize you were famous, but I have nothing to hide and no one in my family or club cares about something alike this. You're the one with something to lose here, not me."

He gaped at her. "They may have taken a photo of me with my hand on your breast. You were left exposed by my neglect."

She rolled her eyes. "You were hardly neglecting me. So what if they got a shot of us? Earlier, you joked about me being a prude, but it's not like this was a sex tape. Everyone has a cell phone. There's no privacy in the world we live in. If anything, you're the one risking your reputation by being seen with me."

"I couldn't care less what people think," he snapped.

She lifted her chin. "Are you sure? Because I'm one hundred percent a biker bitch. It's an important part of my life. And you may not know this, but I'm a sex-positive stylist. I help style women's choice in lingerie and sex toys and empower them in that area of their life. Not exactly high fashion." She put her hands on his chest and pushed, creating space between them. "Our arrangement may be a liability to you."

Here, this girl was watching out for him when he'd failed taking care of her. Jesus, his life was really fucked. As for her being a liability, he'd sacrificed enough to his father's expectations.

Where had that gotten him? Hooked on coke and taking a month off work, that's where. And his work was no fucking joke. It determined whether a person remained free or behind bars. Those were life-changing decisions, not whether he wore a flag pin to a gala. He lost a month of his life to get clean because he went off the rails attempting to satisfy his father. He was determined to leave that shit behind at Tully, along with the other baggage he'd dragged around like a ball and chain since Jax died.

"I don't personally care about any of it. The photos are about my father. He's a state senator and sees himself as a big deal, but I'm *done* with his ambitions. As long as you stay within the bounds of the law, I don't care what you do. I don't care who you are, biker bitch or otherwise. My main concern is that I didn't protect you."

Peals of laughter tinkled in his ears like chimes. "Silly man, I don't need protecting. I have my brother." A slight frown marred her forehead. "Well, not right this minute, but even without him, I have a crew of brothers who take care of me."

He didn't like the sound of that. He wanted to be the only one taking care of her, not a slew of other men. But it was too soon to vocalize that particular desire out loud.

"Plus, I'm pretty tough on my own."

He guffawed. Now, that was funny. She pursed her lips and rapped her nails on one arm.

"That's a good one," he put in.

"What's that supposed to mean?" she said, her eyes snapping like live electric wires.

"Baby, you're curvy in all the right places, but you're a slip of a thing. You've got spunk, I'll give you that much."

"Damn straight," she fired back.

"But you're young, you're inexperienced, and your brother has been over-protective your whole life. The world would eat you alive if you stepped out on your own."

Her gaze slammed into his. "How do you know anything about me and my brother?"

"Have you forgotten that I was in court when he yelled at you because you countermanded his order to stay away. Or what about when he shouted at you not to visit him in jail?"

Her shoulders slumped and he wanted to slap himself for bringing up her brother.

"Yeah, you're right. Puck always took care of me. Since I was young." Sammi unfolded her arms, let them drop, and played with the tab of her zipper.

Alright, this wasn't going in the direction he planned. Everything had gotten intense and it was time to get things back on track. He stood up and dragged her to her feet. "Come on, let's get out of here."

She snapped up her clutch as he prodded her firmly with a palm on her lower back. Walking her toward the entrance, he leaned down and asked, "Are you hungry? I'm going to feed you and then I'm going to eat you out."

9

___

SAMMI

Stanton wasn't lying when he told her he'd feed her.

He took her to a little French bistro she'd known about for ages but had never been to. Sammi knew every nook and cranny of her town. It was her job to know what was going on, from high-end galas and cutting-edge gallery openings to grunge rock concerts and bike rallies.

What, a biker bitch couldn't be a personal stylist? *Yeah, I get that a lot.* Just because a girl was brought up among bikers didn't mean she couldn't appreciate a nice pair of Manolo Blahnik. *I mean, come on.*

Luckily, her clients understood her aesthetic. Being a biker actually paved her way into the niche she'd single-handedly created for herself. A feat she was quite proud of. She started out as a regular stylist, but she wasn't getting many clients. One day, she got a request for help from a woman who wanted to drive her man wild. And out of that was born the sex-positive image niche. Clothing, lingerie, toys.

From there, she'd built a clientele that came back for more routine-type stuff like parties and vacations, but her focus was on the sexier aspects of the event. What started out with housewives looking to re-spark their marriage or new divorcées back on the market morphed into more hard-core body image issues, like burn victims and survivors of breast cancer.

They'd arrived at the bistro without a reservation, but the moment Stanton stepped through the door, the hostess found them a table in a cozy corner. He'd fed her, as in spoon-fed her, the most delicious *mousse au chocolate a la chantilly* she'd ever had. The dessert whetted her appetite and she couldn't wait to repay the favor by licking any part of his anatomy he liked. In fact, she was looking forward to it.

After dinner, he took her to the most luxurious hotel in town. Stanton held the door of the hotel suite open for her. She stepped in, trepidation in her heart, and halted in her tracks. She'd never been in a place like this before.

The place was huge. There were leather sofas and love chairs, with thick beige drapes framing large French windows. Different areas were subtly sectioned off from one another, creating a sense of intimacy. There was a cart with a cheese plate, an array of desserts, and an opened bottle of champagne, condensation lining the bottle as if it had been opened only moments before their arrival.

She glanced over her shoulder as Stanton shut the door, leaned back, and crossed his arms over his chest as if he expected her to flee. She was more intimidated than she'd expected, but she didn't have time to think about it because he hauled her up against him. His mouth crashed down on hers, his tongue thrusting between her lips.

Moaning, she instantly opened for his sensual assault. With a hand holding the back of her head, he plundered deep in her mouth and she was lost. His hand palmed her mound, one finger tracing the line of her panties over her skirt. Damn, he moved fast.

Pulling back, she panted out, "Take it slower."

Stanton loosened his grip, his eyes fixated hungrily on her lips, which felt swollen and red. "Tell me how you want it?"

"Slow. It takes time for me to warm up. Especially to a stranger. I've never been with someone I haven't known half my life," she confessed.

He scraped the four o'clock shadow on his angular jaw. "Fair enough." His eyes lifted and locked on hers.

The grip on his jaw tightened but he replied, "Any way you want it, baby girl. You're in charge."

After a beat, he inserted, "For now."

She graced him with a wide smile. She loved when a man could control his impulses. "Oh, yeah? That works for me 'cause once you're inside me, I'll want you to fuck me hard and fast."

The back of his head knocked against the door and he let out a groan. Having regained her balance, Sammi molded the length of his shaft straining against the front of his dress pants. His eyelids shuttered as he consciously slowed down his breathing.

"You're such a tease." His eyes flashed open, eyes burning a cobalt blue. "So, if I've got this right, I go slow until you beg me to give it to you hard and fast?"

She cupped his balls through the light, fine wool beneath her hands. "And rough. Yup, that's about right. But until then, I'll be teasing you, alright. For your sake, I hope you have a large reserve of self-control because I'm going to test exactly what type of man you are."

She toyed with the button of his shirt as she continued to fondle him with her other hand. Pulling him toward the couch by his balls, she ordered, "Take off your shirt."

His fingers fumbled with the buttons of his shirt. Then, he yanked it off impatiently.

Dear God. That chest. His pecs were so defined she could have outlined them with a pen. And his six pack? *A work of art.* She stifled a whimper and would've bit into her fist if she'd been alone. She was pretty sure she could bounce a quarter off those abs. Then there was the happy trail of fine hair pointing south like an arrow to the hard cock in her hand.

Liquid heat gushed from her core, forcing her to press her thighs tightly together. "God, you must work out a lot."

"I do mixed martial arts."

Her head snapped up. Did he know that the Squad owned and ran a boxing and MMA club.

Her voice dropped. "I can't wait to lick your chest." The nails of her fingers flicked a nipple. "Especially these."

"Fuck me. Just my luck to get a woman with a cocktease mouth as well."

"Oh, you have no idea," she baited him, as she bent her head and laved his nipple with the tip of her tongue. "I've got a cocktease tongue to go with it."

She undid the top button of his pants and slowly drew the zipper down. Reaching in, she touched the satin hardness of his shaft. Her eyelids dropped. "You go commando."

"Only in anticipation of you, little girl. And you haven't let me down yet."

Her fingers wrapped around his thick girth and pulled out his shaft. She dove to her knees. Her tongue darted out and flicked along the underside of his crown. His cock jerked. *Oh yeah, baby.*

She canted her head to the side, watching his hooded eyes and parted lips. His features were so fierce and taut, he looked almost cruel. The sharp angles of his high cheekbones and the ice-cold blueness of his eyes were tempered by the flush on his skin and the heat in his eyes. His shaft bobbed a few times, and she straightened so the crown settled on the crease of her bottom lip.

Her hands skimmed up his thighs and circled his shaft, holding it still to better lick it from root to tip. His hand snaked beneath her hair and clasped her nape, pressuring her to move forward. She inhaled deeply and then nuzzled into his nest of springy curls. Inhale, nuzzle, lick. Inhale, nuzzle, lick, and away she went.

"Fuck, the sounds you make," he ground out between clenched teeth.

A dribble of pre-come coasted down the side of his shaft, and she lapped it up to the tip before taking it into her wet mouth. His fingers tightened around the hair at the base of her skull. He began to pump his cock, so she pulled her mouth off him with a popping sound. "Nuh-uh. I do all the work. You stand there like a good little boy and take it."

"Christ, you're a dirty one, you know that?"

"Only with you," she replied, reflexively. Although it was the truth, she instantly regretted her admission. Sammi usually didn't enjoy giving head and she never swallowed, but the musky scent and taste of him was delicious. She'd barely started and she was already addicted to the power of this man under her sway. She was going to swallow every last drop of him.

To distract herself from her embarrassing confession, she licked down. Stanton wrapped his hand over hers and jacked himself hard in their hands. She watched as she sucked. It was so hot to witness him losing control. Her breasts felt heavy and full, her nipples taut and scraping against the lace of her bra. She pressed her knees together and wiggled her clit on the back of her shoe.

His balls pulled up high and he stiffened.

She doubled down on her efforts. Hot come filled her mouth and jetted down her throat. She sucked and swallowed as much as she could, but some escaped out the sides of her mouth.

After pumping into her until he was empty, his hips finally slowed. He gave a full-body shudder and his back slammed back against the door. Sammi let his shaft slip out and she leaned back on her haunches. Shoulders back and chest puffing proudly, she gazed up at him. *She* had done this to him.

Pushing her come-laced tresses out of her face, he panted out, "Fucking hell, I didn't last long."

"It's okay, I'll still respect you in the morning."

A choked laugh escaped him. Dragging her up, he whispered against her lips, "Don't worry, I'll get a second wind and fuck that mouth of yours until its aching. Now lick me clean."

"Hmmm, promises, promises," she taunted, but didn't hesitate to drop back to the floor and clean him off.

Once she was done, he pulled her up to standing, latched onto the tab of her skirt, and dragged the zipper down with excruciating deliberateness. One last tug, and it fell off her. His hands immediately went to her ass.

"Nice," he commented, moving a little to the side and eyeing her ass. Slapping one cheek lightly, he said, "Now it's my turn to take care of you."

That simple slap reverberated up her side and she started to pant shallowly. "I guess ... since you were *such* a good boy, you deserve a reward."

He butted his head against the door and groaned, "You're filthy mouth is going kill me, woman. You have no idea how much I deserve a reward, and that reward is you." From behind, his finger slipped between her thighs, roughly stroking the wet silk of the gusset of her panties between her lower lips. "So hot and wet."

"Yes, please," was all she could say because if he didn't do something soon, she was going to burst into flames.

10

STANTON

S tanton swung Sammi into his arms and stalked through the sitting room, past a pair of open French doors, and into the bedroom.

They'd barely made it past the door before attacking each other. Holy fuck, that was one hell of a mouth she had on her. He knew she could use it for sassy comebacks, but apparently she was an expert at using for other things, as well.

Now that he got his orgasm out of the way he could get down to business. Pussy business. He was one of those men who loved eating pussy; right this instant, he wanted to grab her thighs, split them open, and devour her. He didn't know why licking pussy held such a powerful sway over him. Maybe he had a refined sense of smell like a canine, adding credence to Cornell's argument that he was a *dawg*.

Although he didn't quite get a good whiff at the courthouse or the lounge, when Sammi slid into the passenger seat of his Maserati, he felt like fist pumping the air because god*damn*. Vanilla, bourbon, and something irrepressibly feminine hit him like a sucker punch to the face.

Stanton was skating down a dangerous path. This young

woman tugged at his heart strings like no other, but *nothing* would stop him from licking her pussy from end to end. He'd deal with the fallout *after* he was done with her. He'd been through hell and back at rehab, and he fucking *deserved* an award for his herculean efforts.

Truth be told, he missed coke, but staying clean was his number one priority, and if tasting her delectable pussy gave him an edge in this life-or-death battle, then so be it. Chances were he'd get hooked. He was an addict; the numbers weren't in his favor. But, like a gambler, it was a play he was willing to make. The reward would be oh-so worth it. He could do this, he told himself firmly: he could tongue her and still maintain an emotional distance.

Laying her on the side of the bed, he took his leisure in stripping her out of the rest of her clothing. He especially enjoyed untying the bows just below her knees and unlacing her shoes before gently lifting them off her dainty feet.

He gazed down at her completely bare and his heart stuttered. Curly ink-black waves tumbled down her shoulders, one strand snaking down her front to tickle at her dusky nipple. His gaze dipped over the canvas of creamy skin, her ample breasts with dime-sized nipples, whose peaks stood proud, begging for his mouth. Her small waist made her flared hips look almost indecent.

But his eyes rapidly zeroed in on the juncture of her thighs. Swinging her legs, she inched her thighs apart to give him a little peek. And peek he did. Spotting the juices glistening her slippery folds, he shuttered his eyes and squeezed them tightly. She was a fucking porn star come to life.

Snapping his eyes open, he drank her in as he quickly toed off his shoes and shucked his pants.

Pulling back the covers, he settled her in the middle of the bed and kneeled in front of her. Her arms were wrapped around her bent knees, keeping herself hidden from him.

"Spread your legs for me, baby girl," he growled with impatience. "I'm going to feast on the dew between your thighs."

She cocked her head to the side, her lips curling up impishly. "You want me to spread my legs for you?"

Tone harsher than he intended, he replied, "Did I stutter?"

"No you didn't, but the answer is no."

"No?" he replied, incredulous. Her eyes were smoldering for him. He wasn't imagining that. Fucking hell, she was teasing him. Taunting and testing him.

"What? Is this the first time a woman turned you down?" she challenged.

"Yes," he seethed. He was too close to her heavenly scent for much more of her games.

"I don't like having a man's tongue down there. It's slimy."

He bit down on a groan at the way she said tongue. So innocent-like. Okay, he understood what was going on. She'd had a bad experience. It happened. Some men had no fucking clue what to do when they had their tongue in a slice of heaven. A sad truth that sometimes made it difficult for the next man down the line.

"Have you ever had a man put his tongue there before?"

"Of course," she huffed out, blowing at her bangs. *So fucking cute.*

"Guess those bikers don't know what the fuck they're doing, huh."

She glared at him. He shrugged. "It's the truth, because when I get my tongue on you, you'll be screaming *and* creaming on my mouth." He turned on his side, propping his head on his elbow, and let his fingers glide down her belly and tap her mound, just above her clit. "I'm a master and I promise you: you will love it."

She was squirming, but doubt still clouded her eyes. "I don't know..."

"Come on, give it a try. If you don't like it, I'll stop." That was an easy promise since there was no chance in hell she wouldn't like it.

"I guess..." she trailed off.

That was enough of a green light for him. He had her on her back and legs spread in one second flat. His hands caressed her from knee to the crease of her thigh, spreading her wider each go-around. Shimmying onto his stomach, he pressed openmouthed kisses on the inside of her knee and gradually moved to the apex of her thighs.

"Oh, wow," she breathed out, eyes riveted on his head.

This is nothing, baby.

Hovering above her, he inhaled deeply and was almost overcome. Damn, she had the most delectable pussy. No lie. There was something sweet and smoky. Vanilla and musk.

He blew across her engorged, pulsing clit and she moaned, twisting her head side to side on the pillows behind her. She arched her back, pressing to get closer to his mouth, but he slipped his palms under her ass and gripped it to keep her in place. Her hips began to grind and her pussy butted against his lips. He clucked against the surface of her clit and her hands grabbed at his hair, yanking hard.

Smiling against her clit, he said, "Thought you didn't like getting your pussy licked."

"Just put your mouth on me already."

He chuckled and then shoved his tongue into her wet, hot hole. He growled deep as he sucked and licked at her entrance and then up to her clit. He alternated for a bit between licks, nips, and suckles. Stiffening his tongue, he thrust inside, making her pussy clench against it. Then he went at her, consuming whatever he could. Lips suckling her clit, he pressed a finger inside her core.

Fuck, but she was tight.

Sammi might have hips that told a man she was getting fucked, but her tightness told him it'd been a while. Another indication of her innocence. She wasn't as experienced as he'd thought, and this goaded him to redouble his efforts. She was so his. His plaything. His fucktoy. His, his, *his*. He added another finger and decided to leave it at that for now. Pumping into her, he twirled around her stiff little clit and she began to twitch and shudder.

Pulling back, he said, "Keep your pussy open with your fingers."

Her eyes snapped open, looking at him, dazed. "W-what?"

He withdrew his fingers and she cried out, grabbing his wrist.

"Sammi," he warned. She quickly let go.

"W-what is it? Why did you stop?" Her eyes were glazed, but she had to learn to follow his commands.

"Listen to me," he intoned. "Take your fingers and curl them around. Keep your pussy lips open for me."

A look of shock crossed her face and she stammered, "Are you serious?"

He traced the lips of her mouth and pushed his index finger inside. "Dead. Fucking. Serious."

She sucked on his finger, moaning around it, and his cock poked against his thigh. He was back to being hard. He dragged his wet finger out of her hot mouth, but she followed to keep it in. Thank fuck, he'd already come, or his willpower would've been shot. But this was necessary. She needed to understand who was boss.

"Come on, Sammi," he coaxed, "be a good girl and I'll go back to licking that sugar pussy of yours."

"Okay, okay," she whispered, and pressed her lower lips open.

Caressing her hair, he praised her fondly, "Good girl, make sure you keep them there or I'll stop until you're back in position."

She nodded frantically, eyes wide with worry and excitement. He settled back in, this time draping her legs over his shoulders, and returned his fingers and tongue to where they belonged.

Bucking against his mouth and chin, she was quickly back where *she* belonged. On the edge. Her pussy tightened around his fingers, her panting increased, and her head swung from side to side. He latched on to her clit, tugging and sucking, fingers speeding up inside her. Shuddering, her ripe ass bucked, but desperate beauty that she was, she managed to keep position.

Stanton felt the grip of her walls around his digits. Keeping up a ruthless rhythm, he smiled when she began keening his name, begging him for more. He hooked his fingers inside until he hit the right angle, and she detonated on the spot.

Grinding into his face, she rode him for broke, completely wild as she chased her climax. He kept his nimble fingers and tongue moving, feeling the echoes of her aftershocks on his mouth until she collapsed against the pillows, her chest heaving for air.

Her legs were splayed wide open.

Best of all, her fingers hadn't moved an inch.

She was magnificent.

He licked his lips, smeared with her liquid heat. One taste. One taste and he was down for the count. She was even juicier than he'd imagined, and he had a highly active imagination. At one point in his life, he'd accepted the fact that he could overdose. He just figured it'd be over cocaine, not pussy.

Of course, he couldn't get hooked on an appropriate woman like Melanie. Of course not. It had to be an adorable little biker girlie with a criminal maniac for a brother. From the same biker club as Sage's husband, who despised him.

It was official: life hated him.

11

STANTON

I t was early, long before the sun began its ascent, when Stanton finally took Sammi with his cock.

His orgasm had almost reached spiritual proportions, it was that good. After riding her until she came a second time, he pulled out and disposed of the condom. He'd be taking her bare soon, but he wanted to have another conversation first.

Returning to the bed, he gathered her into his arms. The scent of her hair beneath his chin was like a good glass of bourbon at the end of a long day.

In the burgeoning light, he gazed down on her and got a good look at two more tats. The first curved over her left rib and looked like a tattoo for her club. Must be meaningful to her. He may not know Sammi very well yet, but he was a good reader of people. It was easy as fuck to see that she was passionate about the people in her life. Her feelings ran deep. There was another tat, the name of her brother and another feminine name drawn in loopy cursive.

His fingers glided over the club tat and dropped down to follow the curly script of Puck's name.

"For a biker, you don't have many tattoos," he remarked. Hell, he had more tats than she did. Of course, his were centered on his chest and back, where they could be easily covered up by a T-shirt. Nothing above the collarbones or down the arms.

Although he always wanted tats on his biceps, he couldn't muddy his father's clean-cut image in photo ops. It was a specific request his father had made when he'd turned eighteen and started his collection. Anything that rubbed up against his father's senatorial races was more decree than request, however.

What he couldn't do on his arms or neck, he more than made up for on his torso, which was covered with ink. At first, it was out of rage at his brother's death. Later, it morphed into the simple goal of keeping people away. If that was still his intention, he was shit out of luck because this girl wouldn't bat an eye at a chest full of tats.

"For a civilian," she retorted, "your chest and back might as well belong to a biker. Why, I believe a little rebel lives inside you, Stanton."

"A little?" he snorted. "That's an understatement. The only difference is that mine are easily covered up by my chameleon outfits."

"Chameleon outfits?"

"Suits," he clarified. "Have no doubt, Sammi, a dirty addict rebel lives and breathes under the image I portray on behalf of the family."

"Family's important," Sammi replied with a light shrug, as if the sacrifices he made were par for the course. "That's why I have a tat for Puck and my mom. He almost didn't make it, you know," she said, her eyes going soft. "Becoming Puck, I mean. He was going down the wrong path before my mother died. He was partying hard and even started dealing. But after she died, he was forced to get his shit together. For me. Prospecting for the club was a game changer. They may like a good party, but the brothers don't tolerate nonsense. The name Puck was like a rebirth for him. Plus, it suits him. He's loyal, but playful and definitely mischievous."

"A little like you, no?"

Sammi's gaze fixed to a spot in front of her. She contemplated his question for a moment before replying. "A little, I guess. I do like to give Puck trouble but, on the inside, I'm a good girl."

Stanton reached down and cupped her mons. "Oh, babe, you have no idea what a good girl you are. A very good, tasty girl. Although, I've seen how naughty you can get when you put your mind to it."

Sammi gave a throaty laugh that shot straight to his balls. Shifting to relieve the pressure of his growing erection, he asked, "Have you read *A Midsummer Night's Dream*?"

"Of course. I even read up on the mythology behind his name. Puck is connected to a Norse demon, which also fits since he's part of the Demon Squad."

"You love him very much," observed Stanton.

"I may not have had a father and I may have lost my mother, but otherwise I'm blessed." Turning over onto her belly, she propped her chin onto his chest, caught his gaze, and asked, "Do you have siblings?"

"Sister. I had an older brother," he answered quietly. "But," he flipped his wrist in a brusque motion, "Jax has been gone for over a dozen years." Sometimes he couldn't believe so much time had passed because he still missed the fucker. His older brother. He'd idolized Jax. He swallowed hard and looked up at the ceiling. It was part of the reason he'd turned to drugs. For an escape, because what does one do when they've lost their better half?

"I'm sorry," she whispered. "I know how it is to lose a family member."

His gaze flicked down to lock with those light brown eyes, golden flecks running through them, reflections from the light of the lamp on the nightstand.

"That's partly why Puck and the Squad mean so much to me," she went on. "It was just the two of us those first couple years, before he decided it was safe enough to bring a fifteen-year-old girl around a clubhouse. He shouldn't have worried. The brothers took me in as one of their own."

She shrugged. "I'm everyone's little sister. Prez, our president, became a surrogate father to the both of us. This tat reminds me that you can get a second lease on life. My mother was big on forgiveness and second chances. Neither of the men she loved were able to reciprocate, but she didn't hold back or wall herself off. She kept on giving herself fully, looking for love. No matter what happened, she'd have your back. I try to live by the same creed."

"Sometimes people don't deserve a second chance," Stanton replied with finality.

"You can't believe that," she challenged.

"I can and I do," he responded gravely. "Thoroughly."

He was talking of himself, of course.

"People deserve more than to be judged by their mistakes. They're so much more than that."

"Not all the time. Sometimes their mistakes reflect exactly who they are," he countered. *Like me, with Jax's death.*

Sammi's eyebrows pulled close and low. "No one is so broken that they can't be fixed."

"My sponsor says something similar." The hair on his nape stiffened. Stanton's hand clapped the back of his neck and rubbed it. Talk of redemption, or in his case, the lack thereof, was like prodding a gashed wound with a hot poker. "Some people don't deserve forgiveness. Not every broken human can be put back together again."

Tipping her head to the side, Sammi watched him carefully and Stanton grew warm under her scrutiny. "Is it because you're a prosecutor? You believe in the system of justice and incarceration."

"I certainly believe in justice. Not so much our system of incarceration, but until we have better, I work with what I have. No, I was talking about my personal belief about human nature. We have free will and we make conscious choices. Choices that can lead to harm." His voice dropped an octave. "Choices that can lead to death."

He swallowed around his constricted throat. "Those need to be taken with the utmost seriousness."

Sammi reached out and gently laid a hand on his cheek. "People need love. If we open our hearts and give people the love they crave, then they will change. In forgiveness and understanding, people can be healed. They can turn their lives around. Live meaningful lives. Lives that bring joy to others. People deserve a second chance."

Again with this second chance nonsense. If she knew who he was in his core, she wouldn't be so quick to talk that. Then again, it fit with who she was, with the innocence that called to him. But it was a Pollyanna worldview. He knew better. He knew some people did *not* deserve forgiveness. He was one of them. His sin had been forged in crushed metal, exploding airbags, and his brother's blood.

He squeezed his eyes tightly shut against the images that assaulted him.

So, so much blood.

His flaws were embedded so deeply that nothing could extricate them from his soul. They were bonded to him like metal because his brother shouldn't have been in the driver's seat when they'd been mowed down by a drunk driver.

Stanton wasn't about to get into a philosophical discussion with Sammi, no matter how much her words plucked at his heartstrings. It was false hope. He had to remember that. Sammi was like a precious little porcelain doll that one kept protected in a glass cupboard. The brothers had miraculously shielded her from the filth of life and preserved a pure soul. It was a marvel, her purity. Not only had her goodness survived, but it had been nurtured. An incredible feat, really. Coming from a supposedly privileged world, he had an exhaustive grasp of the pain and agony, the simple badness underlying the girdle of life.

A pit in his stomach yawned open. This girl needed his help. His protection. He felt compelled to preserve the goodness within her. Not for himself. He was beyond saving. Beauty such as hers was rare indeed. It was meant to be safeguarded and coddled for its own sake. At all costs.

If it wasn't for that urge to save her, and the fact that he was too desperate to turn down the chance of forgetting himself in her body, he'd have run for the fucking hills without a backward glance. He had the tendency to ruin anything good and pure, like Jax. Always striving to do the right thing, but never quite managing to pull it off. Sure, he wasn't sniffing an eight ball of lines off Sammi's ass cheeks after he was done fucking her. But by no means did that suggest he was *healed*. Christ, brooding tired him out.

Sensing his mood, she shoved him down on the tousled bedsheets and crawled over him. Swinging her hair to one side, she planted her palms on either side of him and licked down the midline of his chest. His eyes were glued to her tongue, the feel of the soft rasp on his skin like the best extravagance.

"I sense you straying. Maybe this will bring you back to me."

"Oh, I'm back, baby."

Rocking from side to side, she let her full breasts sway, mesmerizing him like a pendulum. She smirked. "Thought this might get your attention."

She sat on his abdomen, spreading her wet pussy on his skin, and stretched her arms to lift her thick hair above her. Fuck, she looked like Aphrodite, coming out of the sea, glorying in her sexy nudity. He cupped her tits and lifted to take a dusky, fat bud into his mouth until her writhing pulled him off her nipple.

"You can punish me for letting my attention stray. That was a goddamn crime I committed."

"Oh, I intend to prosecute you to the fullest extent of the law. *My* law."

"Do your worst," he replied in a low growl, "as long as you lick it all better afterward."

And so she did. Tortured him until he came into her mouth and then cleaned him off with one thorough licking.

12

SAMMI

S ammi finished up with her client and strode down the street toward her favorite French café to join Abby for lunch.

She clocked a new prospect leaning against a lamppost outside the café. Huh, that was a bit strange. Then again, Loki was a fanatic when it came to Abby's safety.

Peeking through the large bay window of the restaurant, she caught sight of her best friend's bright blonde hair. Physically, they were quite different, yet they'd shared an unbreakable bond in having lost their mothers as teens, having overbearing brothers, a love for bad eighties music, and being obsessed with all things *Sex and the City*.

The hostess led Sammi to Abby's table. She plopped down on the black-and-white wicker chair. Groaning with relief, she eased off one of her Jimmy Choo heels. They were fantastic, but one of her feet was slightly larger than the other and it pinched her pinky toe like a mother.

"Hey, girl," Abby gushed, grabbing Sammi's shoulder and leaning over the short distance to give her a hug.

"Hey, bitch," she replied fondly, returning her embrace.

She took off her plaid coat, looped her Givenchy leather tote bag—the one she only used for client appointments—over the back of the chair, and settled in. "How are you doing?"

"Great!" Abby shone like a sunflower. Truly. Her blond curls bobbed at her chin and her golden eyes were bright and lively. Probably the pregnancy hormones.

Abby pushed a glass of chilled white wine her way. "Since I can't drink right now, I thought I'd live vicariously through you. If you're too tipsy to drive, I'll take you wherever you have to go, and Loki will pick up your car."

Sammi threw her head back and laughed. Abby always knew how to make her day

"Anything for you, babe." Taking a sip of the cool, crisp beverage, she hummed. "Very nice. Chardonnay."

Abby shrugged nonchalantly, but her face lit up with pleasure.

"So, how's the father-to-be doing? Still driving you crazy with his overprotectiveness?"

Abby looked down and played with the napkin on her lap. "Things are good. You know, I'm tolerating it since he's being particularly useful at this time."

"Okay, speak English, woman. That was way too mysterious for the likes of me."

"Well, you may not know this, but it seems that some women get very needy when they're pregnant."

A frown formed between Sammi's brows. No, she didn't know this. For the first time, Abby was experiencing something different. Not that she wasn't thrilled for Abby because, of course, she was. Abby had been attacked by a club enemy and suffered a miscarriage. She barely wanted to admit it to herself, but ... well ... between her and Sage's pregnancies, she was feeling a little left out.

Abby grabbed the menu, snapped it open, and inclined

her head to the side, huffing, "Sex, Sammi. I need lots and lots of sex. The only thing that takes the nausea away in the morning is an orgasm. Hopefully, this will pass after the first trimester, but I'm feeling particularly benevolent toward Loki and his shenanigans." She leaned over and confessed, "Because he's satisfying me, oh, so very well."

"Pfft. It's not exactly a hardship for him. You don't need to give him special favors for doing what he'd do naturally."

"I don't know … it's been way more, lately. I mean, we were pretty active before, but now, it's like I can't keep my hands off him. I have no control whatsoever, and I'm feeling a little guilty about it. He works crazy hours and then I keep him up half the night."

Sammi lifted her gaze from the menu. "Only you would see it as a problem. That man adores you. He worships the ground you walk on, and if you told him to kneel, and keep his tongue on your clit all day, he'd do it without a second's thought."

"But he's working so hard at the Box. It's busier than ever. He's organizing MMA competitions throughout the entire month. By the time he gets home, he's exhausted and then he has to take care of me."

"Abby, he's a former Army Ranger, Special Ops, whatever. He's been trained to endure difficult circumstances, and I can assure you, there is no way he thinks of this as anything other than a godsend."

"If you say so …," she trailed off.

"Oh, trust me on this one. Go at him as hard as you can. And tell him I said so. He'll feel he owes me a marker and I'd love to have one over on him." Taking another sip of her wine, Sammi asked, "Any wedding bells soon?"

Abby waved her hand dismissively. "There's no need to rush."

Sammi dropped her menu, mouth gaping. "I beg to differ. Loki will lose his shit if he's not named father on the birth certificate."

"He can be named the father without us being married," Abby replied airily. "Either way, the baby will have his last name. I'm never giving mine up, married or not. My parents were never married. Love and commitment don't require a piece of paper from a Justice of the Peace. Why is that, you ask? Because love is love." She pressed her hands together and gave Sammi a dreamy sigh.

"You want to crush his spirit? Okay, I can get behind that agenda," supplied Sammi. "I'm always down with torturing a brother when the opportunity presents itself."

Abby frowned at her. "That's not what this is about. My parents had a beautiful partnership, full of love and *unmarried*. Sure, as a kid, I lied and told everyone they were married because people are judgmental, but I fundamentally agree with their philosophy."

"Do you even know who Loki is?" asked Sammi, dryly. "Like, do you know who your man is? He's a possessive asshole is what he is. Not a hippie." She shrugged and picked up her menu. "Just sayin'."

Abby's laughter rang out, making Sammi grin. "It'll be fine. We'll get around to it eventually. There's no need to rush."

"Hmm. If you say so. And what's up with your guard dog outside?" she asked, tilting her chin toward the bay window and the prospect outside.

"Oh, Loki's paranoid. Ever since Puck beat up Kerri's ex, he's had someone on me. You know, with what happened last time I was pregnant, he's taking every precaution. I'm allowing it because he's so busy at the Box, and I don't want to stress him out by fighting him on it. Like I said, I'm feeling especially benevolent lately."

The waitress stopped by and they gave her their orders. Sammi ordered a *salade niçoise* and Abby chose the special of the day, a *sole meunière*. Talking to the waitress, Abby confided, "This is only because I need to eat, but what I'm really waiting for are the desserts." The waitress laughed and gave them a preview of the desserts.

Handing off her menu, Abby eyed Sammi with a playful tilt to her lips. "So, how are things going with you? Your date went well earlier this week, and I'm so proud of you, stepping outside your comfort zone."

She flicked her index finger up. "One, he's not someone you know."

She flicked up a second finger. "He's not a biker."

A third finger. "And Puck hasn't vetted him. I'm duly impressed."

Just the mention of Stanton brought her back to what it felt like to be surrounded by him in bed. Her head pillowed against his bicep. His arm over her waist, cupping her breast cupped in the palm of his hand. His spicy scent wrapping her in a cocoon of languid arousal.

She snapped out of her daydream and focused on her friend, who was looking at her with expectation.

"Yeah," she breathed out. Anxiety ricocheted in her chest. Abby was her best friend, and if she couldn't confide the truth to her, then she shouldn't be doing what she was doing. "It's a bit more complicated than that. You know me ... when I do something, I go all out."

Abby's eyebrows raised up and took a prim sip of her ice water.

"He's the prosecutor in Puck's case. He sought me out after the trial and asked me out."

"Oh, wow."

"It gets worse." Her gaze strayed to the window and then

back to Abby. She took in a huge gulp of air and blurted out, "It's Stanton. Sage's ex-fiancé." There. She'd said it.

Abby's eyebrows hit her hairline and her mouth hung open. "Holy shit."

"Bad, huh?"

Abby joggled her head a little, as if to get her vision back. "No, no. It's just the shock of hearing it. I'm processing." After a moment, she continued, "Okay, so the sex was unbelievable, but are you seeing him again?"

"Yup. He's busy with cases because he'd been away for a while so we agreed on Friday evening."

Abby gave her a sly look. "What's going on between the two of you?"

It was Sammi's turn to be taken by surprise. "Sex, obviously."

Abby slapped the palms of her hands on the surface of the table in exasperation. "Besides sex."

"Besides having the best sex of my life?" Her eyes glazed over for a second as she recalled his head between her legs, piercing blue eyes riveted on her. Goosebumps broke out on her arms despite wearing a suede-trimmed cashmere turtleneck. God, she couldn't wait to have him and his talented tongue there again.

Shaking her head to dispel the image, she said, "My plan is to influence him to go easy on Puck. There's no way Puck can avoid jail time after running his mouth, but maybe Stanton won't go full Rambo on him. I mean, I'm not sure if it's even possible. Sage already warned me that the judge is a hard-ass when it comes to bikers, but I'll try my best. I wish I could strategize with Sage on how to sway him..." she pondered aloud. Looking up at Abby, she asked, "What? Why are you giving me that look like someone ran over your dog?"

"The first time you talk about a man in a special way—"

"What *special* way?" she cut in.

"This guy is the first man you've ever gotten excited about. You just sighed when you talked about how good sex was with him. When we talked earlier this week, you seemed to genuinely like him. He's obviously smart and attentive. You texted me from the car he ordered *to pick you up in*. He wants to flaunt you on his arm and throw gifts at your feet. I thought he was a gentleman, although now that you tell me it's Stanton," Abby's pert nose crinkled in distaste, "I might have to rethink this."

"He's changed," Sammi explained. "He got out of difficult situation and he's turning his life around."

Abby threw her hand out. "See! That's my point. You finally find a guy who might be worthy of you and all you want is sex and to use him to free Puck."

"What's wrong with that? Those are two very sensible reasons."

"Yes. But they shouldn't be the *only* reasons."

Sammi fell back into her chair as if she'd been smacked. She wasn't Abby, who'd fantasized about having a man and a boatload of kids since she was super young. Maybe it was the way their respective mothers died, when they were both thirteen years old. Abby had years to spend with her mother teaching her about life as she battled cancer. Abby had a doting father and twin older brothers. Not that Sammi was suggesting Abby had it easy. It was only that Sammi's mom died in a sudden hit-and-run accident. She only had Puck. Which she was forever grateful for, but she'd grieved alone since Puck was busy busting his ass to support them and prospecting with the Squad. Her tiny, sad world only expanded once Puck brought her to the clubhouse, and she'd always feared even her adopted family might be taken away. Why tempt fate by demanding too much from life?

"Don't you deserve love? Abby prodded gently. "A relation-ship with a fine-looking, grown-ass man who can take care of you and treat you like the queen you are?"

"Of course, but those things don't happen in real life."

"It happened to me. It happened to Sage and Greta."

"You guys are special. And lucky. I'm neither of those things."

Abby cast her head to the side, a pucker marring the smooth skin between her brows. "Why not?"

"For one thing, most men are dogs. Look at the brothers. Look at Puck."

"Look at Kingdom, Cutter, and Loki," Abby countered. "I mean, Loki had abstained from sex for years, but Kingdom? And *Cutter*? If Cutter wasn't the man-whore poster boy, then I don't know who was."

"Well, I'm sure despite his gentlemanly façade, Stanton's a dog just like the rest of them."

"He's turning his life around. Either he is or he isn't. Which is it?"

"Okay, fine, he's working on himself at the moment."

"Good, so he's a dog in recovery. What's your next argument?"

"Love isn't in the cards for me."

"What?!" Abby exclaimed. "That's the most ridiculous thing I've ever heard. You're one of the most beautiful, loving women I know and, mind you, I work with a stellar group of women. You're a creative and you work your ass off. You're loyal, strong, and giving. There are no downsides to you, Sammi. You're the total package."

Sammi reached out and grabbed Abby's hand, swallowing around the lump in her throat. "Thank you, and I love you back just as hard. But I'm focused on building a career, not a relationship. I'm all about living my best life and not turning away opportunities that fall in my lap, but I'm not ready to settle down. To do that, I'd have to find the love of my life, and as hot as Stanton is, he's not the type of guy to let your guard down around. He'd crush my heart. Some men crush, some men build. He's a crusher. No doubt about it. Anyway, I don't know if I'm built for any long-term things." Her heart twisted on that last point.

Abby's face filled with horror. "Why would you ever say that?" she whispered.

Sammi glanced away from her friend, who was staring at her with unabashed shock.

"I've had three parents in my life, Abby. Where are they now? I'm only twenty-one and Puck has been the only blood relative in my life since I was thirteen years old. My father left soon after I was born. Puck's father came back to my mom when I was three, but he didn't last long. My mom died. And look at Puck. He's been my rock, but he has the attention span of a flea. Even now, he's fucked up and abandoned me. If my family can't make it, how can a complete stranger be trusted?"

"Oh, Sammi, don't do this. You're talking as if you're cursed or something. Terrible things happened to you. They didn't happen *because* of you."

"Even if you're right, love is too risky. I can't put my heart out there to get stomped on. I'll have sex with Stanton. I'll allow him to woo me because he's clearly good at it and it's the kind of thing he likes to do, but he doesn't want anything more than sex." *Even if, in my heart of hearts, I can imagine it.* "We're on the same page. He's no more interested in a relationship than I am."

Abby stamped her foot. "I don't believe you. Tell me you're scared all you want but you can't convince me that man doesn't *want* you, in every meaning of the word."

The back of her eyes and nose were starting to burn up.

"Oh, Abby, you're just ... you see what you want to see because you love me."

"Bullshit," she replied, vehemently. "I see reality. I'm not blind. Mark my words, Sammi, that man *will* fall in love with you."

"You haven't even met him."

Abby smacked the marble tabletop, tears sprouting from her eyes. "I've met *you*. I know *you*."

Sammi swallowed hard. "You don't easily stay in your lane, you know that, right?"

A wide grin spread over Abby's lips even through the tears. "Yeah, I know, but you love me anyway, even with these pregnancy hormones kicking my butt." She fluttered her fingers at Sammi. "Go do your thing. Fuck your brains out. Get spoiled by a rich man. But I've got one last thing to say to you. If he falls for you, don't shut yourself off."

Her smile dropped and her eyes turned serious. "You deserve love and happiness, hearts, roses, and chocolate truffles. The whole nine yards. The big kaboodle. You deserve it all, and I will fight you for it till the bitter end."

"Damn, bitch, you're making me tear up. That is wrong, on so many levels." Sammi's eyes darted left and right. "If anyone films this, it'll go viral as a meme: Teary-Eyed Biker Bitch. My reputation will be wrecked. Wrecked, I tell you."

Abby chuckled, wiping her tears with the back of her hand. "Relax, your reputation is safe with me. Now, drink up. I already ordered another drink and we have got to work on Sage's baby shower. If we don't get cracking, she'll go into labor before we get the show on the road, and *that* would be a tragedy."

"For sure," confirmed Sammi, taking a big gulp of wine, the crisp tanginess in her mouth cooling the upheaval in her chest. "I've scoured the internet for ideas, and I've already chosen ten activities for the shower. Ordered party favors and decorations. I may have gone a tad overboard."

She rummaged through her tote, dragged out a plastic bag, and shook the contents out onto the table. Heart-shaped measuring spoons, yellow bath poofs in the shape of baby rattles, mini champagne bottles, soaps, hair ties, bottle openers, and ribbons tumbled out.

Abby's eyes lit up as she poked at the array of favors, picking up a rattle and waving it in the air. "There's no such thing as overboard. Plus, we've got to knock this one out of the park. Set the bar high so when my baby shower comes around, it's lit."

Sammi rolled her eyes. "I should have known this was about you," she teased.

"What? Like you're not going to have one in the future? I'm doing this for all the bitches out there that are going to carry at some point in their lives." She shook a poof rattle at Sammi. "That includes you."

"Are you trying to scare me off?"

"You talk about not wanting a man, but the signals you give off tell me you're ready for more than just a solid relationship in your life."

"Puh-lease, girl," Sammi scoffed, "that's ridiculous. I'm in the mood to celebrate, that's all. I already explained to you Stanton isn't a keeper."

"Doesn't seeing me and Sage make you want one too? Just an itsy teensy bit?"

Damn, that bitch is perceptive.

"*Abbyyy*," Sammi warned, "don't make this more than it is."

Her eyes widened and she blinked up at Sammi innocently. "What?"

"You're doing it again. Making stuff up."

"Okay, okay," Abby replied but pointed her index finger at Sammi. "I'll back off but mark my words. Whatever's going on between you and that hot prosecutor billionaire is going to explode."

Sammi threw a champagne baby bottle at Abby and said, "Oh, hush. Now let's get back to planning that shower before Sage goes into labor."

13

STANTON

Stanton bent down and kissed his mother's cheek, covered in foundation, before moving on to Amy, seated around their regular table at their country club in Hyde Park.

"You look fantastic," Amy murmured as she buried her face in his shoulder for a fierce hug. "I missed you terribly, you know."

"I know, sweetheart. I missed you, too."

Amy was one of the few unadulterated joys of his life. A talented fashion designer who lived in New York City, she opened a store in Poughkeepsie and came up on a regular basis. He'd had a hard and protracted battle with his father to procure her the freedom to follow her dream instead of going into politics or pursuing an academic legal career. Public service or academia were the only appropriate choices. Their family was filthy rich, but working on Wall Street was considered gauche. That's what financial advisers were for, their father always said.

It had been worth every minute of the drag-down argument to be able to watch Amy flit around her store, rearranging clothes. Of course, Benjamin Edward Prescott III only allowed it because she was the baby of the family. That fact alone wouldn't have saved her if Stanton hadn't fallen in line after Jax's death.

Now that Stanton was a disgrace, he guessed that Benjamin regretted his decision, but it was too late to force Amy out of her career. She was *that* much in demand.

Turning to his father, he reached out for a handshake.

"Good to see you, son," his father said, although he made no effort to get to his feet. Simply a twist of his torso to accept his only surviving son's hand. His father's silver hair was combed back in the same classic style he'd worn Stanton's entire life, along with a navy blazer over a crewneck and a pair of dress slacks. The Yale signet ring winked at Stanton from his father's little finger.

Before showing up, Stanton had gone through the internet and newspapers with a fine-tooth comb. There were no photos of him and Sammi, but he was mentally prepared for an attack of some kind. Perhaps his father would go easy on him because of his recent release from rehab. *Doubtful. Old habits die hard.*

Taking his seat, Stanton shook out the pristine white cloth napkin and placed it over his lap. Having done this since the age of ten, basically as soon as his mother had deemed Amy old enough to sit through an entire meal, Stanton knew the menu by heart.

After ordering with Fred, the same server they'd had for years, Stanton settled in for the long haul. Without a drink to wrap his fingers around as a talisman, he fidgeted them on his knee.

"How's the office since you've been back after your little ... hiatus?" began his father, intense blue eyes turning on him.

"Busy, but I'm managing," he answered tersely.

"Any cases I should be aware of?"

His father always asked about any cutting-edge litigation or potential scandal. Studying the patriarch of his family, Stanton wondered, not for the first time, how he could simultaneously love and hate the man. He knew the feeling was mutual. After all, he was responsible for Jax's death.

"None that I can think of," replied Stanton.

Jax, the son of his father's heart. The golden boy valedictorian and star athlete, who was on his way to Yale with dreams of one day running for president. Jax, whom he never once felt jealous or resentful of because his perfection allowed Stanton, the second son, to do whatever the hell he liked.

Which had worked out fine for everyone until the night Stanton had sneaked off to a party where there was underage drinking. Too drunk to drive, he'd called Jax to pick him up. One of the boys from the same party ended up ramming into their car, going ninety miles per hour. Waking from a coma, Stanton was confronted with his father's tear-stained face and the knowledge that his favorite son was gone. Been struggling to make up for it ever since.

Like his tats, he'd managed to cover up his transgressions until his coke use spiraled out of control. A few fuckups had slipped out of his grasp before that, like cheating on Sage and having to call off the wedding *after* his mother had sent out the wedding invitations. Thank fuck there hadn't been a repeat of that particular *faux pas* when he broke it off with Melanie. Desperate for at least one of her children to settle down, each failed chance at marriage hurt his mother.

Amy shot him a concerned look. Preoccupied, he must have missed his father's question. "Would you please repeat your question, sir?"

"If you'd been listening to me instead of daydreaming, I wouldn't have to repeat myself," his father grumbled.

"I apologize, sir."

Damn, but the man put his teeth on edge.

"The Chamber of Commerce is having their annual black-tie gala in three weeks."

"I'll be there," he responded promptly.

"Good," his father replied. "George and the family will be there, as well."

Stanton stiffened.

Melanie.

"Perhaps you'll have a chance to resolve your little spat. George told me how concerned she's been about you and pressed for details about your ... condition."

You mean addiction, don't you, sir?

He shot a look at his mother, who was inspecting the napkin on her lap intently. So, she wasn't coming to his aid in this attack. He could hear her words in his head: *You're past thirty years old. It's time to settle down and have kids. Melanie's a splendid woman, and I know she'll stop working at that silly law firm to raise your children.*

He sighed. His mother was completely sane until it came to the topic of offspring. She lived with the fear that neither Stanton nor Amy would have any. She wasn't too far from the truth, because Stanton was adamantly against breeding the darkness he saw in himself and his father into a future generation.

Time to settle this, once and for all.

"If you're suggesting that Melanie and I reconcile, that will not happen, sir," he stated rigidly.

There was no way in hell that he was going down that rabbit hole again. It wasn't only the image of a certain shapely little sexpot that stopped him. His relationship with Melanie had been forged in lies. Everything about their relationship was tainted. There was also the little matter that he didn't love her.

"You were so close to getting married. Although, thank God your mother hadn't printed the wedding invitations before your unfortunate incident."

Stanton's back molars ground together and only narrowly managed to bite down the exasperated sigh that was about to escape.

"My point exactly. I won't marry Melanie. Or anyone, for that matter," he replied, impressed by his calm tone, considering the roar in his ears. A week out of rehab and his father was butting into his life again.

"Not ever," he muttered under his breath.

He wasn't cut out for what constituted a relationship in his father's eyes. A relationship meant marriage. Nothing less. Like so many of his father's expectations, they didn't fit him. Was there any wonder he didn't want kids? The waiter and a busboy came around with their plates of food, pausing the conversation.

He didn't give a shit if George was his father's oldest friend or that he'd grown up with Melanie. One thing they had in common was their mutual love for Jax. She'd crushed on Jax since she was a girl. It took Stanton a long time to believe her when she swore her affections had transferred to him.

And he'd been disappointed by it. Even so, their relationship was doomed, having started as an affair while he was engaged to Sage. Things went downhill after Sage left him, and fixated on drugs, he stupidly fell into a relationship with Melanie. Despite knowing that he didn't reciprocate her feelings, she insisted on trying to build a relationship with him. From there, he'd spiraled further into drugs.

Amy and his mother found him sprawled on the bathroom

floor unconscious. And that was how he found himself being transported to Tully Rehab Center.

On the ride there, he somehow found the courage to call Melanie. Once he got to Tully, he'd be incommunicado for thirty days. He grabbed onto the token excuse to end the charade with her. Everything was going to shit, but it gave him a get-out-of-jail card and he used it without hesitation. A clean slate. When he walked back out into the world, he'd walk out clean. No drugs. No fiancée.

"She misses you, Stanton. The least you can do is stop by her apartment and see her," counseled his father.

"I will certainly visit her to apologize for my behavior and for how things turned out between us but let me be crystal clear on this one point, sir, we will *never* be together again," he intoned fiercely.

Cupping the vase in the center of the table, Amy interrupted, "My, isn't this bouquet of flowers ravishing?"

Her eyes darted from him to his father.

Stanton stifled another sigh. He hated it when his sister got anxious and felt she had to fix their broken relationship.

His father stopped eating and laid his silverware fastidiously on the porcelain plate. "You insist on being stubborn and breaking her heart."

Between gritted teeth, Stanton snapped, "Breaking her heart? I'm no longer sure she has one. But no, I'd end up hurting her more if I married her. I'm saving her from future heartache. Although, it's refreshing to see what little consideration you have for my own happiness."

His father's left eye squinted. A sign of his growing rage.

"There's happiness and then there's duty. You must get married. To the right woman. Melanie is that woman," he concluded with a tone of finality.

"Love is the foundation of a happy marriage. I. Don't. Love.

Her. There's no glory in fulfilling my duty only to guarantee her misery and having us divorce within the year."

"You're being purposely provocative—"

"Enough," came a soft murmur.

His mother. Fucking finally. His fury and Amy's distress couldn't stop his father, but one word from his mother would.

"We can revisit this conversation in the privacy of our home," she pronounced in a cool tone.

That was the end of it. Until the next round.

Jaws clenched tight, his father picked up his utensils with deliberate precision and methodically cut into his poached halibut.

Stanton had been a fool to think anything would change, even after a stint at rehab. His father's expectations hadn't softened one bit. At Tully, he learned that honesty and sobriety were linked, and he refused to veer off the new path he'd set for himself.

His father's wishes be damned.

Stanton was used to being a disappointment, but at least he'd attempt to stop being a disappointment to himself.

※※※

"YOU LOOK PLEASED WITH YOURSELF. What did you do?" Cornell asked Stanton suspiciously, twirling a spoon of sugar in his cappuccino. They'd met up at a coffeeshop after work instead of the bars they used to frequent.

"Huh?"

·   ·   ·

STANTON DECIDED TO PLAY DUMB, although he doubted he'd get away with much. His friend wasn't one of the best trial attorneys on the East Coast for no good reason.

Cornell's spoon halted mid-turn. "Don't deflect. I know you inside out or have you forgotten?"

Goddammit. Shrugging like it was no big deal, he mentioned, "I got me some."

"Ah, that explains the idiotic expression on your face."

Cornell raised and extended his hands to the ceiling like in prayer. "Hallelujah."

Then he pointed at Stanton. "Told you sex would help. Sex always helps."

"Yeah, yeah. You know everything, Captain Obvious."

"We may have both graduated summa cum laude, but we both know who's the brighter one between us," Cornell gloated.

"Hah!"

Taking a careful sip of his hot drink, Cornell asked, "So who's the lucky lady?"

"You don't know her. Met her outside the courtroom. I'd just finished prosecuting her brother, as a matter of fact, but obstacles like those are only make the victory taste sweeter. And oh, is she sweet."

"Impressive," Cornell replied dryly.

"It was an all-nighter and I'm nowhere near done with her," he finished, with a contented sigh.

Stanton couldn't wait for a repeat. He was swamped with work, and after a long, hectic week, he couldn't wait to see her in the evening.

"There are a few issues. Well, there would be if this were going to be anything more than sex. Which it's not. She's close friends with Sage and part of the motorcycle club that Sage is affiliated with."

Cornell barked out a laugh. "Only you, my friend, would end up in a situation like this."

Stanton was shaking his head. "She's worth the potential hassle. Believe me, I wouldn't have gone for her if she weren't beyond fucking sexy. I repeat, beyond sexy. She's incredible."

Cornell's eyebrows raised up his forehead. "You sure this is just sex? You barely remember, much less discuss, your random hookups. And I have yet to hear you heap that kind of praise on a woman before today. Sage was smart, hard-working, and loyal, but you never spoke of her in those words."

"Of course I'm sure. This isn't a mere hookup. We have an agreement."

He frowned. Was he sure? Yes, yes he was. He'd had the same internal dialogue since late Saturday afternoon, after he dropped her off at her house. Like a broken record, he reiterated to himself that it was just sex. It had to be.

"First of all, I'm in no position to be in a relationship. Besides the catch-up I have to do with work, I have Narcotics Anonymous meetings to attend and other tools that my sponsor makes me use. I have to call him every day and make three calls to other recovering addicts. I have daily writing exercises. Recovery's like a part-time job, bro. I'm drowning in shit to do. I think the point of recovery is to keep me so busy, I can't pick up coke, even if I wanted to."

"Yeah, and the most ironic part is that, after two failed engagements, you're in a better position than ever to have an authentic relationship. One built on a bedrock of honesty," noted Cornell.

"Even if I were in the position to be in a relationship, it wouldn't work," he replied. "For one thing, Sage would kill me. While her fury wouldn't bother me much, it might stop Sammi. And Sammi's young." His brows drew together.

"Although, the truth is that she's mature for her age. She

has her shit together. Much more so than the socialites I knew at her age."

"There you go," said Cornell.

"But there's the issue of the Demon Squad and her brother. Her brother will hate me on principle. And a biker club? That would be the straw that broke the camel's back with respect to my father. I'd be disowned, and there would be nothing my mother or sister could do to redeem me. I'm already skating on thin ice, as it is."

"You've always been skating on thin ice," Cornell threw in, taking another careful sip of his drink.

"Hell, I'm surprised I haven't drowned in the lake of daddy disappointment."

"Seriously, though, you underestimate your father."

Stanton's spine slammed against the back of the wooden chair. They'd had this delusional discussion before.

Throwing up his hands, he burst out, "Christ, just because he's nice to you doesn't mean he's tolerant of me or my choices. After all these years, how do you not see that?"

"He loves you," Cornell stated simply.

Stanton put out his hand, palm face out. "Stop it. You defending him is pissing me off."

Cornell pressed his lips closed. "The wack-ass shit between you two has got to get sorted out, and you know it."

"You're spouting bullshit. This past Sunday, he told me he wanted me to get back together with Melanie," Stanton scoffed.

"Okay, that's ridiculous, but putting Melanie aside, you demonize the man—"

"Stop. Just stop right there," he cut off his closest friend with a low growl.

It was beyond the pale. He took in a long breath. Cornell hadn't been around when Jax was killed. He hadn't witnessed his father's descent into drunken hell. Putting his mother and Amy through a living nightmare.

While his father may have stopped drinking after his mother packed the car with Amy and threatened to leave him, the man never bothered to go deep and fix himself. He'd simply controlled his intake of alcohol. Didn't stop him from raging, especially that last year he lived at home. The year of broken-ass grief.

He swore he'd never have the children and risk repeating the shit he'd gone through. Drawing in a long inhale, he exhaled it slowly to regain his temper. No, he wasn't going there. Not today. Thankfully, he was meeting Sammi later and he could fuck his anger and frustration out with her.

Time to change subjects.

"So, how's your latest case going?" he asked.

Cornell gave him a look indicating that he knew exactly what Stanton was doing. So what if he was deflecting? If nothing else, he was being utterly transparent.

"Alright, I'll play your game, but I'm warning you, we'll be returning to this conversation. It's that important." He leaned over the table and caught Stanton's eyes. "You know why, Stanton? Because I'm going to help you get over this, whether you like it or not. It's part of why you turned to drugs and have no doubt that I'll do whatever it takes to keep you off that poison."

Stanton's eyes dropped to his coffee. "I don't deserve you."

"Of course you do. Just because you can't be my bitch doesn't mean you get to throw your life away."

Stanton laughed deep from his belly. "Yeah, okay. Go on, tell me about your case."

STANTON

G od*damn*, she was gorgeous.

Stanton stood up as Sammi sashayed her fine hips through the restaurant door. She'd agreed to meet him for dinner at his favorite brasserie on the Waterfront. Better yet, she didn't fight him on sending a car for her.

This time she was dressed in a strapless red cocktail dress with a plunging sweetheart neckline. He got something pretty and sparkly to put around her neck, to hang just below her tat. During one of his rare lunch breaks, he found an Art Deco necklace, dotted with garnets and diamonds, in a jewelry store by the courthouse.

"Hey, gorgeous," he murmured in greeting as he bent down to kiss her cheek. That was another thing about Sammi. Her skin was so soft. Christ, he was sounding like an idiot.

Dozens of fairy lights of different sizes dropped from the ceiling, illuminating her glowing skin.

He pulled out the pale-blush velour-covered chair for her, which gave him an unintended glance down her neckline. He bit back a groan when he caught sight of her tits, nestled in a red bra matching her dress.

"It's a crime to wear lipstick like that," Stanton observed as he sat down.

"Is it? Hmm," she replied, daintily laying her napkin over her lap.

She canted her head to the side as if considering his suggestion. "I'll have to keep that in mind."

"Every man in here sees that hot red lipstick and thinks of one thing and one thing only."

"I'm not interested in the other men."

Placing her palms on the two-tone wooden table, she leaned forward over her plate and said, "I only want to know what you think."

Oh, fuck, and that did it. Now he was hard in public.

The waiter popped out of nowhere, startling him out of his obsessive focus on Sammi. He quickly ordered a bottle of champagne, wanting to watch Sammi's lips sipping delicately from a champagne glass. Yeah, he was clearly an animal when it came to her. Fucking sue him. He'd gone an entire week without touching this woman.

Once the waiter left, Stanton toyed with the knife at his side and said, "Your lips wrapped around my cock. That's what I see."

"Do you see that happening here? Because that can be arranged."

Closing his eyes briefly, he let out a groan. "No quickie for you in the restaurant bathroom, naughty girl. I'm going to treat you to a nice, long dinner while I tease you with all the things I'm going to do to you. Then I'm going to take you home and fulfill every single fantasy, both yours and mine. Once I finally get my tongue on you, I'm taking my sweet time."

Across the copper tea-light holders on the table, he enjoyed the pink tinge that raced over her face and chest. *Nice.*

"For dessert, I'm thinking ... you spread out on my bed,

braced on your hands and knees, while I take you from behind, nice and deep. But, till then, let's keep it civilized, shall we?"

Fanning herself rapidly, she cocked a brow and asked with deceptive sweetness, "You do civilized?"

He smirked. "Most people see me as such."

"Oh, but I know the truth and the truth is there's a savage beneath that expensive Italian wool suit with what? 180 super count? I mean, who even wears a suit to a date nowadays? But as hard as you try, you'll ever be fully redeemed," she replied. "And that's the way I like you best."

He smirked. "Is that right?"

Sammi shrugged a shoulder. "People don't notice much of anything beyond themselves. I guess, doing what I do, part of my job is to observe people. Their likes and dislikes. So much is left unspoken."

"Tell me more about what you do," he prodded. She had become animated as she talked; her eyes had lit up and she'd gestured with her hands as she spoke.

"I help women curate themselves in a way that makes them feel sexy and comfortable to act upon their desires."

"I'm not sure what that entails. Spell it out for me."

"In man-speak, I style women to dress in ways that make them feel feminine and sexy. Whether it's part of seducing someone or simply prepping them for a sexual encounter. I help them dress for dates, parties, clubs, hookups—any event where a woman wants to showcase her sensuality. I style them from head to toe, and from the outside in. That includes lingerie, in case you're wondering. I also help them choose toys if that's what they're into. Set up their apartments, hotel rooms, or what have you."

"I had no idea," he replied.

"My clients aren't only recent divorcées or housewives who

want to spice up their marriage. I have a client with third-degree burns and scars from a terrible car accident. A few breast cancer survivors who've gone through double mastectomies. There are a variety of things that can undermine a woman's confidence."

"Most of the women I've been with have been confident. I can't imagine them needing to seek help."

"You'd be surprised. Many people fly by the seat of their pants when it comes to meeting men. They follow their instincts, or simply get drunk and hook up. But there's a certain type of woman, usually one with a disposable income, who seek my services."

A popping sound came from his left. Stanton glanced over to find the waiter pouring Dom Perignon in their flutes.

He raised his glass, clinked it against hers, and said, "*Salut.*"

Stanton put the champagne down, picked up his glass of water, and took a sip. Then he pulled out a rectangular jewelry box from the inner pocket of his jacket, laid it down carefully, and pushed it across the table.

Sammi's eyelashes fluttered over the rim of her flute. She slowly lowered her glass, then hurriedly placed it on the table before snatching the box up with both hands. He laughed at the giddiness on her face. She was goddamn perfect in every way.

Batting her long, dark lashes at him, she grinned and said, "A present. For me?"

"Of course."

Clutching it tightly to her chest, she asked, "What's the occasion?"

"No occasion. I'm simply taking full advantage of the opportunity to give a gift to a woman who'll appreciate it."

Flipping the long rectangular box open, she covered her

mouth with her hand. Her fingers caressed the necklace lovingly as her gaze strayed up to him.

"I've never received a gift before. I mean, guys have bought me drinks before but this ... this is beautiful," she confessed.

He rose to his feet and went behind her chair to clasp the elegant necklace around her neck.

"It goes well with the dress you're wearing. I'm pleased," he confided against the curve of her ear.

He let his fingers linger on the base of her throat and saw the goosebumps run down her arms. He caressed her shoulders and warmed her arms before stepping back to his seat.

She repeatedly touched the large gem. Whipping out her phone, she snapped a few photos of herself. He waited patiently as she uploaded it onto her social media.

Placing her phone face down on the table, she shrugged apologetically. "Sorry about that. I couldn't help myself. It's not every day I get a gift from a sugar daddy, so it had to be put on public record. I'm going to get so many likes and comments."

"Sugar daddy?" he repeated with an arched eyebrow.

Sammi gave him a saucy wink. "Do you have a problem with the term?"

A chuckle resonated from his chest cavity. "Not in the least, I've just never been blatantly labeled as one. There's not such a huge difference in age between us."

"True, but I like the extra-ness of calling you my sugar daddy. On a serious note, though, you're more of the protector type."

"That label I definitely approve of," he replied, taking a sip of water.

"It was one of the first things I noticed about you."

"Before the incident at the Champagne Room with that fucking pap?"

Sammi nodded her head, her black curls catching the low light of the restaurant. "It was at the courthouse when I got upset about Puck. The look of distress on your face was almost laughable." She gave a husky laugh. "You seemed to be cursing silently, and then you touched my cheek."

Her eyes sparkled. "Protector."

Stanton leaned back and folded his arms over his chest. He noticed Sammi's gaze going to his biceps bulging under the stretch of his fine wool jacket. His jackets were getting a little tight. He'd have to get them altered, because he wasn't about to risk losing muscle mass after catching the look in her eyes. "Not sure I like the idea that I'm an open book."

"My brother has been overprotective of me almost my entire life. I can spot a protector in the blink of an eye."

She reached out and caressed his jaw line. His abdomen clenched at the surge of desire that rushed through him. His cock, which had calmed down, definitely took notice as well.

"And I like it." Her eyelids dropped and she gave him a bashful look from under her lashes. "Very much."

Fuck, he felt like a Viking warrior from the way she talked. Protective was also a code word for domineering. He was equally both. The little submissive in Sammi was preening under his display of dominance, proving what he'd already long suspected: they were a perfect match.

The waiter returned, and asking for her permission, Stanton ordered for the two of them. "Ever have classic French mussels?"

She nipped her bottom lip with her teeth, which made him want to lean over and capture it between his own teeth.

"No," she replied in a breathy tone.

"Then you're in for a treat. I kid you not, they make the best mussels in Upstate New York."

"Do you always treat women to dinner?" she asked curiously, although she was watching his reaction carefully. As if the answer mattered to her.

"Little girl, you're one of a kind. The answer to your question is that I do not. But tonight, I need to make sure you're well fed because I intend to put you through your paces." He leaned over, captured her chin, and locked eyes with her. "All. Fucking. Night."

Sammi licked her lips in anticipation and he bit his lip to stifle a groan. Quickly, he let her go and folded his arms again. Otherwise, they'd never make it past the appetizers.

15

SAMMI

No hotel, this time.

Instead, Stanton drove her to his apartment. If Sammi didn't know her city so well, she wouldn't have known where he was taking her. She was that hot and bothered with the anticipation of touching him again.

The week had felt long, what with missing Puck and worrying over his case. She was primed for the workout Stanton had promised. She'd long recuperated from the battering his cock gave her the night they'd spent together. Now all she could do was clench and release her thighs in eagerness.

They drove into an underground parking lot. He helped her out of his car, and then they were in the elevator, where he finally made a move. His demanding tongue pushed inside her mouth, turning her on, yet not nearly enough.

She clawed at his jacket until it was stripped off his arms, landing on the floor.

The elevator doors opened suddenly with a little *ding*. They kept going until the elevator doors almost closed. Stanton finally broke their kiss and flung his hand out to keep it open. In no mood to talk, Sammi picked up his jacket and followed him silently down a long, marbled hallway. The sexual tension between them was as thick as a cloud of hookah smoke.

Finally, he unlocked the front door and held it open for her to precede him. Instead, she took a fistful of his shirt and shoved him inside. Hard.

Stanton chuckled as he walked backward. Taking no notice of his apartment, she dropped his jacket and stalked him until the back of his knees hit the couch. Standing in front of him, she slowly unzipped the side of her dress. Peeling it off, she slowed down deliberately as she exposed herself. Her entire body tingled with need. Her black lace panties were so wet they were ruined for good.

His blazing eyes roved over her with greed, his teeth scraping over his bottom lip, causing her nipples to pop as hard as diamonds. The necklace looped around her throat rose and fell to the rhythm of her heaving chest.

"I need you. Now," she demanded, in a raw voice.

Her own gaze fell to his pants and she smirked at the clear outline of his thick erection.

Sammi had never felt such desperation before, but it drove her to be bossy.

"Strip," she commanded as she took the zipper of his pants.

She was about to lower it when his hand landed on top of hers, halting her action.

"Tsk, tsk. This isn't how we play," he chided softly.

Her brows gathered in uncertainty. She was frantic for him. What more was there to do?

Instead of explaining, he simply pulled back and slapped the side of her breast with the flat of his hand. A surprised gasp escaped her. The sting reverberated like a zipline straight down to her clit.

Taking her wrists, he held them at the small of her back and licked the pinkened flesh of her left breast. Thank God, on the ride to his apartment, he'd alerted her to the types of games they'd be playing and had gone over the stoplight method. If she didn't like something, she was to call out *red* without hesitation.

Cool air left goosebumps on the wet spot he'd finished licking.

Languidly propping his butt on the arm of the tan leather couch, he slapped her buttock. Sammi instinctively stepped back with a hiss, but she couldn't go far with her wrists clamped in his hand.

Releasing her, he walked around to her back, letting his fingertips glance over the edge of her panties. "You're fucking gorgeous, you know that?"

She shrugged lightly. Compliments would get him nowhere. She wanted his cock, nothing less. Spreading her legs, she arched her back to tempt him.

His hand slipped over one buttock and rubbed as he ordered, "Bend that fine ass over the couch."

It's what she wanted to do, of course, but she was a biker princess at heart. She wasn't used to orders.

Raising an eyebrow at her, he unbuttoned his crisp shirt with businesslike efficiency and stripped it off. His hand landed on his belt and fondled it. "Are you going to do what you're told like a good girl or do you need further incentive?"

She hopped to it, hooking her fingers into the sides of her panties, beginning to shimmy them down her hips when he stopped her with his hand.

"I didn't say take them off," he intoned. "Hmm ... we're going to have to work on your listening skills. Every command

I give you is done with intention, Sammi. I know what I'm doing. Your *only* job is to listen and follow my exact commands."

His finger glided up her throat to the nape of her neck. Then he grasped a fistful of hair and dragged her head back. "Understand?"

She nodded.

"The words, Sammi."

"Yes, I understand. I'll try my best."

"You'll do more than try your best," he warned, "because I'll exact a punishment for any missteps. Pay close attention to whatever I tell you."

He softened his tone. "You're a good girl at heart and what you want to do is please me. I have complete trust in you, so relax, baby. You can do this."

Her nervous energy wilted, her heart melting at his confidence in her.

"Okay," she breathed out, a shiver of thrill coursing over her skin.

"'Yes, sir' is the proper response," he advised.

"Yes, sir." *Finally, I've said them.* Those two words were the culmination of so many fantasies.

"Good. Now, bend over."

Sammi did as he said, the butter-soft tan leather smooth beneath her bare belly. Her skin crackled with anticipation as she heard Stanton undress behind her.

"The reason," his hand landed on her lace-covered cheek, "I want your panties on is because I want the privilege of checking them."

His fingers danced over her hips.

"Do I have your permission?"

She nodded frantically.

He glided his fingers to the front until he was at the apex

of her thighs. The friction of wet lace against her clit caused her hips to twitch.

"Just as I suspected. How long have you been walking around in soaked panties, Sammi?"

"Since I sat down to dinner."

A groan resonated above her bent head. "When at dinner?"

She shifted under his caressing tone. Having trouble focusing, Sammi had to rewind the evening in her mind before she came up with the answer. "When you came behind me and laid the necklace around my neck. Then you clasped it on. Your breath was on my neck."

A low growl vibrated in the shell of her ear, and her panties were ripped off her. She teetered on her high heels and had to grip the back of the couch harder. Her pussy felt slippery and her clit was throbbing so hard it could've tapped out Morse code during battle.

From behind, she felt his hand cup her butt cheek and jiggle it a little. If she wasn't so turned on she would've been embarrassed and shifted away from him, but she couldn't distract him from touching her in any manner he chose. He'd already proven himself a consummate master of her body, and she was dying to see what he'd do next.

Crack!

She inhaled harshly through her nostrils. The spank was so hard it echoed off the walls.

"Christ, you should see what your ass looks like, bouncing back from my hand."

He smoothed the pain away and even dropped a kiss or two her smarting skin. "So fucking pretty in pink, your ass."

He spanked her repeatedly on both cheeks and the crease where they met her thighs. She had to bite down on her bottom lip to prevent from crying out. After half a dozen slaps, he rubbed the abused flesh, and she couldn't help squirming under his ministrations.

"Stop moving," he commanded

"Can I take my shoes off?" she asked, holding her breath for his response. She heard him move behind her. He lightly wrapped his hand around her ankle and lifted her foot. She slid farther down the couch as Stanton removed one of her heels and then massaged her arch for a little bit.

"I should forbid you from wearing these if they bother you so much," he muttered. "Even if they're sexy as hell."

Forbid? No one's used that word with me before. Not even Puck, when he used to lay down ground rules before going to a party.

She silently rolled it over her tongue. *Forbid.*

Her fingers curled into the leather. Yes, yes, forbid it. Then she could be naughty and purposely defy him.

"They don't hurt much. It's just hard to keep my balance when you're walloping my butt."

Stanton chuckled behind her. "This is nothing, certainly not a wallop."

He placed a kiss on the arch of her foot and then removed her other shoe, giving that foot the same treatment. Both feet back on the ground, she curled her toes into the plush rug. Sooo nice.

Stanton was back to kneading her butt, and she wiggled it a little to communicate her impatience. Did he think she was made of glass? Because she'd been waiting for this kind of play for a long time and she was anxious to speed things up while he seemed to want to take his time and savor it.

Stanton patted her bottom and she waggled more overtly.

"Something you want, Sammi?"

"More," she said into the cushion of the couch.

"What did you say?"

"I. Want. More," she punctuated the words in a clear voice.

Stanton muttered, "'More,' she says, but does she use 'sir'?" as he calmly adjusted her, exposing her flank.

A palm cracked over her buttocks, knocking the breath out of her. *Oomph.*

"Address me properly," he intoned.

The stinging lash coupled with his command triggered an avalanche of ripples in her pussy.

"Feel that, do you? Here comes another."

"Yes, sir!"

Fuck, he was putting power into his smacks. After all the stuff she'd watched, and the blogs and books she'd read, she was finally, *finally* living it for real.

He turned her head so that her cheek lay on the cushion, and said, "I want to watch your expressions to make sure how you're doing."

Stanton returned to searing a path of pleasure-pain the likes of which she'd never experienced before. She shuddered with each contact of his hand. Her nose ran, her eyes stung, and her ass smarted. Her initial yelps began to run together until they came out as long moans.

Eventually, the rhythmic paddling subsided, and his hand became an instrument of comfort.

He soothed and kneaded her flesh till it was a slow burn as he crooned, "Such a sexy red."

She sighed in relief, but then gasped as he wrapped her tresses in his fist and pulled her head up.

Unabashed, he grinned down at her. "So fucking proud of you. You're going to do so well with me."

Stanton released his hold, and she let her head drop as she regained her breath. Behind her came the sound of a crinkling wrapper. Anticipating him, she spread her legs wider and arched her back to give him greater access. The wide crown of his cock nestled at her opening and smeared in her pool of juices.

"Oh, babe, this needy little pussy wants to be filled with my big cock, doesn't it?" he asked as he swiped his cock back and forth between her lips, spreading her wetness all over. Her pussy was throbbing to be taken.

"Yes, dammit, hurry up, Stanton. You're such a pussy-tease," she griped.

He swatted her ass and pulled away. His condom-covered cock slapped between her ass cheeks.

"Patience," he advised.

Sammi gritted her teeth and tamped down the urge to scream only because she thought he'd delay it further. Breathing in and out deeply, she stilled her body and waited with bated breath. Eventually, the tip of his shaft was back where she wanted it.

With one hard thrust he was inside her, filling and filling her, until he bottomed out and his balls slapped against her clit. She moaned and bit down hard on the leather cushion.

"Don't fucking move," he ground out, withdrawing and then rocking himself back in. "Don't you dare come until I give permission."

Pushing back into him, she moaned, "Oh, God, you're so hard and hot."

"You've got a dirty mouth on you, little girl. I should wash your mouth out with my come."

"Yes," she pleaded.

"Christ*fuck,* woman, you're desperate for cock, aren't you?" he grunted as he slammed into her with brute force. By now, her inner muscles clamped down on his shaft in a hopeless attempt to keep him from withdrawing. "You've got one hot cunt. Fucking love how your walls cling to me."

She huffed out a laugh. "I don't think that's me. That's your massive dick. And I don't fuck a lot," she panted out. He filled her to the hilt, not a millimeter of space to spare.

"Explains why your hole's so tight," he mused as fucked her, his pace relentless.

One of his hands snaked to her front and grasped her breast, pinching an erect nipple while his other hand slipped down and tweaked her clit. She jolted from that combination on top of the raw pounding he was giving her. Her insides twisted tighter and tighter, her belly clenching so hard she was cramping.

Her eyes snapped to his, pleading for release.

Please, please, please, she begged silently.

"Not yet," as he snarled as he pumped harder.

She squeezed her eyes, biting down on her bottom lip. *Don't come, don't come.* She clenched down tight, holding herself rigid despite his cock and magical hands, fighting to keep the on-coming climax from overtaking her.

"You may come," he granted.

She popped off instantaneously, screaming out his name.

"You're milking me. Oh, God, fuck."

His cock thickened as he rutted inside her, thrusting hard and deep. No holds barred. It triggered aftershocks through her core.

She opened her eyes in time to see his face crumble in unabashed ecstasy. Seconds later, he seized up, grunted and dropped on top of her, pitching her forward until her toes left the ground.

She grinned into the leather. What a ride.

They didn't move for a while. Panting in her ear, Stanton was heavy. Not that she minded. She enjoyed the motions of his chest, heaving against her back. It showed how she'd stripped him of his self-possession, even if he was the one ordering her around. Her first time playing a game of domination and it had been fucking fantastic. She'd never be satisfied with vanilla sex again.

$\sim$

STANTON FELT INCAPABLE OF MOVING, all the while knowing he was heavy as fuck on top of Sammi.

"Give me a second," he implored.

Beneath him, face buried in the cushion, he felt her nod. Shit, she couldn't breathe. He withdrew and simply let gravity do its thing, sliding him down to his knees behind her delectable ass propped up in the air.

She rolled over to her side and inhaled deeply.

Yeah, he'd been suffocating her.

Stanton had to hand it to her. She was incredible. He spotted handprints on her skin, *his* handprints, and couldn't help but smooth them over one last time before stumbling to his feet.

Grasping the couch, he stood up and disposed of the condom.

Returning, he found her lying in the same position. He drew her up to sit on the arm of the couch and helped her onto her wobbly feet. With an arm clasped around her waist, he led her to his bedroom. She plopped down at the foot of the bed. Pulling back the sheets, he then guided her to the middle.

Crawling in on all fours, her ass swayed in the air, placing her wet pussy right in his line of sight. He had to fist his hands to prevent from snatching at her again.

Crashing down beside her, he took hold of her hips and shifted her until her ass was nestled nicely against his crotch. Once she was in the proper position, he took a deep breath and relaxed. It was like a boil of aggression had been defused and siphoned off, and he was free from the relentless drive to be useful.

He was at peace. So fucking simple with Sammi. Something about her gave him permission to be himself, to just fucking *re-lax*.

He hadn't intended to take her quite so hard, but the moment she'd demanded *more*, all hell broke loose. The reins snapped and he did what he'd been wanting to do since the first time they had sex. If normal sex with Sammi was incredible, this was certifiably mind-blowing. The first time, he was convinced her pussy had been molded to fit his cock. This time, he was a full-on convert, a supplicant for life. The way she fucked was tailor-made for him.

Mind and body suspended in a hush of blissful peace, he glided his lips over her glossy hair and dropped a gentle kiss on the crown of her head. Inhaling the mint and herb fragrances from her shampoo, along with the undertones of her own woodsy scent was incredible.

Smoothing his lips over her locks, he marveled at the ebony coloring of her hair. Something moved through his chest, and his heart seized. Clenching his eyes shut, he let this new feeling sweep over him until it dissipated.

Focusing his attention back to the present, he asked, "Are you sore, little one?"

She wiggled her buttocks against him, and his eyes rolled back a little. Just a little wiggle and he was getting hard.

"Why? Are you ready for more?" she teased.

"You and the word *more* is a dangerous combination, woman. Be careful, because the last time you said more, it had me pounding into you like an animal."

"Did I look like I didn't enjoy your so-called 'pounding'?" she quipped. He groaned into the side of her throat. "Or did I scream in pleasure and come harder than I've ever come in my life?"

"Stop it," he demanded.

"Just saying ... I mean, I've heard that men peak in their twenties, and you're past thirty. Maybe you can't keep up anymore," she replied with barely suppressed laughter.

"I know psychological manipulation when I see it, but that won't work with me. Go ahead, squirm that ripe ass on my cock all you want, but hear this," he took her chin and turned her to face him, "I'm in total control of my body. Even a perfect, tight pussy as pretty as yours won't get the drop on me."

A pretty blush flagged her cheeks.

"So, no, you won't be getting my cock until I say so."

Apprehension flittered across her face. Giving him an adorable pout, she asked quietly, "Should I go?"

He chucked her chin and huffed, "Hell no, did you hear me order you to leave? I'm nowhere close to done with you, but we'll proceed on my timetable, not yours."

"So bossy," she griped as she pulled her face out of his fingers, but she didn't make a move to distance herself.

Eyes squinting a bit, she asked, "Are you tired? It might be the lack of lighting, but I see shadows under your eyes."

Warmth flooded his chest, accelerating his heart rate till it hammered against his ribs. At her concern, a wave of exhaustion swooped over his body. "I didn't get to bed until three in the morning. Crushed it at trial this morning, but it's been a long day."

The pads of her fingers lightly caressed his eyebrows and eyelids, forcing him to shut his eyes.

"Go to sleep," she told him in a soothing tone. "I'll be right here."

"Alright, but I meant to ask if you to the annual gala hosted by the Department of Commerce," he slurred as he tightened his arms around her and burrowed deeper into her neck and the pillows.

"Sure, Stanton. Sweet dreams," he half heard before he slipped off to sleep.

16

SAMMI

Stanton pulled open the shower door.

"Starting without me?" he queried as he stepped in.

His irises were a dark blue, smoky with desire and a hardness that made her soul sing. His broad chest rippled with every slight move, emphasizing the cut of each slab of muscle as he came closer. He was already hard, his shaft jutting out from the juncture of his thick muscular quads.

Studying him, she turned slippery wet with more than the water running off her body.

Slapping her palms on the wet tiles, Sammi gave him a come-hither look over her shoulder. He pulled on his cock and gritted his teeth as he flicked the tip of his crown.

Oh, God, he likes a bite of pain with his fucking, too.

Riveted, her eyes focused on the movements of his hand, and a moan slipped out from between her lips.

"How do you want it?" he demanded harshly, curling his fingers around her hip.

"Hard," she breathed out. "I want it hard."

"Perfect, 'cause that's how I'm going to give it to you. I need to get a mirror installed in here because I want you to watch when I push into your tight sheath and stretch your pussy around my big cock."

He placed the bare head of his cock and slid it through the cream of her slippery folds. "I'm going to take you bare, baby. Feel you all wet and hot and clenching down on my cock."

Sammi's eyes flared wide, her mind struggling to catch up with what he'd said. "Wait. What?"

They'd talked about unprotected sex but, after the last two times, she wasn't expecting it to happen right this instant.

"I told you I'd fuck you raw. Haven't fucked without a condom in years. We've gotten tested recently. How about you?"

"Sex without a condom?" she squeaked. "Never done it before."

His cockhead swiped against her clit. Then he notched it between her inner lips, pulsing gently.

"It's not something you want to miss, the sticky heat of my come inside you." He kept his prodding gently, his cock spreading her open as the flared tip pushed in a bit. "Christ, the way you stretch around my cock. Fucking beautiful. So wet and pink and slippery."

She swallowed. There was a first time for everything. She'd heard the feel was incredible, and damn, it was true. *Relax and enjoy it.* He was clean. She was clean. She wasn't getting pregnant.

There was a seismic shift in her chest. Pregnancy. The thought was back.

Discomfort snapped over her skin.

Feeling this way with *this* man was not smart. No way was he *the* guy. It was only sex. Granted, the hottest, wildest sex she'd ever experienced.

Over her shoulder, she nodded her assent. His eyes were

like a polished azure blue, his lips twisted in pleasure as he shuddered against her.

His hips punched forward. She doubled down on the extra two inches of cock lodged inside her.

"Babe, you're clenching." He chuckled low. "You trying to keep me out?"

No point denying it.

"You want this, then work for it." She was wrangling a bit of control and couldn't wait to see how he responded.

His hand slid up her back, took hold of her hair, and yanked. She gasped, her neck arched, thrusting her chest out. Her pussy gushed around his cock, adding more lubrication.

"Little girl, if it's rough you're asking for, then rough is what you're going to get." He thrust through her resistance until he was seated deep inside, stealing her breath. Oh, sweet Jesus, she'd never felt anything so good. She was so full. Deliciously so. His hands swept up her ribs to cradle her tits. He tweaked them and she arched into his aggressive touch.

"Feel that, do you? My big, dirty rich man cock is going to take good care of this tight little pussy." He pulled out and then his hips snapped forward, pumping back in.

"With the way you're fucking me, it won't be tight for long." Again, he withdrew, almost to the tip, and slammed right back inside. The *slap, slap, slap* of skin on skin as his cock laid siege to her, all rough and demanding, made her feel irresistible. Here was this big man behind her, plowing into her like he couldn't get enough. She no longer knew where she ended and he began.

"Damn, woman, you're a goddess with that filthy mouth of yours. You should see your pussy lips pulled taut and weeping around my shaft."

His dirty talk had her clenching down on his shaft again while his fingers found her clit and massaged. Angling his cock just so, he hit the magic spot that he'd discovered the first night. The speed and the glide of his velvety, hard rod, with no rubber between them, edged her closer and closer toward her peak.

"Oh God, oh my God, Stanton!"

"Scream my name, baby. Scream my name while your sweet pussy comes. I feel it suctioning my dick, sucking down on it like your mouth when I fucked it." She bore down on him *hard*. His grasp on her hair tightened, pulling her head back as he swore beside her ear, "Oh, no you don't. You're not winning this round, Sammi." He clasped her hips roughly to restrain her, hammering into her with his ever-swelling cock. Braced against the wall, she used her weight to push back against his hold and fought him for every inch as she met him thrust for thrust.

"Look at your tits bounce. Eyes on me," he commanded. Sammi struggled to turn her head, but too soon pleasure steamrolled over her.

"Look at me, dammit," he shouted. At the gravel in his tone, her head whipped around, gaze shooting to his. Mouth open wide in a soundless scream, she exploded.

"Come on, baby girl, that's right. Chase it down." He sped up, each thrust more brutal than the last. "Gimme what's mine. Gimme my prize. Ah...*fuuuck*."

Body shuddering, she milked him for all she was worth.

"Yeah, baby, I've got so much come for you, you'll be dripping for days." Liquid heat spurted inside her, the new sensation sparking off another wave of pleasure. His mouth landed on her shoulder and bit down hard as his cock pulsed. He'd leave a mark, but she didn't care. Nothing could surpass the feel of his seed spurting inside her; knowing it hit the walls of her uterus. *Sublime.* She clamped down on his cock for a long moment. An animalistic sound vibrated between the teeth lodged on her skin. She wanted every single drop. It was *hers*. She'd *fought* for it. She'd *earned* it.

An image flashed before her. She was in this same shower, bent over in the same position, with Stanton inside her and around her. Except, his hand coddled her full belly.

Shocked, Sammi's feet lost purchase on the wet tiled floor and she slipped.

Stanton secured her waist, his defined forearm laying right at the spot she'd imagined.

Fuck, what the hell was happening?

So intuitive, he sensed the sudden shift in her and demanded, "What's wrong?"

Ducking her head, she brought her hand up and cupped the side of his face on her shoulder as water pounded down on them. "Nothing, nothing. I just slipped."

"Damn, sorry, baby. I didn't realize I was putting so much weight on you." He flashed her a grin. "What can I say? You brought me to my knees. That was fucking incredible. *You're* fucking incredible."

With excruciating care, he pulled out of her and she immediately felt the loss, her inner walls throbbing around the ghost of his cock as she shuddered. *Get yourself together.* Sammi smoothed a hand down her hammering heart, imploring it to calm down. The image that had popped into her head unbidden was not to be trusted. She shouldn't want something deeper with this man, no matter how good the sex was. He was not the keeping type, no matter how delicious he was. It was Abby and Sage's pregnancies that were at fault for putting the thought of pregnancy in her head.

Suckling the bite mark on her shoulder, he caressed her sides. Sensing her emotional rawness, he was taking care of her. Her heart practically cracked open at that realization.

Stanton reached past her to grab the soap from the holder

indented in the marble wall. Stepping back, he gently turned her around to face him.

She watched the shifting play of light and shadow on the bones and ligaments of his large hands as they lathered up the soap. Then he glided his soapy hands over her, washing off his and her come.

Having managed to force down the well of emotion that image had triggered, Sammi faked it till she made it and giggled airily when he paid extra attention to her pussy.

"Just making sure it's thoroughly clean," he murmured with a slight uptick of one corner of his mouth.

"So gallant of you," she teased back, releasing a pent-up breath as his gentle touch massaged away the tension left from the terrifying, yet exhilarating, image seared in her mind.

Then it was her turn and she took her time, focusing her attention and energy on exploring the masculine beauty of his carved body, from the sharp angle of his jaw to the ripples of his abs and the thick slabs of his thighs. He moaned when she began kneading into his shoulders. After she was done, she pressed down on his shoulders until he was kneeling. He nipped at her mons but she batted him on the cheek and took the shampoo in her hands. Lathering his hair, she rhythmically massaged his skull with her fingers, treasuring the sensation of having this big, powerful man melting under her touch. Finally, she pulled the showerhead out and rinsed him off completely. He rose to his feet as she returned the showerhead to its hook.

He placed a tender kiss on her lips. "I need you here for my morning shower every day."

Her heart stuttered. She breathed through the moment, smiled up at him, and replied, "It was my pleasure, not only yours."

17

SAMMI

Despite the nippy weather, Sammi preferred to wait for Stanton on the patio of the empty house she shared with Puck.

Ever since his arrest, she limited her time there. Which was an ongoing struggle considering she worked from home. Clothing and lingerie were stored in one of the spare bedrooms of the house Puck had bought for them once he'd patched into the Squad and was financially stable.

Surprise couldn't begin to describe her reaction when Stanton asked her to accompany him to the Winter Gala. At first, she thought he was delirious from the shower sex and would forget the following day.

Since his text to confirm, she'd been grinning so wide her cheeks ached. He was picking her up to shop for a cocktail dress with her. Normally, she'd be slightly insulted that he didn't trust her to dress herself, considering styling was her business, but he'd explained it he wanted to go shopping with her. He wanted to spoil her. She couldwork with that.

Minutes later, Stanton drove up in his Maserati. She jumped in and gushed, "Yay, shopping trip."

Grasping her nape, he pulled her in for a long, deep kiss.

With a smirk, he said, "Glad to see you so excited."

Casting a look in his direction, her belly flip-flopped. When not in a suit, Stanton didn't go for polo shirts and slacks. Instead, he wore a pair of tight, worn jeans with holes and a long-sleeved Henley under a black leather jacket. That man was sin personified. Even his hair was tousled.

If she didn't know better, he'd fit right in with the brothers at the clubhouse. But, of course, there was the whole Sage situation. Sammi cringed a little at the thought of her friend. She'd been avoiding Sage, dreading when she'd have to confess that she was fucking her ex-fiancé.

Sage was head over heels in love with Kingdom and carrying his baby, no less, but she still couldn't imagine the conversation going well. Five years had passed since their breakup, and Sage was no fan of Stanton's.

Looking over at him, with the scruff on his sharp jawline and the tuft of hair flopping over his forehead, she thought he was stunning. She knew what those fingers, clasped lightly over the steering wheel, could reduce her to. The way they could caress her cheek softy or grasp her chin roughly, depending on his mood.

Stanton glanced over to her. "Why are you looking at me like that? It's the clothes, right? I'm letting you down with my less-than-dapper image."

Sammi laughed out loud. "You look good," she confessed. Taking the opportunity, she gave him a languid look-over. "More relaxed."

"It's the weekend, I got a full night's sleep, and we're going to meet my favorite sister, so there's every reason to be relaxed."

"Your sister?" she squeaked, spine snapping straight against the leather seat. Her eyes dropped to what she was wearing. Tight black jeans, a sheer black embroidered shirt opened down to her bra, and her Demon Squad leather jacket.

"You did *not* mention your sister," she accused. "Turn the car around. I'm changing my outfit."

Stanton dropped a hand on her knee and squeezed. "Babe, you look fucking beautiful. We don't have time for that. Amy's returning to Manhattan right after we're done. We're going to her shop to get your dress."

A pucker formed between her brows. "Her shop?"

"Yeah, she owns A La Cloche."

Sammi's mouth fell open. "She owns Cloche? Like *the* A La Cloche?"

"Yup, Amy Prescott," he said with pride. "My sister."

"She's a superhero in the Poughkeepsie fashion world for her debut at New York Fashion Week three years ago. She's like one of the youngest female fashion designers to break through and she opened a store here, in our small city. She's a complete badass."

His lips twitched. "I'm aware."

"And you want to bring me to meet her dressed *like this*?" she practically shrieked. "Have you lost your damn mind? Turn around, Stanton. I can't meet her dressed like this."

"Babe, you look gorgeous as fuck."

"I'm dressed in a beat-up leather jacket and a boring pair of jeans. For the love of all that's holy, Stanton, it's like meeting the governor in a ratty white T-shirt."

"I've met the governor and I can assure you he doesn't give two fucks about how people dress." She rolled her eyes at his ridiculous response. "

My sister's going to be far more interested in who you are, not what you're wearing."

Panic was starting to set in, and fast. "That statement only proves you know nothing about women or fashion designers. Now, be a good boy and turn around."

"Little girl..." he warned in a soft baritone.

Slamming her head against the back of her seat, she bemoaned, "Don't you *little girl* me. This is my career. I don't get to make an impression on someone like her every day. Or, like, ever." She narrowed her eyes at him. "You could have told me earlier. You know that, right?"

"I'd only mentioned it to Amy this morning. I didn't expect her to postpone her departure, because she's got a deadline or something, but she said she wouldn't miss this for the world."

She shook his hand off her knee. "Oh, just shut up. Every word out of your mouth is only making me mad."

He chuckled darkly.

She glared at him. "What exactly did you tell her that makes her want to meet me?"

"She's intrigued by the woman who's taken up every spare moment of my life since I've met her."

"That's such an exaggeration. You don't have spare moments."

"Exactly, but I do for you." He gave her a quick side-look. "Since you've accused me of holding back, I should probably mention that my parents will be at the Gala."

Sammi threw her hands up in the air. "Oh, for the love of God!"

He burst into a laugh. The sound was so wonderful. It rippled down her spine, leaving her feeling heated. And flustered, because ... *uhm* ... his parents. Seriously, she couldn't deny feeling a tiny bit thrilled at the way he nonchalantly mentioned introducing her to his *entire* family. "You're enjoying yourself at my expense, I see."

His fingers drummed against the steering wheel and he shook his head.

"Sorry," was all he said, but a bemused smile lingered on his lips.

"I want to make a good impression on her for you, not just because I'm a stylist. I want to look good for you. To represent you."

His blue eyes softened, but his brows gathered into a slight frown. "You do please me. Have you no idea how much you, baby girl? Because I'll park the car right fucking now and prove it to you."

She rolled her eyes. "I'm not talking about sex."

"Neither am I." His lips curved upward. "Well, not *just* sex. Seriously, Sammi, if I thought you'd undermine me in any way, I'd have warned you ahead of time." He gave a blasé shrug. "Besides being drop-dead gorgeous, you're smart and funny. I'm a good judge of character and I saw you when you shouted at Puck in the courtroom. Listen, if I had any doubts whatsoever, I'd never let anywhere near my little sister. After Jax, she holds the other half of my heart so when I say I trust you, it's not a meaningless compliment."

Sammi's heart stopped and then stuttered back into working order. *Holy. Mother.*

Whatever walls she'd erected against this man disintegrated to dust in the wake of his confession. Her hand crept delicately onto his thigh; the muscle flexed under her touch before relaxing again. The man wasn't a master of words in his profession for nothing because he'd stunned her into silence.

A flash of herself pregnant flickered in her mind's eye again and, for once, she didn't thrust it away or try to reason it away. Staring out the window, she let it flutter around for a bit before gently shooing it along. There was no denying it; she felt something for him. A neon sign reading "Danger" should be flashing in her mind's eye, but instead, a low hum of anticipation tripped through her.

18

SAMMI

"**O**migod," Amy breathed out, her eyes wide and her arms flung out for a hug. Sammi floated into her embrace like in a dream.

Caressing her hair lightly, Amy murmured near her ear, "It's so nice to meet you."

Pulling away, she held Sammi at arm's length, her mind seemingly ticking away as she scanned her body.

Glancing up at her brother, she scolded, "You didn't mention how beautiful she is."

Stanton leaned back against the back of a loveseat, ankles crossed and arms folded over his chest.

"It's to be assumed," he drawled. "If you don't yet know how sophisticated my taste is, then there's really nothing to say."

Amy rolled her eyes before returning to Sammi. "You've got your work cut out for you with this one." She thrust her thumb in his direction. "Are you sure you're up for it?" She tilted her head, giving Sammi a long look. "Never mind, you're clearly up for it."

Amy was a slim, tall woman with features that reflected

Stanton's. The same strong, angular jaw, refined nose, and piercing blue eyes. Her hair was a few shades lighter and she wore one of her iconic button-down dress shirts with a thick, leather belt.

Sammi scanned the boutique, her gaze flittering around excitedly like a butterfly on crack. There was so much to see. She could spend hours inspecting the different high-couture garments and accessories disbursed around the boutique. The handbags and matching shoes artfully piled next to each other on a series of shelves set at different levels would take an hour, at the very least.

Amy waved over a stunning model-thin young woman from behind the jewelry counter. The woman moved elegantly toward them, extensions that brushed the top of her butt swaying from side to side.

With a bright smile, Amy introduced them. "Sammi, this is Amber, my assistant. I may have to leave a little early, so she'll take care of you. Amber, this is Sammi. Please bring the measuring tape and we'll choose a selection of dresses for the Gala."

At the word *Gala*, Amber's eyes skittered to Stanton, who was busy poking away at his cell phone, and then swung back to Sammi. Her eyes slitted and pelted Sammi with daggers dipped in poison. *Whoa, an ex-lover.*

While she knew Stanton had been promiscuous, Sammi hadn't expected to interact with an ex- quite so soon. The woman's irritation was completely understandable. Not only was she no longer with Stanton, but she had to suffer seeing him with another woman. That would make any woman froth at the mouth with jealousy.

Amy had left to go to the back of the store, where the racks of evening wear were located. Deciding to play nice, Sammi turned her warmest smile on Amber, who stuck her nose in the air and twirled away, snapping her skirt out of the way.

Amber returned with a thin white measuring tape and took Sammi's measurements, muttering under her breath. Once she was done, she took off to join Amy.

Left alone, Sammi wandered over to Stanton and leaned into his side. His arm immediately snaked around her shoulders and pressed her closer.

"I just have to reply to this email," he explained and returned to his cell phone. Just as he pocketed it, Amber called her to the fitting rooms. Sammi nuzzled into his throat and took a deep breath of his delicious, masculine Stanton scent before stepping away.

As she turned away, he gave her butt a little swat and she yelped.

Glaring at him, she warned, "I'll get you back for that."

"I'm counting on it," he gloated.

Stepping into the fitting room, Sammi reached for the first hanger, which displayed a classy little black dress.

By her ear, a low snarl startled her. "You know, he'll never love you," hissed Amber with such vitriol that she was almost spitting. Her eyes flashed hatred and her lip curled up. Sammi's stomach crashed down to her ankles.

"He will tell you he does, but he's incapable of feeling anything for a woman. And of honesty." She flicked her hand. "Totally depraved, that one."

Heat flagged Sammi's cheeks. How dare this woman throw Stanton's past in her face? Especially when he and his sister, her *boss*, were standing right outside the dressing room. The nerve of her. For once, Sammi was speechless.

"Humph. You'd do best to heed my warning. He's a user. I was game for whatever he wanted. He didn't have to declare his love to get me in his bed. And I'm his sister's shop manager.

His father would've never approved of someone like me, so I don't know what he was thinking."

He wasn't thinking. He was high.

Of course, Sammi zipped her lips. It wasn't the girl's business to know or Sammi's business to tell. While she didn't doubt that Amber was speaking her truth, this wasn't the Stanton she knew. The one who was determined to hold on to his sobriety, the one who was committed to honesty.

"I'm sorry about what you went through, but I'm not you," Sammi replied coolly.

"You think you're, what? Special?" she spat out. "Not possible. The man's a sociopath."

Enough was enough.

"Hey, chill with the nastiness already," Sammi burst out.

Realizing she'd gone too far, Amber pressed her lips together and hurried to complete the laces of the dress's bodice. Once she was done, she ripped the curtain open and stalked out.

Stanton glanced up from his phone across the floor. His eyebrows puckered as Amber stormed past him without a word.

Sauntering over to her, he gave her a nice, slow look-over.

"Is there a problem?" He cocked an eyebrow casually, although there was a dangerous glint in his eyes.

A smile spread across her face. "No problem. Just staking my claim. She didn't like that very much."

Stanton expelled an audible sigh. "I should have mentioned Amber. Honestly, I'd forgotten. It was years ago," he finished, with a dismissive flick of his hand. "Didn't think she cared enough. Certainly never acted like she did."

"Oh, she cared alright. She still cares. Whether it's you or her bruised pride, I'm not so sure."

"I'll talk to Amy."

Sammi grabbed his forearm. "No, please don't. It's done, and I'm not one to tattle on people trying to make a decent wage. Especially in this industry."

Reaching out to brush lint off her dress, he shook his head. "Never thought I'd say this to a biker chick, but you're too nice, you know that?"

"I doubt it" she scoffed. Spreading her outstretched hands over her hips, she asked, "So what do you think? Is black my color?"

"Every color is your color, little girl," he replied, his tone husky and low. His fingertip glanced over the neckline of her bodice. "This is it. I don't need to see another one."

"Oh, no you don't. I'm not leaving without trying on every possible version of a cocktail dress that I can manage to shimmy my ass into."

He slanted his head to the side and mused, "What a fine ass it is, too. I'm game, so long as I'm the one helping you in and out of your outfits." He cast a dark look in Amber's direction. "I don't want her near you."

"There's the protector coming out again."

"Fuck that," he growled.

"Have it your way," she teased as she sashayed back into the fitting room, Stanton hot on her trail. A swoosh of curtains and they were enclosed in the hushed quiet of the dressing room together.

His hand cuffed her throat, caressed down her chest, and then moved to the zipper on her side, dragging it down ever so slowly. The dress parted and she stepped out. She turned around and heard his breath catch behind her. Then a heavy sigh brushed against the sensitive skin of her back. She could feel his gaze lingering on her backside and the boy-cut pink panties she wore.

"Damn, you're exquisite," he said, his fingers trailing down her spine to rub one cheek. "It's tempting to give you a nice round of smacks for wearing such a pretty pair of pink panties." His fingers cupped her ass cheek and flexed.

Breath coming out rapidly, she watched him from the mirror with bated breath to see what he would do next.

There was a soft rap on the wooden pillar of the dressing room, and Amy's voice called out, "Stanton, are you in there?"

"Yes," he grunted, and after giving her a light squeeze and a nip on her shoulder, he slipped out from the closed curtains.

"Thank you," said Amy, in an amused tone, as she switched places with Stanton and took down another dress hanging in the dressing room.

Poking her head back out, she rebuked him, "You're so naughty. Stay outside and sit down on the sofa over there."

Turning back to Sammi, she shook out the dress and huffed, "He's incorrigible." Her gaze met Sammi's in the mirror, and she added softly, "Don't let him fool you. He may be cocky, but he's actually really sensitive for a man."

"I know," she replied, keeping her gaze on Amy's. "I love my older brother as much as you love yours. Believe me, I understand."

A small whimper escaped, and Amy pressed her fingers against her mouth. "I want him to know happiness. He's been through so much, and our family continues to harass him. I found a way to escape to New York, but he's so dedicated to his work here. He'd never leave so he'll always have them to contend with, along with the Prescott image to live up to. I know it sounds like I'm tuning the violins for the poor little rich boy, but he's under pressure from so many sides. It's a wonder he hasn't drowned yet."

Hearing Amy's desperation had Sammi swallowing around the lump in her throat. "You don't have to worry about him with me, Amy. I'll take care of him."

At that moment, Sammi knew she'd spoken the truth. Stanton had become hers, whether he could reciprocate it or not. He had become a part of the tight inner circle of family and friends she kept close to her heart.

Amy's eyes welled with tears and she swiped at them with her knuckles. "You know, he's never come here with a girlfriend before. Nor did he attend with his fiancées, for their bridal showers or their entire trousseaus. Yet, here he is with you, for one single dress."

Shaking out the dress, she helped Sammi get into a slinky gold-colored number and zipped her up.

"I hear you, and I don't what you've shared with me lightly," she said in an attempt to comfort Amy.

"What do you think I'm telling you?" Amy asked, with a sardonic twist of her lips.

"That I matter."

"Yes, that's it." She cast her gaze at the closed curtain of the changing room. "I'm not sure he realizes it, but it's obvious from the way he's talked about you and the fact that he's brought you here."

Amy's gaze returned to Sammi. "I've been frightened for him. I'm still anxious and worried, but since he met you, he's more relaxed. It gives me h-hope," she broke off.

Sammi enveloped Amy in her arms and shushed her quietly. "It's going to be okay, sweetie."

Amy's back shuddered. "I hope so because I've already lost one brother. I won't survive losing another. Especially this one. This one is so much more fragile than the last."

"I promise I won't let anything bad happen to him. You don't know me well, but I can tell you, I'm a force to be reckoned with when it comes to people I care about."

Amy hiccupped. "I believe you, Sammi. I do." Closing her eyes, she took in a deep breath and confessed, "He doesn't believe anyone can love him for who he is. He's fucked up so many times and he thinks he's beyond redemption."

"No one is beyond redemption," Sammi replied fiercely. "If that were the case, my brother would've been lost long ago."

"Hey, what's going on in there?" questioned Stanton from the other side of the curtain. "This girl talk is getting out of hand."

"Commm-ing!" singsonged Amy, dabbing at her eyes with the sleeve of her shirtdress. Sammi reached out and touched Amy's hand one last time. They shared a glance of acknowledgment.

Nodding, Amy put her game face on, thrust the curtains open, and presented Sammi with a *ta-da!*

Stanton's eyes smoldered.

"See," Sammi teased him. "It was worth the wait."

19

SAMMI

The ballroom of the luxury hotel was filled with a couple hundred members of the highest echelons of Poughkeepsie society.

There was an open bar, a large dance area with a small orchestra playing classical music, and waiters flitting in and around groups like determined hummingbirds. One entire wall, facing the back of the hotel, consisted of half a dozen French doors that were likely kept open in the warmer seasons.

Stanton had his hand on Sammi's lower back most of the time they were at the gala. It had been more than half an hour, but he was clearly reluctant to leave her alone.

She'd spotted a few of her clients, who were generous in acknowledging her, although they registered shock on their faces upon seeing who was by her side.

And by her side Stanton stayed, with one hand on her somewhere. Her lower back, her hip, her arm. Sammi wasn't sure if it was meant to provide her comfort or simply a show of possession. She didn't need the comfort, but she appreciated the display of entitlement.

Stanton's jaw tightened on one or two occasions, nodding to various older men, most likely friends of his family. He pointed out several politicians and celebrities, giving her their bios. Then they mingled. He seemed prepared to dominate the conversation, ready to swoop in and save her, but Sammi had enough experience with this stratum of society. Feeling at ease, she laughed easily and asked what she hoped were interested questions. She only hung back when Stanton got involved in a detailed legal discussion with another attorney.

An introduction to his parents was imminent.

Having stalked his father online, Sammi was now privy to the depth of his power over their region. Benjamin Prescott was kicking off a new re-election campaign, and big money was pouring in from his party and wealthy donors. Stanton's family was no joke. She marveled at his boldness in bringing her to this gala, much less continuing his involvement with her. It made her ever more grateful for Amy's instantaneous support of their relationship.

While they hadn't explicitly redefined their relationship, Stanton had once told her to pay attention to his actions because they spoke the truth. His action of walking into the ballroom with her on his arm was loud indeed.

An hour of conversation and another champagne glass later, Sammi was standing alongside Stanton when she felt him stiffen beside her.

Glancing around, she caught sight of an elegant older woman approaching them. She dressed in a beige taffeta sheath dress with intricate embroidery on the sides. Even from a distance, Sammi recognized the Chanel dress, and her resemblance to the man standing beside her. Nodding from side to side and stopping to make comments, his mother worked through various groups of people like a pro as she made her way in their direction.

Sammi straightened her spine and raised her chin. She wasn't one to cower, no matter what impression she hoped to make on this woman. Stanton had made this decision, and she trusted his judgment.

"My mother," was all Stanton said. She knew close to nothing about his relationship with his mother, although Sammi did semi-stalk her on the internet and learned that she came from an old, monied family from Newport, Rhode Island.

As his mother finally reached them, Stanton released his hold on Sammi to air-kiss his mother on both cheeks. "You look stunning, Mother."

Her eyes gleamed. "Always the charmer. Your father's wrapped up in a discussion with Senator Richards. He may not be able to tear himself away any time soon. You know Richards," she stated with an arched brow as if that was explanation enough.

"If he wanted to, he'd most certainly find a means of escape," Stanton returned, although there was no frown or other indication that he was upset by his father's dismissive conduct.

From what he'd told her, Stanton engaged with his parents on a fairly regular basis. Yet, his manner was more reserved than she'd expected. She was honored that he'd revealed the other side of himself to her. Like earlier that afternoon when he climaxed with her lips around his cock. His facial muscles slack, his mouth gaped open, and his big body shuddering with release. Or in the aftermath, when he spooned her, nuzzling into her neck, his muscles relaxed against her back, praising her on what a good girl she was and how well she sucked his cock.

"Who do we have here, my dear?" she asked Stanton,

although she stared straight at Sammi, a subtle tilt to her lips. No outright laughter for one Marie Prescott.

"Mother, this is Sammi Rossi."

"Mrs. Prescott," Sammi said, as she reached out her hand.

Stanton's mother took it calmly, although her sharp eyes watched like a hawk, likely wondering what her son saw in a young commoner like her.

"Call me Marie. Everyone does."

"Thank you," Sammi replied, a broad smile on her face, "Marie."

"I now understand what my son sees in you. Not only pretty, but you have a charming way about you. An innocence. She has quite the allure, Stanton."

"No one could claim I'm an innocent," he noted, as his hand slipped around her waist. "Sammi's more than her beauty and innocence. She's smart, generous, and far more mature than the average twenty-one-year-old."

His mother raised her brows.

"Don't pretend you're surprised by her age, Mother. I know you've done your research."

"Yes, Stanton, but that's not the kind of thing one brings up in public or admits to," she chided, a touch of dryness to her tone. She sighed. "But you weren't the obedient one, were you?"

His fingers dug into Sammi's waist, but he chuckled with a shake of his head. "There's no disputing that point. I never seem to make the proper choices for either you or Benjamin."

Marie's eyes softened and she cupped his cheek. "It's not your fault."

A deep undercurrent thrummed beneath her seemingly simple phrase.

After a brief moment, Maire dropped her hand, and said, "Well, I must be off to perform my duty as your father's better half while he's fending off Richards. Mingle and converse. A few of the many inanities one must endure during campaign season. I'll try to stop by again before the end of the evening, but no promises."

"Not necessary, Mother. There will be future occasions to spend time with Sammi."

Her heart soared at hearing the promise of a future in those words. His mother's eyes sharpened and coasted over Sammi, as if taking inventory for a judgement she'll make at a later date.

"Very well," she said evenly.

She kissed Stanton's cheek, smiled a goodbye at Sammi, and drifted off, only to be stopped within a few feet by a woman of her own age and stature.

"That went much better than expected," Sammi offered. "My mother's the easygoing one. You took it much better than Sage the first time she was dismissed by my father."

"He's a busy man," she supplied.

"Not an excuse," he countered, "but it is what it is. The man won't change for anyone or anything. As they say in the twelve steps, expectations are premeditated resentments."

He brought her closer into his side and nipped the lobe of her ear discreetly.

"I'll meet him eventually, but from what you've told me so far, I don't expect him to approve of me."

"We did our part. Honestly, I can't wait to get the hell out of here and strip this dress off you. It'll be like unwrapping a present on Christmas Day."

Sammi nestled closer and said, "I'm going to get a drink at the bar." She glanced down at his half-empty seltzer water. "Need a refill?"

"I'll go with you," he declared.

She placed her palm on his bicep, feeling him flex underneath the woolen fabric. "Stanton, you're hovering and I don't need a bodyguard. Seriously, go find someone and talk about work or law or whatever?"

"I don't want anyone to come on to you," he argued.

Sammi pursed her lips together. "Riiiight. Or is it that you're afraid someone will make insult me? I can take care of myself. I'm not made of glass and I promise you no one can hurt me." She pointed to the bar. "I'll be right over there for five minutes and I'll be back. I swear, you're worse than Puck."

"Puck's not a fool."

"No, he's not, and even he would give me the freedom to walk around on my own."

"These people—"

"Are just people, not sharks, Mr. Protector. I'll be fine."

"Fine," he huffed. "But I'll be right here. *Watching*."

"You do that," she threw over her shoulder with an air kiss and a wink as she sauntered away, giving her hips an extra little shake. His eyes narrowed with a promise of retribution for her teasing.

At the bar, she waited for the bartender to finish serving a throng of young men at the other end.

"I'd heard he'd gotten a new one for his collection," a woman sneered, her eyes raking Sammi from head to toe with a curl of her lips.

Sammi smiled at her. Guess Stanton was right. The sharks were waiting for an opportunity to pounce, but Sammi wasn't easily rattled by a little cattiness. Bitches at the club could be catty as fuck, even if their insults were rarely lobbed at her. A bitter little rich girl was nothing for her.

"Honey, you have nothing to keep that man's attention," the elegant woman continued, lazily twirling a cocktail straw in her mixed drink.

Another sleek, razor-thin woman in her late twenties

plopped on the bar stool next to the catty one. "God, I can't wait until this is over. I've just arrived and God, do I need a drink. Stanton's here, with new arm candy hanging off him." She grimaced as if sucking on a lime. "I heard he had the nerve to go to Amy's and pick out a dress for the slut, but I don't see her anywhere."

The first woman's gaze locked on Sammi. "You mean this slut, Melanie," she spit out, with a flop of her upturned hand in Sammi's direction.

Melanie wasn't that common a name. This could only be fiancée number two. Sammi's heart pounded against her ribcage, but she slid a blasé mask over her face. Her first impression was that Melanie was pretty, sophisticated, and rail thin, but let's face it, the woman had no tits to speak of. Stanton had only spoken of her as a mistake, and Sammi could see why. She and Melanie were exact opposites. So different, in fact, that it was unlikely for a man to be intensely attracted to both. It was either one or the other, and Sammi had no doubt of Stanton's desire for her.

The look on Melanie's face indicated that she'd come to the same conclusion. All evidence pointed to this quickly devolving into a dramafest, and the chance of a confrontation dumped adrenaline into Sammi's system.

"What?!" Melanie cried out, her eyes flaring wide. "What the hell?"

Slitting her eyes, she scanned the ballroom and landed on Stanton's profile, who was engaged in a conversation with another man, hands flying around as he dramatized whatever he was describing.

Melanie's gaze whipped right back to Sammi. A bitter, lurid grin spread over her face, cracking her practiced perfection.

"Hi, slut," she sneered.

Sammi's belly dropped, her throat tightened. Passive-aggressiveness she could easily handle. Blatant hatred, not so much.

Clearing her throat, she found her words. "Wow, I didn't expect that from someone like you. And they say you have class. Not true, is it now."

"You're a rebound, that's all you are," she snarled. "A rebound from *me*."

"Hmm-mmm, like you were a rebound from Sage?" Sammi threw back.

She laughed tightly but, by a miracle, her chest loosened. One order of outright disgust, coming right up.

Checking her nails nonchalantly, she drawled, "Yes, Stanton told me. Stanton tells me *every*thing." Flicking her eyes up and down Melanie's skinny frame, she was getting into a groove. *Badass biker bitch in the house, yo.*

"If calling me petty names makes you feel better, go for it. Still won't change the fact that you lost the best fuck of your life to my bed." *Take that, bee-atch.*

Melanie gasped, but Sammi forged on, "He does fuck good, doesn't he? This would be a good time to invest in Duracell since you'll be needing lifetime use of your vibrator." She gave Melanie a wink. "Think about it."

"You trashy little bitch. How dare you? You're nothing, nothing I tell you. You will never be worth any—"

"Shut the hell up," Stanton snapped as he wrapped his fingers around Melanie's thin arm. "You're making a fool of yourself."

20

STANTON

Dragging his ex- off the stool, Stanton first order of business was to get her away from Sammi.

Goddammit, he let Sammi get away from him for one minute, and there was Melanie, claws out and scratching.

He managed to get a hold on his fury in the time it took him to haul her around the bar and behind a column, cutting off the public spectacle he knew she was gunning for.

Twisting her arm out of his hold, Melanie turned on him and sneered, "Is this part of your incessant campaign to humiliate me any manner possible? Have you not done enough to degrade me?"

He sighed. *So fucking self-involved.* Until he heard her call Sammi a trashy bitch, he'd thought Melanie was redeemable, but it was official: she was selfish and spoiled as fuck. Blood pumped in his veins because he was pissed as hell. It felt good and natural, dare he say *easy*, to be at the gala with Sammi, and Melanie wasn't going to ruin it for him.

Folding his arms over his chest, he casually propped a shoulder against the column and inquired with a strain of mockery, "How, pray tell, is me dating Sammi humiliating to *you*?"

"Because she's not one of us. She's a b-biker!" she stuttered, flinging her arm out in Sammi's direction.

From the side of his eye, he saw Sammi tip her head to the side. She'd clearly overheard the outburst. The woman was worlds away from Sammi in terms of compassion and, obviously, basic human decency.

The corners of his eyes tightened as he glared down at his ex. "You want to have this out right now?"

"Yes," she seethed.

"Not happening, Melanie," he said in a hard tone. "I'm not leaving Sammi to hash out your feelings about the woman I'm dating."

A gasp flew out of her gaping mouth as her hand clutched her flat chest in horror. "Are you in a ... a *relationship*?" she spat out. "Not possible."

"Yes, the word dating is self-explanatory, is it not?"

Damn her, Sammi was ten times the woman she was. He'd forgotten about Melanie's notorious snobbery. A knife twisted inside his chest because, at one time, he'd harbored such thoughts towards Sage and her man.

It's different, dammit. Kingdom was a fucking criminal. Yes, it was common knowledge he'd cleaned up his club for Sage's sake. Kudos to him, but Stanton doubted Kingdom had suddenly developed a love for abiding by the law. Sammi was nothing like the Demon Squad president. She was an innocent, growing up among bikers, sure, but she herself was about as untainted as they came. Pure, compassionate, tender. *None* of those labels applied to Melanie.

"Why, Stanton? What could she possibly give you that I can't? I did *everything* in my power to make you happy. Does she fuck you dirty, is that it?"

Now her nasty side was coming out. Tears of fury rimmed Melanie's eyes.

Stanton let out another exasperated sigh.

"Don't be crass," he reprimanded her. "Unbelievable as this may seem, it's not about you. It would've never worked out between us, despite what our parents want. Nothing was premeditated or arranged between Sammi and I. That's the problem with our social circle, we behave as if we're part of the English aristocracy. This isn't *Downton Abbey*. We may have seemed compatible on the surface, coming from old families that are rich as sin, but I never fell for you."

It wasn't ideal, but he'd make his amends right here. There was no way he'd seek her out and endure being alone with her again. Hard pass on that.

"I regret how things ended between us. I tried to do what was expected of me, and I hurt you. I formally apologize for that, but we're done," he added to make sure she didn't harbor any fantasies about them ever getting back together again.

"You can't do that! If you got rid of her and came back to me, we could make this work," she pleaded, plastering herself against him. Her touch felt clammy on his skin and her smell was all wrong.

"No. I'm not that man," he replied as he firmly placed her away from him. "Been there, done that, and I have a thirty-day NA chip to prove it. I had to be on drugs to keep up the charade of my life. On. Drugs. Do you not get that?"

"You had to be on drugs to be with me? To have sex with me?" she asked in tiny, defeated voice.

"Well, not the sex, no, but I had to be on drugs to maintain the veneer of my life. I was in rehab for *thirty* fucking days. Fuck the fact that I couldn't get high, I couldn't even work. I sat around and talked about my feelings in group and indi-vidual therapy. It was one of the hardest things I've ever done and I'm never going back there again. Not for you. Not for anyone."

His eyes burned and his chest felt tight.

"Babe," a gentle voice pulled him off the cliff.

Soft, cooling fingers curved around his forearm and he glanced over to see Sammi, eyes concerned, shaking her head softly. "Come on, let's get some fresh air."

Melanie's face turned white.

"People were turning their heads," Sammi explained. Tugging him, she said, "Let's go out on the patio and take a breather."

Stanton let Sammi drag him from behind the column that had done little to conceal the shit-show with Melanie. With Sammi's hand in his, they passed a station for the waitstaff and slipped out onto a wraparound flagstone patio overlooking a manicured lawn with a scattering of bare trees.

Glancing from side to side, he was relieved to find it empty. Strains of music and the hum of conversation could be heard in the quiet of the evening. He guided her down a series of wide stone stairs and along a retaining wall below the patio and main floor.

Leaning back against the stone wall, she drew him close until their chests were touching. Her fingers lightly glided along the side of his face and tilted his chin down until their lips touched.

Grabbing hold of her ass with both hands, he plundered her mouth. God, he needed this. Needed her. That had been fucking awful, and he grabbed at the chance of losing himself in the wet heat of her mouth.

Out came her tongue, playing with his, and he drowned in the taste of her, the feel of her soft, cushioned lips slanted over his. After a thorough exploration of her mouth, his anger was drowned out by arousal and his breath quickened for all the right reasons.

He broke off their kiss before they sped past the point of no return. Understanding his mood, she didn't push him to talk. Instead, she wrapped her arms around his waist and laid her head against his shoulder. Wisps of raven-black hair got caught in the breeze and feathered over his cheek.

Nuzzling her tresses, he whispered, "I'm sorry."

She lifted her face toward him, gaze challenging him. "There's nothing to be sorry about."

"Not true. I have an ex who said some fucked-up things to you. Got into what could've turned into a public shouting match if you hadn't interrupted us. Christ, you can't take me anywhere, can you?"

Her head dropped again, and she laid her cheek against his heart. He felt her chuckle through the cotton of his tuxedo shirt. "I heard you stick up for me."

His palm glided up her cheek and hooked onto the back of her neck. "I'd never let anything happen to you. Never allow anyone to disrespect you. I have a past, so brace yourself. This won't be the last time someone goes after you."

She dropped a kiss on his chest and laid a palm on his solar plexus. The warmth and stability of her hand suffused him with calm. It was like being hit with a cocktail of opiates. He shuddered out a breath.

"They couldn't hurt me if they tried."

Bending his head, his lips grazed hers. "You're too fucking sweet, little girl. I want to hide you away so no one can touch you and hurt you. I want to protect you from the big, bad world. Coddle you and spoil you and keep you near me, always."

"You can't protect me from life, and I don't need you to,

Stanton. You don't have to worry so much about me. I can hold my own."

"I do worry," he insisted.

Her palm glided beneath his jacket and scratched against his nipple. He groaned and took a swipe along the side of her throat with his tongue.

❋❋❋

ALL SHE HEARD WERE the deep growls beneath his words. They sparked a cascade of tiny shivers down her arms. The deep rumble of his voice lit her up inside like a flash of lightning. With his hair tousled in several directions, he already looked half-crazed. There was an abrupt shift in his mood, coming on so quickly it left her feeling whiplashed, but she reveled in the delicious danger.

His hand shoved up her dress and then swooped into her panties. His head slumped into her shoulder. "Fuck, your panties are soaked."

How it be any other way after he'd stuck up for her?

He ground the stiff cock she longed for against her belly.

"You remember how my cock feels, huh? Remember howling in pleasure the first time I thrust up inside you? That was nothing compared to what I'm going to do now. But first, I need your taste on my tongue. Spread your legs for me, little girl, and whatever you do, do it quietly. We don't want to alert anyone to the fact that I'm going to tongue-fuck you right now."

The sound of the French doors opening echoed through the quiet. A couple of waiters stepped out on the patio above them, taking a cigarette break. The scent of tobacco and phrases from their conversation drifted down to them.

Stanton's gaze crashed into hers. He placed his finger over his lips, and then slowly dropped to his knees.

Unhurried, he bunched her dress up to her waist. In contrast, he tore her panties down her legs. Cold air hit her skin, causing goosebumps to break out on her thighs and belly. She quickly stepped one foot out of her thong to give her the freedom to open her legs.

Taking the back of her knee, he guided it over his shoulder, and without further ceremony, buried his face in her pussy. She bit her fist to keep her moan at bay as he took a long, languid lick at her.

While the waiters were complaining about their supervisor above them, Stanton took his pleasure at torturing her with his tongue.

She fisted his hair, mussing up his pristine style, and murmured as low as she could, "I want your cock, Stanton."

He ignored her, which was pretty easy to do since she had absolutely no leverage, and kept up his ministrations, lapping at her entrance and nipping her clit.

"*Please.*"

He pinched her inner thigh and she let out a little yelp. By chance, it had been covered by the sounds of the waiters getting ready to return inside.

Thankfully, he was in a lenient mood and rose to his feet. Towering above her, he thrust his tongue in her mouth, and grasping the backs of her thighs, lifted her up like she weighed nothing.

His bare cock rubbed against her mound, and she rocked against the ribbing of that fat vein on the underside of his shaft.

Holy hell, no way would she last.

There were sounds of the French doors closing, and every-thing was quiet again. His fingers found the top of her bodice and yanked it down, freeing her bouncing breasts.

"Feed me," he commanded.

She lifted one breast and brought it to his lips. He latched on immediately and sucked down on her nipple, forcing her to sink her teeth into the shoulder pad of his jacket to absorb the scream hurtling out of her mouth.

Hitching her up a few inches, his cock nestled between her lower lips. Wet arousal coated the crown of his shaft. Stanton let her drop an inch and the flared tip spread her open. Another inch and, damn, did that feel so good. The stretch burned a little, but she reveled in it, writhing her hips in figure eights, taunting him to take her fully.

"Your cunt is so tight, little girl. Tell me no one will be in here but me."

"No one but you," she gasped.

"Fuck yes," ripped out of his mouth and he impaled her on his massive cock.

She sunk her teeth in the shoulder of his jacket, barely aware her mouth was full of wet wool. His silky hard cock throbbed against her inner walls. Holding her thighs open, he paused to give her the chance to adjust to his size. Then he lifted her and slammed her clenching pussy back down. Her head swiveled to the side and she released a low moan.

His patience snapped. Nothing but savagery was left in him.

Lifting and dropping her as he thrust up, he demanded, "Look at me."

She pried her eyes open, barely seeing through the narrow slits. He was in total control, and it felt so good to be used by him.

"Goddammit, Sammi, look at me when I'm fucking you," he growled.

She forced her eyes to snap open and focus on his face. The skin around his mouth was stretched taut as he bared his teeth. His jaw jutted out, tension gathering in every line of his face.

"Please, Stanton," she begged as she rolled her hips. It had the required effect because his thrusts got rougher and faster.

He grabbed the outsides of her thighs, spreading her even wider until her knees scraped against the wall. Battering her G-spot, sparks scattered through her body, his pelvic bone grinding against her clit with each upward thrust.

Pleasure coiled and snapped inside her. Without much notice, she flew over the edge and an orgasm ripped through her. Sammi screamed into his neck, tearing at his collar with her teeth as he roared out *fuck* and followed her.

His knees bent as his body gave a big shudder and then stilled as his cock continued to spurt liquid heat inside her. Straightening up, his thrusts returned, but shallow this time, and come trickled out to paint the sides of her inner thighs. His hot breath gusted against her throat and she reveled in the feel of him surrounding her and inside her. She skimmed her fingers over his flanks, loving the feel of his ribs and the definition of his muscles.

As if on cue, the strains of classical music drifting out of the ballroom came to an end.

"Wish we could get the fuck out of here, but I have to stay and listen to my father emcee the award ceremony. Once it's done, we're going home so I can take my time licking you from end to end. Then, I'm going to fuck you."

"You've already done that."

His eyes hardened. "Again. I'm doing it again, but this time long and slow. I want to take my time and savor you."

Her body shivered at his words. He was killing her. He introduced her to his mother and stuck up for her with his raging ex. After thoroughly fucking her into oblivion, he was waxing lyrical about savoring her.

She wasn't falling anymore. She was crashing headlong into him. Her stomach fluttered with nerves. There was no point in denying it. She could only hope the same was somewhat true for him. Again, his actions. His possessiveness and care told her he might be in the same ballpark. *Please, let it be true.*

Bringing her down to her feet, Stanton dug out a handkerchief and cleaned her up. He grabbed her ruined panties and stuffed it along with the handkerchief into the pocket of his tux. Quickly arranging his clothing, he helped her shimmy her dress down over her hips.

"I'm holding you to that promise," she murmured against his lips as she fixed his crooked tie and smoothed down his shirt.

Stepping away, he swept his arm out in a gallant gesture for her to precede him. They slipped back inside just as the *ping* of a fork hitting the crystal of a champagne glass resounded in the crowded ballroom. The warm hum in her blood that had begun during their car ride to his sister's store had grown into a full-blown operatic aria.

21

SAMMI

S ammi slunk down onto the old beat-up black leather couch of the clubhouse where Abby was knitting a yellow blanket for Sage's baby.

Not the color she would've chosen, but since the happy couple didn't want to know the sex of the baby ahead of time, the choices were limited.

After giving her friend a hug and her belly a rub, Sammi launched into what was preoccupying her since the night before.

"His father didn't come up to us during the entire evening. I mean, who doesn't meet his son's girlfriend?" Sammi asked with a pout, angry on behalf of Stanton more than herself.

She might not have a father, but Prez was like a father to both Puck and her, and she had many surrogate uncles. No one would've pulled that shit in the Squad. They'd be asking for a beating for such a sniveling little bitch move.

Abby raised her head from her knitting and gave Sammi a speculative look. "Is that what you are?" There was a twinkling her eye that Sammi did not appreciate.

"We don't need labels for whatever's going on between us,

but that's how *they* view it. I think Stanton was embarrassed or ashamed for his father's behavior because he fucked me endlessly throughout the night. Not that I'm complaining, but I'm angry on his behalf. Those people may be rich, but they're soulless. He's their only son, and yet, they couldn't make the time to meet his new girlfriend. And don't get me started on his ex. A real piece of work, that one. She ripped into me, and then into him."

Abby shrugged. "I'm sure you were able to handle her easily. If I were in your shoes, I wouldn't judge her too harshly. Sounds like he wasn't honest with her and the shock of seeing you put her over the edge."

"You should've seen how he came to my rescue." A goofy smile spread over her face as she remembered the fury lining Stanton's face, the telltale muscle in his jaw ticking away like a time bomb. He swooped in like an avenging warrior. And the way he fucked her in the garden afterward. Oh, Lordy.

"You haven't talked to Sage yet," she mentioned with a raised eyebrow. "If he's introducing you to his parents, then it's about time you come clean with Sage. And Puck."

Touché.

Sammi cringed slightly. "Okay, okay. I'll talk to her today. As for Puck, I'm not worried about him. He'll accept anyone I'm with."

"Sure about that? You haven't exactly had a chance to test out that theory since you've never brought a guy around. The extent of his involvement in your love life has been to threaten the men you've hooked up with behind your back. This is most definitely a first and, besides the obvious fact that Stanton is prosecuting his case, Puck already vicariously hates him through Sage. Sprinkle that onto the fact that Stanton isn't exactly Puck's type ..."

"He may not *seem* like Puck's type on the outside but,

believe me, they're terrifyingly similar on the inside. Puck will accept anyone who protects me the way Stanton did last night."

"So, this is a thing, then," declared Abby.

Sammi squirmed a little in her seat. Fiddling with the pleats of her skirt, she nodded. "I think so."

Abby placed a reassuring hand over Sammi's fidgeting one. "Why are you embarrassed?"

Sammi met Abby's steady look. "I-I thought at first that this was about helping Puck and a few nights of scorching-hot sex, but something switched last night. I mean, things had been moving fast, but when he stood up for me, I had a glimpse of something more. I'd assumed we'd have an affair and I'd be the kept woman in the shadows, but yesterday we became a couple. Sometimes, when I look at him, I feel giddy and scared at the same time."

Abby's needles clicked together in the lull of her declaration, blending with the background sounds of clinking glasses mingled with the low hum of the brothers and bitches by the bar and the pool table.

"Could you see yourself bringing him here?" Abby's voice punctuated the comfortable, familiar sounds.

"I don't have a choice. He did it for me."

"That's not an answer. Let me rephrase my question. Are you ready to take that step?"

Was she?

This morning, as she came out of the bathroom, her gaze landed on Stanton. His long body was propped against the headboard, one arm folded behind his head, his bicep bulging out in ridiculous sexiness. She knew for a fact that those biceps were strong enough to lift her up and fuck her against a wall. Lust curled in her belly as she sailed past him. Her gaze dripped down his chest, bumping over his six pack like a surfer over choppy waves, and followed his happy trail to the growing ridge of his cock. His long fingers wrapped around his shaft and moved up and down in a languid pace as he watched her with hooded eyes.

An instant later, she was crawling onto his king-sized bed, swatting his hand away and wrapping her lips around his velvety steel rod. Yeah, there was no way was she giving him up. Which meant she had to integrate him into the club. The club was family.

Sammi snapped out of her memory and replied, "Yup, I'm ready."

Abby giggled. "You're blushing. You're thinking about sex."

Sammi broke into a wide grin. "Am not."

"I'm going to trust you and assume this decision isn't based on some sex-induced brain fog or because you feel obliged to return his gesture."

"Please, bitch. Since when do I feel obliged? As for sex, I may not have experienced this level of gratification before, but I wouldn't bring a guy around my family unless I meant business."

"Good," Abby replied with a firm nod. "That's what I want to hear. I'll support you in any way I can. The bitches didn't make it easy for me in the beginning. I don't imagine the brothers will make it easy for Stanton, especially with Puck gone. They're going to be compelled to take on his fight."

Sammi chuckled. "I don't think the brothers will be as bad. For some reason, the bitches are more territorial."

"Okay, stop right there. You're like the little princess of the club, and Puck isn't here to play gatekeeper. Don't expect things to be easy. These men," her hand swept over the main floor of the clubhouse, "don't play."

Sammi's gaze scanned the clubhouse, touching on Cutter throwing back a shot at the bar, across a row of heads, and then over to Tank bending over the pool table to take aim. These men had known her since she was a needy young teenager.

She grimaced. Abby was right. It wasn't going to be easy. They didn't take things like protection lightly. Any man she brought around would have a fight on his hands, especially an outsider.

Yeah, this wasn't going to work without getting Sage, Kingdom's old lady, on her side. It'd be a tough conversation, but she trusted Sage. Step one, convince Sage. Step two, introduce the topic to Kingdom. This is where things could get sticky. Kingdom hated Stanton on principle, and he wasn't tender-hearted like Sage. It would take a concerted campaign to convince Kingdom.

"I'll go with you to talk to Kingdom," Abby spoke, breaking Sammi's brooding. Her heart expanded. Abby was like a ray of sunshine; she shone warmth on any cold corner of one's life.

"Yeah?"

"Of course. I said I'd help and Kingdom won't stand a chance against two pregnant old ladies," she replied confidently.

Sammi only hoped she was right.

22

STANTON

The door of Stanton's office slammed open and bounced off the wall.

"Are you out of your ever-loving mind?" came a voice, trembling with rage.

His gaze lifted off the memorandum he was working on and landed on Sage, clenching her briefcase against her chest as if to prevent herself from launching over his desk and attacking him.

"Is this some sort of revenge?" she ranted. "You go after a woman that's like a little sister to me as payback for calling off the marriage? I swear, Stanton, I knew you were twisted, but this is beyond the pale."

Sammi had texted him yesterday about her "talk" with Sage and Kingdom, so his only surprise was that the confrontation had come so late in the day. He glanced at the wooden clock on his desk. Just past noon.

His jaw ticked at the thought of Sammi dealing with the two of them alone, without him to support her. After a back-and-forth via text, he conceded her point that she knew them better as a couple, and therefore, he supported her decision to go alone. Didn't mean he liked it, though.

Bringing her as his date to the gala solidified them publicly as a couple, and he was more than satisfied with the result. Let every man and woman out there know who Sammi belonged to.

Eyeing Sage with ennui, Stanton leaned back into his high-backed wing chair. Once upon a time, he would've reveled in this scenario. Although he'd cheated on her with Melanie, in his delusion, he was crushed when she'd jilted him. The drugs had twisted his mind and he'd pursued her relentlessly for a time, but she'd shut him out completely. Back then, he would've been thrilled if Sage barged into his office, her fury on full display. Although it no longer held any allure for him, she'd always been hot when riled up.

"I've been honest with Sammi every step of the way," he drawled.

"You wouldn't know honesty if it bit you in the ass, Stanton. The idea that you can behave with an ounce of honesty is the height of absurdity," she replied in a condescending tone.

"I've explained what this is between us—"

Sage cut him off with a palm in the air. "With your emotions, Stanton. Honest with your emotions. Sure, you can be verbally honest with her, but it's a lie if you continue being dishonest with yourself. How about you answer a simple question since you're so gung ho on truthfulness? You couldn't adequately answer that question with me, even though you were prepared to bind yourself to me in holy matrimony, but let's try again, shall we? What do you *feel* for her, Stanton? How the hell do you really feel about her?"

Alive. As alive as he'd ever felt since Jax died. Exhilarated. Hopeful. And ... complete. She filled whatever hole had been left in him the night Jax died.

Sage dropped into the chair facing him. Her briefcase slid off her lap and toppled to the carpet as she white-knuckled the armrests.

Jaw dropping, she gasped, "Oh my God, you're in love with her."

Stanton's gaze met hers. He didn't bother to deny it. Not only was Sage intelligent and perceptive, but they'd been together for years. She knew him better than most.

"You'll never be able to do it, Stanton. Her mother may have died when she was young, but Puck and the club have protected her. Cosseted her. There's no way *you* could give her half of what they've given her. It's too high a bar for you. You'll fall flat on your face, and when you crash, you'll crush her along the way. I'm begging you. Walk away now. You'll fuck up, *like you always do*. For once in your life, think of someone besides yourself."

He barked out a laugh. *For once in his life.* Nice touch. As if in the years between Jax's death and meeting Sammi, he'd ever done something purely for himself? Even the drugs had started as a pick-me-up for the extra jolt of energy required to work harder and faster than anyone else in his department. To be the best. So that his father wouldn't regret the decision to approve Stanton's career in law enforcement instead of politics. To prove that *he* was the best. Not Jax.

As Sage spewed her assumptions, his body temperature began to rise.

Glaring at her, he went on the attack. "Fucking seriously, Sage? I'll take the brunt of our fucked-up relationship, but don't act like you're so perfect. Don't put what happened between us on my relationship with Sammi. She's a completely different person and I'm a different person with her."

"Are you, though?" Sage leaned forward, glints of challenge in her eyes.

He rose to his feet. "You have every right to hold a grudge against me, but let's be real here, you don't have an open mind when it comes to me. Nothing I say can change your opinion of me."

"Okay, fine. You're right." She crossed her arms over her chest and huffed out a breath. "I'll try to listen to what you have to say. At the very least, it seems like you genuinely care about her. At least within your limited ability to care, of course."

"Of course. How generous of you," he retorted.

Her eyes narrowed on him. "If you care about her, then explain yourself. You know the club is like a family, so think of me as an older sister and Kingdom as her uncle."

Fine, she'd made a valid point. He wanted to *eventually* win these people over. Stanton slowly resumed his seat. Elbows on his desk, he steepled his fingers together.

"I'm assuming Sammi didn't speak about my personal issues," he began. Sage confirmed with a shake of her head. "As you know, I took a month off from work. Have you ever known me to take that amount of time off?"

She shook it again, slower this time as a realization dawned on her. She always was quick on the uptake.

"I went to Tully. A drug rehabilitation center."

"I know of it," she replied with a slow nod of her head.

"I was already long past dabbling in drugs when we were together. If you think back, you may recognize certain erratic behaviors. If I had been more mature and not trapped in a cycle of addiction, I should've been honest about the fact that I never wanted to get married or have children. I should have dated casually, but I had my father breathing down my neck with his political campaigns and the picture-perfect image he was touting of our family."

Threading his fingers together in a prayer-like gesture, he continued, "It's of little use to you now, I know, but I apologize for the pain I caused you. For being dishonest. For asking you to become my wife when I wasn't prepared to reciprocate. I apologize for cheating on you. The drugs were elemental in that, but the underlying problems were all me. I made amends to Melanie, although I'm not certain she heard my apology. She was beside herself with anger at the time. But I'm trying to fix the wreckage of the past."

Sage fell back against her chair, arms limp at her side. Her mouth opened and closed a few times.

"I see my apology has taken you by surprise," Stanton commented dryly.

"I'd say that's an understatement," she replied and then fell silent again. Her brows gathered low on her forehead. She was clearly sifting through his confession. Eventually, her forehead smoothed out and she cleared her throat.

"There were times when you seemed out of it. I remember one specific conversation at the courthouse, a couple of years ago. You seemed so unlike yourself. Then again, you have the propensity to act like an asshole, so I chalked it up to that." Shaking her head slightly, she drew in a long breath. "I never would've thought you ... of all people."

"Had a secret as dark as an addiction," he finished for her. "If I hadn't met so many other addicts, I'd concur in your surprise. However, thirty days of hearing people regurgitate the tricks they played on their loved ones put my own conduct in perspective."

Her eyes shot to his. He made a disgusted noise in the back of his throat. "I'm not suggesting that my behavior was excusable. What I mean to say is that I'm not the only one. Far from it. Perspective allowed me to overcome my shame about everything I'd done. I'm now able to admit it and apologize. Look, I don't expect you to forgive me. I'm simply providing you with context."

Sage's gaze drifted around his office, pausing on various objects, like the award for best attorney of the year from AILA that he'd shoved to the back corner of his bookshelf.

Grabbing his NA coin in his desk drawer, he rubbed it as he waited for Sage's reaction.

"This is a lot to process. I can't say that I accept your apology, but I respect it. I appreciate how difficult it must have been for you to confide in me. Putting that aside, let's turn to how this affects you and Sammi."

"I'm not the same person with Sammi that I was with you. My change began before I met her and it's continued since then. There are no guarantee that I won't go back to using, but it's a one-day-at-a-time philosophy. I have awareness and a set of tools to help me when I get the urge to text my dealer. The answer to your unspoken question is that yes, I do get the urge. Certainly, it helps that the physical dependency is no longer there. I'm trying to live an honest life and I've been open with Sammi about everything."

He raised his hands and concluded, "That's about the gist of it."

Sage sat calmly, listening to him. Then again, she wasn't a ranter by nature. Her poker face was always good because he couldn't get a read on exactly what she was thinking. But regardless of what she thought, he and Sammi were an item. He only cared so far as it made Sammi's life easier.

"Took the wind out of your sails, huh?"

"Something like that," she replied. It was a good sign that her facial muscles relaxed and her hands lightly rubbed her protruding belly.

Stanton gave an internal shudder. Another reason it would've never worked out between them. Sage was meant to be a mother while Stanton cringed at the thought of parenthood. He loved Wesley, Cornell's son, of course. Truth be told, he loved kids, but he'd sworn to never perpetuate the relationship he had with his father on offspring of his own. Witnessing his mother's breakdown after Jax's death only reinforced the perils of parenthood. There wasn't enough love in the world to prevent the inevitable heartache of bringing a child into this world.

"Alright, you've given me quite a lot to mull over." Sage's voice broke into his thoughts. "I'll go back to Kingdom with this information. I'm not sold on you, but, for Sammi's sake, I'll get him to back off and not destroy your relationship with her."

"I'm sure you'll can manage to convince him. He seems quite smitten with you," Stanton said.

A brief smile flitted over her lips.

Slapping her hands over the armrests of her chair, she said, "I will expect Sammi to bring you to the clubhouse this weekend for a party. Family friendly, so there won't be any bloodshed."

Her brows puckered together. "Hopefully," she muttered low, but he heard her.

Bracing herself against the armrests, she struggled to her feet and bent down to pick up her briefcase.

"Despite our past, I'm going to give you a chance. But Stanton, don't prove me wrong."

"Fair enough," he replied as he stood up, crossed the room, and opened the door for her. Closing it behind her, his shoulders slumped. He was not looking forward to being tested by a clubhouse full of bikers.

23

STANTON

Ever since the gala, Stanton had anticipated a summons from his father, which he'd finally received in the form of a straightforward text stating a date and time.

So here he was, handing his briefcase and coat to Mariah, his parents' housekeeper. She'd been with his family for decades and had become a confidante of his mother's.

He greeted Mariah and asked about her family.

"Oh, you know, now that the children are all grown up, it's the grandchildren that take up my every waking thought. Not that I'm complaining, mind you," she replied.

After putting his things away in a large closet, Mariah slipped through a door off the grand marbled foyer of his familial home. A wide wooden staircase led up to the first floor of the house, the family wing to the right and guest rooms to the left.

Stanton bypassed the stairs altogether, took a left to one of several rooms off the main foyer, and ducked through the dining room to a small sitting room in the back. One wall of the room was lined with floor-to-ceiling glass doors that opened into a glass-enclosed sunroom.

His mother sat, with her feet tucked beneath her, on an overstuffed paisley chaise lounge, a book propped on her bent knees. She was surrounded by love seats, small sofas, and round tables covered with potted plants and other knick-knacks. Beside her, on a small table, lay her after-dinner coffee with an array of small pastries. It was past seven o'clock and there was no light coming from the acre of land surrounding the house, but the faint trickling of the fountain outside could be heard in the still quietness of the room.

Not having yet eaten dinner, Stanton scooped up a mini éclair and stuffed it into his mouth.

His mother glanced up at him, a gentle smile playing on her face. "Hello, darling. Have you not eaten yet? Should I get Mariah to bring you a sandwich?"

Stanton swallowed and bent down to kiss her cheek. "Don't bother. I'm sure Father will cut my appetite with whatever he has to say to me."

She swatted his arm. "Hush, now. Your father has your best interests at heart."

"Hmm," he replied noncommittally, and took a seat across from her. Her response told him that she knew the reason for the summons, and more importantly, that she was in full agreement with his father. There was no point in getting into it with her. She never argued. She didn't like it and said that she found it uncouth.

His mother never pushed an agenda. If there was pushing to be done, she left it to his father. Division of labor, she called it. On the upside, if things didn't turn out as she'd hoped, she'd let it go. In that way, at least, she respected Stanton and his decisions. This quirk of hers salvaged their relationship, time and time again.

There was one exception to this iron-clad rule: the subject of children. Once Amy passed the age of twenty-five, and probably after Mariah started bringing up her own grandchildren, his mother became anxious. As for him, he'd told her on several occasions that he had no intention of having children, but she was deaf to his hints. If he had to guess, he'd say that this summons had to do with this.

"What are you doing here anyway? Isn't there a soirée somewhere? A dinner or play?" he teased lightly.

"One can't go out every night of the week, Stanton. It's a Wednesday in the middle of winter, and I'm not as young as I used to be."

"Nonsense, you'll always be young," he replied glibly, and popped another mini éclair into his mouth.

Checking his watch, he stood up, smoothed down his shirt, buttoned his jacket, and pulled on his cuffs. "Well, I'm off to the execution squad. I'll stop by on my way out."

"Listen to what he has to say," his mother called out behind him as he strolled back into the house.

He paused, keeping his back to her, and answered, "I always do, Mother," before continuing on his way.

Stanton passed the foyer where he'd arrived, crossed to the other side of the house, and knocked softly on the heavy oak door of his father's study. Hearing his father's invitation to enter, he took a deep breath, turned the brass handle, and pushed in.

His father's study was decorated in red leather and mahogany, like a quintessential study of academics of old. The scent of lingering cigar smoke mingled with the old leather-bound books encased in the bookshelves behind his father's desk. Stanton remembered hiding underneath that desk for hours, playing hide and seek with Jax. It was before he learned that his father regularly swept the room for bugs because he used this study as an inner sanctum for his political deals. Honestly, at a certain point Stanton made a conscious decision that the less he knew, the better.

"Good evening, sir," he greeted his father, reaching across the massive desk to offer his hand.

His father rose and shook his hand. "How are things?"

"Well enough, sir. And you?"

"As can be expected." His father motioned to one of the seats facing the desk. "Come, sit down."

Stanton opened his jacket and seated himself in the stout, wooden armchair with leather-covered padding on the arms.

His father stood and refilled his drink at a small bar to the left of his desk. "Can I offer you anything?"

"Do you have soda water?"

"Yes," he replied, taking a cut crystal glass, and placing a couple of ice cubes inside. Picking up the metal seltzer bottle, he pressed the release valve and there was a hissing sound as seltzer water shot into the glass. Returning the bottle to its exact place, he handed the glass to Stanton and then sat back down.

Swirling his drink in his hand, his father immediately got to the point. "Your mother described to me her meeting with your newest," he paused for a long beat, "girlfriend."

Stanton didn't respond. There was no need to. His father was not one to mince words, but any potential extraneous niceties were put aside in his study.

Not expecting an answer, his father continued, "I had her investigated. Other than the fact that she's a member of a motorcycle club, I was surprised to find that you are the prosecutor on her brother's criminal case."

His father glanced up from his drink.

Now an answer was expected.

"This is true."

"She must be quite a girl to forgive you for your involvement."

"She's quite exceptional, yes. You would have found out yourself if you'd taken the time to meet her."

His father waved his hand as if batting away an annoying insect. "I had my hands full and your mother's more than a capable judge. She was pleasantly surprised, considering the girl's background."

Stanton's teeth clenched briefly, but he released the tension in his jaw, and stated, "The girl's name is Sammi."

He was still in the realm of calm, but his pulse was starting to tick up. It was ridiculous for a man his age to have a discussion like this with his father. He'd been brought up to understand that his family was unlike others, that there were a set of expectations and demands to be adhered to. Complicating things further was Jax, which kept Stanton tethered to this infantile need to make up for the part he played in his brother's death, but Stanton was a grown man and this was a chastisement the likes of which only children endured.

"Let's cut to the chase, Stanton, shall we," his father declared.

"Yes, let's," he replied. "You don't know her, but that fact doesn't stop you from disliking her. She's not from the right family or even the right stratum of society. Let's not pretend otherwise."

"If you know how I feel about it, and I've never hidden my expectations for you, then why are you with her?"

"Because, sir, my private life is exactly that. Mine. I'm willing to toe the line, but there are limits. Whom I bed or date is none of your business. If you don't want to meet her, then so be it, but know this, she will continue to be in my life."

His father stared at him from over the top of his steepled

fingers. "Stanton, you're too old for adolescent rebellion. You did it once before and look at the chaos it caused."

Stanton's heart stalled. Bringing up Jax was low, even for his father. His parents didn't speak of Jax, and Stanton respected their decision, but to bring him up a dozen years after his death in *this* context was unacceptable. Gripping and releasing the arms of his chair, Stanton glared at his father. He would not be pressured to do the man's bidding. No more.

"I assure you, sir, this relationship was not caused by angst, adolescent or otherwise. I've deemed that my actions will not hurt the family, so I will live as I choose."

He knew he'd laid down a gauntlet in front of a formidable opponent, but it was time to fucking man up. Jax or no Jax.

"I see," his father replied quietly. Leaning back in his chair, he held the silence between them.

Stanton refused to break first. It was an old trick he'd used many times with juries. Releasing the arms of his chair, he leaned back and mimicked a relaxed pose, even if every muscle in his body was clenched with tension.

"If you don't cut her off, then I will cut you off. Do you understand? You won't get a dime from me. Yes, you have your grandfather's inheritance." He made a scoffing sound. "He was a weak man. Outside of that, you will get nothing."

"Not this crystal," he said as he held up the antique cut crystal glass, a family heirloom.

"Not this pen," he added as he picked up his Mont Blanc fountain pen.

"Nothing. Do I make myself clear?"

Fuck. You. I don't need your fucking glass or your Mont Blanc pen, asshole.

Stanton raised to his feet, ready to leave before his head exploded. The one fucking time he did something for himself, and his father cut him off at the knees.

"Very well, sir. Is that all?" he said coolly.

With a disgusted flick of his hand, his father drawled, "Yes, that is all."

Spinning on his heels, Stanton took measured steps to the door, calmly opened it, and shut it quietly behind him. What he really wanted to do was slam the damn door and punch a hole in the fucking wallpapered wall, but he held firm. Not trusting himself to speak calmly, he decided against saying goodnight to his mother and stalked to the foyer. Retrieving his coat and briefcase, he flung the door open and slammed it shut behind him.

In the frigid air, he heaved out breaths, the condensed air hovering for a moment before dispersing in the thin night air, and punched the air with his fists.

Fuck. Him. Just fuck him. I'm done.

24

SAMMI

The Squad cookout didn't begin until the afternoon, giving Sammi a chance to lounge in Stanton's bed to her heart's content.

Over the past month, they'd fallen into a pattern. During the week, Sammi came over to his apartment the nights he didn't burn the midnight oil. They had the entire weekend, uninterrupted.

Mondays were the hardest for her; she suffered from Stanton withdrawal. But today was a glorious Saturday morning, and she had the whole weekend to revel in his presence and take advantage of his gorgeous body.

Sounds of a pan landing on the stovetop and the *click click click* of the stove being lit carried through Stanton's loft in the newest luxury apartment building in the city center.

Throwing on one of his T-shirts, she padded into the kitchen and spied Stanton frowning into a large blue porcelain bowl with a whisk in his hand. He hadn't bothered to put on a shirt, and the muscles of his chest and shoulders were on glorious display. His nipples, flat and round, tightened as he watched her stroll over to him. She wanted to follow the midline between his pecs with her tongue and lick his abs. But, they had to get ready for the party.

"Morning, babe," he said, his voice smooth as bourbon.

She returned his greeting with a huskier voice than his and had to clear her throat. Propping her hip against the counter, she asked, "What are you making there?"

"Pancakes."

"Hmm, yum."

His eyes darkened to a shade of blue she easily recognized.

"Don't say that word unless you're saying it with your lips around my cock," he replied, his voice a whole lot tighter than it was before. The fact that she could take him from zero to a hundred in a matter of minutes had her laughing.

His gaze flicked down the worn T-shirt that ended at the juncture of her thighs. Closing his eyes, he said, "Christ, do you seriously want to eat? I can put this in the fridge, carry you back to bed, and feast on you for breakfast."

A flush of heat whooshed over her as she considered his suggestion. No, they'd never make it out of the loft if they went back to bed.

"I'm hungry," she replied.

The instant she confessed to hunger, he was all business. He finished whisking, put it aside, and dropped a dollop of butter in the pan. It hit the hot metal with a sizzle and soon he was flipping pancakes. It was so fucking hot to watch him cooking for her that she had to turn to the fridge and busy herself with rummaging through it.

"No whipped cream?" she asked, turning around just as a pancake slid off the spatula and fell to the floor.

"Dammit, Sammi. Whipped cream? Really?"

"For the pancake, silly," she teased.

She preferred whipped cream with her pancakes, but she did a mental fist pump for flustering him.

Batting her eyelashes, she asked innocently, "What? Little girls can't like whipped cream with their pancakes?"

Stanton's eyes raised to the ceiling. "Such a cocktease, this one. What did I do to deserve this?"

"Very, very bad things, I can attest to that," she tossed back, although his brand of badness felt oh so very good.

Shutting the fridge with the heel of her foot, she carried the maple syrup and a bowl of blueberries to the counter. Stanton poured them orange juice, and they settled on a pair of high stools around the counter.

Moaning, Sammi complimented, "Good job on the pancakes. Even without whipped cream."

His eyes cut to her lips, which had closed around a forkful of pancake. "I'll make certain to keep some from now on. I can think of a few uses besides pancakes."

She poked her fork in his direction and winked. "I like the way you think, buddy."

He guffawed and shook his head. "Too fucking cute," he mumbled low to himself, triggering a pool of warmth in Sammi's belly.

Watching him carefully, she asked, "Are you nervous about going to the club? You shouldn't be, you know. I'll make sure people treat you right."

"You're going to be my protector, little girl? Must I give you a reminder of exactly who's the daddy in this relationship?"

Instantly, her pussy got slippery. It was not a word either of them had specifically used before except in jest, but there was no doubt it was a running theme in their relationship.

"I've been through worse things in my life than a clubhouse of bikers," he quipped.

Curiosity piqued, she tilted her head to the side and blurted out, "Like what?"

His fork halted midway to his mouth. There was a shift in the air. His eyes grew serious. His gaze darted away and then slowly returned and locked on her. She'd felt a shift in him a few days ago, but chalked it up to the stress of his caseload. A rush of coolness slithered down her spine.

"I've told you about losing Jax, my older brother. What I didn't tell you was that I caused his death."

Sammi felt the color drain from her face.

Holding her gaze, Stanton went on, "I was the fuckup of the family."

Sammi shook her head in denial, but he nodded in confirmation of his statement.

"He really was fucking perfect, but that was okay. It suited us both," Stanton insisted. "There was never competition. First, because he was the apple of my father's eye and nothing I did would change that. The thing was, imperfection accorded me the freedom to be myself. While my brother scored a perfect SAT and gunned to be valedictorian, I lived as normally as possible for the offspring of one Benjamin Prescott, the Third. Unfortunately, I fucked it up."

"No you didn't," Sammi bit out.

A tender smile graced his lips. "You haven't even heard what I did."

"I don't need to," she huffed out and then stuffed her mouth with a large piece of pancake. Swallowing, she went on, "Whatever you did wasn't on purpose, that much I already know. You're not a malicious person."

"Malicious or not, my actions led to death and heartbreak. Listen to the story, at least, before judging me as innocent. It was the summer I'd turned sixteen, and I'd sneaked out to a party. Too drunk to drive my ass back home, I called Jax to pick me up. A drunk driver rammed head-on into our car. I survived and have failed miserably at filling his shoes ever since."

Hearing the ache in his tone had her reaching over the counter to clutch his hand. Stanton may have been born well-off, but his life had by no means been easy. She knew what it was to lose someone, the agony and damage around it, and she hadn't been forced to witness her mother's accident, survive it, or blame herself for it. Those were heavy burdens.

"It's true, Sammi. It's the defining moment of my life, and to understand me, you must accept that truth. It devastated my parents and changed the course of our lives permanently. Not for the better, I might add."

"It may be *your* truth, but that doesn't make it the *whole* truth," she replied forcefully. "You're not your brother so it doesn't surprise me that you feel like a failure. Of course, you'd fail at being him because you're you. Living up to the memory of a dead boy—because let's face it, he was still a boy and we have no idea how he would've turned out—is pointless."

"Being me is no great achievement," he scoffed.

The Stanton of this confession was so different from the cocky, arrogant man she was used to. The one who would stop at nothing to get what he wanted. This was a broken Stanton, and she'd do anything to relieve him of this crushing weight.

She stood up and moved around the counter to him.

"Babe, you can't change the past or make up for it, no matter how much you try. Believe me, I did some crazy things after my mother died, hoping to recapture the past or change the future. One day, Puck sat me down and told me that, dead or not, the only thing she'd want is for me to be myself. Same goes for Jax. He loved you for who you were.

He wouldn't expect or want you to fill his shoes. You," she laid her hand on his bare chest and felt his heartbeat pound against her palm, "are who you're supposed to be. Hell, I didn't fall for some dude named Jax. I fell for Stanton, and he's loyal, protective, and smart as a whip. Oh, and hot as fuck."

She raked her fingernail over his nipple. "No man touches me like you do. I wouldn't trade you for the world, and it's not like I'm blind to your faults."

He pulled back, a frown between his brows. "What faults? Who could make pancakes like these for his bitch?"

She grinned. "Oh, so I'm a bitch now, am I?"

"Yes, *my* bitch. And that was said with the toughest, sexiest connotations in mind," he clarified sternly. Slipping his fingers beneath the hem of her T-shirt, he grasped her hip and drew her between his legs.

Grazing his lips over hers, he murmured, "You fucking complete me, babe."

Her tongue slid into his mouth and tangled with his. Pushing his chest, she stared into his eyes. "Promise me you'll stop chasing empty dreams."

"You'll have to do a little more to convince me of the error of my ways," he suggested.

"Hmm, is that right? Anything in particular you have in mind?"

Her fingernails scraped down his chest and her hand landed on his package. Squeezing, she felt him grow hard beneath her touch. She loved how she could affect him so quickly, could turn him on, and get him to focus back on what mattered. Them.

"I have a vivid imagination when I put my mind to it," he confided.

"Is that right?" she crooned.

Lifting the bottle of maple syrup, he grabbed her hand and dragged her toward his bedroom.

"You're going to mess up the sheets," she warned.

Casting a heated look over his shoulder, he tugged her behind him. "Oh, babe, you underestimate me. My tongue is a precise instrument. I won't let a single drop go to waste."

25

STANTON

"Hot damn, that's a fine piece of ass."

The comment boomed out of the biker standing behind Stanton, at the clubhouse. He seethed with possessiveness. Sammi was *his*. He was the man who split her open earlier that day, withdrawing his cock smeared in her juices, like the traces of lipstick on his dick when she deep-throated him. The fucker was begging for a broken nose if he kept talking about Sammi like that.

Stanton was already more irritable than usual since his conversation with his father, but he had every intention of behaving. Unfortunately, almost upon arrival, the men lobbed taunts and tests at him like it was open hunting season. The last time he had to endure this kind of nonsense was when he pledged for his father's fraternity at Yale. A few fraternity brothers tried hazing him; one ended up in the emergency room. Only his father's influence saved him from getting suspended.

His fingers twitched by his sides. Twisting his head, he glared the big man down. The asshole had at least fifty pounds on him, but he wasn't in as good a shape as Stanton.

Problem was that Stanton was the outsider in this shithole. Chances were high they'd gang up on him, and he'd get his ass handed to him.

"Look at her tits. Bet they'd fly when I bounce her on my dick."

Without another thought, Stanton whirled around, pulled in his balled fist, and slammed it into the man's face.

Doubling over, the man held his bleeding nose and bellowed, "What the fuck?"

"Don't you dare speak about her like that. Matter of fact, you don't look at her," he threatened, fists up.

"Why the fuck didn't you say she was yours?" the biker growled, suddenly standing tall and hovering over Stanton. "Instead of standing there like a fucking pussy and letting me trash-talk her It's not like she has a cut on that claims her as taken?"

Stanton ground down on his back molars. What the hell was wrong with these people?

"If you don't claim her, then she's free pussy. You claiming her?" he asked, peering closely into Stanton's face.

Christ, another test. A few brothers milling around halted their conversations, blatantly listening to the confrontation.

"Not sure what you mean by claiming her, but I'm the only man who touches her. Anyone have a problem with that?" Stanton spat out, glaring at the men that shifted into a tight circle around him and the huge, questionably human, monstrosity.

"Enough," thundered a voice as a pair of large hands parted the crowd. "Knock it off, Tank."

Stanton recognized Kingdom, the president of the Demon Squad and Sage's husband. Sammi slipped out from behind Kingdom's back and hugged Stanton.

Glaring up at Tank, she said, "What the hell, Tank? I can't

leave him alone for a moment without you getting all up in his face?"

Tank guffawed and displayed his open palm smeared with his own blood. "Your old man just punched me."

Sammi's eyes narrowed into slits. Between clenched teeth, she seethed, "He's not my old man."

Tank's grin widened. "Sure about that?"

Sammi stamped her feet a little. "We're not doing this right now. My relationship is none of your damn business."

"It sure as hell is my damn business. I'm like an uncle to you. Puck's not around, so it's up to me to make sure this fucker treats you right."

"Uncle?" Stanton sputtered. Seeing red, he grabbed the front of Tank's shirt and twisted it. "You fucking pervert, talking about her like taht."

Swatting Stanton's hand off his shirt, Tank edged closer to him and gave a self-satisfied chortle. "I do whatever it takes to make sure that Sammi doesn't get hurt. You got played, son."

Stanton squared his shoulders, ready to beat the bastard down. They were insane, every one of them.

Kingdom cut in between them, planting a hand on both of their chests, and shoved them away from each other. "Tank, since when do we treat visitors like this?"

"What-fucking-ever. I did what I had to do."

"I had it under control, brother, till you stomped all over my plans with your size fifteen shoes," Kingdom grumbled.

"My bad," Tank replied, with an unconcerned shrug of his broad shoulders.

Sammi crossed her arms over her chest and tapped one of her feet impatiently. "Seriously, people, I can handle myself. I don't need a dozen big brothers trying to take Puck's place. I'm a grown-ass woman, thank you very much."

Ignoring her, Kingdom gave Stanton a chin lift and said,

"Come with me." He waved away the crowd of brothers. "The rest of you, go back to whatever the hell you were doing."

Fucking finally. He'd wasted enough time on the others. Kingdom was the main opponent. If he hammered out his differences with Kingdom, the others would step in line. That much was obvious.

"Where are you going with him?" Sammi asked, the corners of her lips slanted downward.

"Stanton and I have to talk," Kingdom replied.

Sammi stepped forward. "Then I'm coming, too."

Without bothering to reply, Kingdom turned his back on them and walked away. Sammi grabbed Stanton's hand and followed through the parted crowd. He could handle Kingdom on his own, but he liked having Sammi with him. It was reminiscent of how they'd worked together at the gala. They made one badass team.

Once in Kingdom's office, he gestured for them to take seats on a couch set against the back wall. Going around his desk, he sat down on a swivel chair, leaned back, and propped his boots on the tabletop.

"So," he began, "my first concern has been taken care, thanks to Tank."

Sammi rolled her eyes. "Since when do you care who anyone goes out with in the club?"

"Since when have you been with anyone, Sammi?" he returned, mimicking her exasperated tone. "Puck is locked up. He expects us to watch over you, and we don't let our people down."

His eyes cut over to Stanton and held his gaze.

Stanton tamped down the surge of irritation that threatened to spill over. He was close to wrapping his hands around Kingdom's throat and choking him out. Somehow, he thought that was a predictable reaction to these assholes.

"If you're suggesting that I would treat Sammi badly, rest assured that's not going fucking happen. I'm not the same man I was when I was with Sage."

Linking his hands behind his head, Kingdom replied, "Glad to hear that. Don't get me wrong, I'm glad you fucked up with Sage. She was meant to marry a guy like you, live in a big fancy mansion with two-point-five kids. I would've never had a chance in hell if you hadn't screwed up so goddamn badly. You did me the favor of my life."

"Glad to be of help," Stanton replied sardonically.

"Thing is, though, her experience has raised red flags. The first one is loyalty. The fact that you brought Sammi to your fancy-ass gala and stood up to Tank are good signs, but the jury's still out."

"For fuck's sake," Sammi burst out. "He doesn't have to prove himself to you. He's proven himself to me, which is enough! Yes, Kingdom, we are in a monogamous relationship. No, he hasn't cheated on me."

"How the fuck would you know if he's cheated or not?" Kingdom snapped. "Cheaters don't advertise their affairs."

Sammi's face turned bright red. Jumping to her feet, she hissed, "I know you're trying to take care of me, but this is bullshit. I'm a grown woman, and whatever arrangement Stanton and I have is between the two of us. We don't need to run it by you. We don't need your approval. Since when is monogamy a thing that is so important in this club anyway?"

"Point taken, but look at it from my position. I don't want to be all up in your business and cause stress between you and your man, but he doesn't have a good rep. Now, if he were a biker, I'd have the power to threaten his ass and make sure he treats you right. But I can't put the fear of God in him." He implored, "I'm in unchartered territory here. And I don't have the years of experience Puck has in dealing with your ass."

"Puck wasn't so great at it, let me tell you. How about you trust me? I know that seems like a novel idea, but I'll say it again. I'm an adult. It's my life. I understand that Stanton is not your first pick, but it turns out that he fits *my* requirements perfectly and I'm the only one that matters. Trust me, you don't want the details of why he's so perfect."

"Christ," Kingdom grumbled, swiping his hand over his face. "You sure about that, Sammi? I know he doesn't eat pussy. Just sayin', is that the kind of life you want for yourself?"

"Oh. My. God. You did not just say that," she said with a gasp.

Despite himself, Stanton burst into laughter. "Is that truly what's concerning you?"

Kingdom swung his arm out in her direction, palm up. "I want Sammi here to have the best. Hell, it was an uphill fucking battle to get Sage to spread her legs for my tongue, thanks to you. You did a real mind-fuck on her. Can't imagine you know how to satisfy a woman."

Sammi made gagging noises, and Stanton had to press his lips together to hold back the laughter bubbling up in his throat. "Let me put your mind at ease. I have no issues with eating pussy. In fact, I had the same problem with Sammi as you had with Sage. Ironic, that. Thing is, Kingdom, I love going down on my woman. I love hearing her scream my name and creaming all over my face. I love it so much that I made sure never to do it with Sage, because I didn't want to fall for her. If I'd tongue-fucked her, I would've never been able to get out from under her, and I wasn't ready to commit. Currently, it's a non-issue. Isn't that right, sweetheart?"

Stanton wrapped his arms around Sammi's shoulders, bringing her in tight against his side. Mouth parted, she blinked up at him a few times.

His lips twitched. Glancing down at her, he prompted, "Do

I do right by you? Tongue-fuck you until you scream? Go on, tell your president."

Shoving her palms against his chest, she sputtered, "You men are ridiculous. I can't believe we're having this conversation and there's no way I'm talking about my sex life with the husband of one of my best friends. No thanks, but I'm out."

She stood up and marched to the door. Twisting around, she jammed her finger in Kingdom's direction and warned, "This conversation never happened."

Her gaze swung to Stanton and she declared, "I'll meet you outside. Finish up with him, but for the love of God, keep our private life private."

Yanking the door open, she stalked out and let it slam behind her. The door shook in its frame for a moment before silence returned.

"If you hadn't hurt my woman and this wasn't about Sammi, I wouldn't give two fucks what you do. But we're dealing with Sammi here. When Sammi walked into this club, she was a sad kid. Never seen a girl so damn sad. Her moms had died a couple years back and she had no one but Puck. Now she has a whole club behind her. Haven't seen that sad look in a long time, and I don't want to see it there again, feel me?"

"Understood."

The one thing this club family cared about was her emotional state of mind. The exact opposite of his family life, where emotions didn't factor in.

"I didn't do right by Sage so there's no way for me to prove it, but loyalty is important to me. If you ask Sage, she'll tell you I've always been loyal to my family and my work. I'm not going to sit here and pretend I didn't fuck up majorly in my life. More than you can imagine, and I bet you've seen quite a lot. The thing is, I came out of rehab—"

"Sage mentioned," Kingdom cut in.

Stanton nodded. "Good, then I don't have to go into details. Point is, I'm doing everything in my power to live right. That includes Sammi. Looking from the outside, it seems insane. Just out of rehab and falling for a young woman who comes from a different world. But the truth is, we're compatible in ways I never knew a couple could be. Every past relationship was a struggle, but with Sammi, it's simple and easy. It works and I feel good with her. Whole. I can only hope I give her the same feeling."

There was a long moment of silence. Kingdom's boots thumped to the ground. He leaned over his desk and stared Stanton down over the steeple of his fingers. "Christ. Puck is going to kick my ass for letting this come to pass."

"Let him think Sammi's with me to influence his case," he suggested. "It was one of my selling points to convince her to go out with me."

His eyes sharpened. "Are you?"

"Of course not. I already told you, I'm loyal about certain things. It's a short list, but it's unbreakable. Sammi's on that list now. What I will tell you is what I told Sammi and Sage. Puck painted himself into a corner with his confession, and with Korman holding the gavel, his choices are limited. But am I going all out? Hell no. Was I planning to before meeting Sammi? Not in the least. I don't have an ax to grind with the Squad or bikers in general. Puck doesn't have a record and I saw the victim's arrest sheet. That guy's a piece of shit."

"Have you found him? Kerri's ex?"

Stanton's ear pricked up at the sudden hardness to Kingdom's tone. "No, he hasn't come forward, and I haven't made an effort to search for him. Why?"

"No reason," he responded vaguely. "My last concern is that you're an officer of the law."

"I'm not a fucking policeman, I'm a lawyer. And I have no intention of making a citizen's arrest on my day off," Stanton assured him.

"Good, then we're on the same page. I don't need any trouble. Especially for my woman. If you have a problem with anything you see, I ask that you come to me first and we'll resolve the issue together."

"Fair enough, but I'm no saint, and I don't make it a habit to cast stones. I'm here for Sammi because you're her family. That's it."

"Brah, good luck with taming that wildcat. I don't envy you," Kingdom said with a smirk. "I've got a docile one compared to you."

"Bringing a strong woman in hand is part of the game." Stanton rose to his feet and walked over to the entrance. Hand on the knob, he threw over his shoulder, "The best part."

26

STANTON

"I'm taking you to my favorite spot, so hush and be a good boy," Sammi said, patting Stanton on the cheek.

Grabbing her hand, he dragged it down to his crotch, and inquired with an arched brow, "Does this feel like a boy to you?"

Releasing her hand quickly, he pushed open the door of her favorite French bakery, La Boulangerie, and the bell attached to the handle jingled. It was past breakfast—hell, it was past brunch—but Sammi convinced him that they'd find breakfast treats waiting for them.

Apparently, the owner put several croissants aside for her when she didn't show up at her usual morning time. He didn't want to burst her bubble by telling her there was no way a few measly croissants were going to satisfy his hunger after the night they'd had. He bet he dropped a pound in weight just in come. At this point, he could eat a fucking horse. With a side of her pussy, of course. Always a side of her.

Holding the door open, he swatted her bouncy ass as she sailed past him, eliciting a small yelp from her.

"Bonjour!" boomed a voice from behind the counter. "I told Madame Vachon our *cherie* would stop by."

A round, jovial man in a white apron rounded the corner of the counter, holding up a paper bag.

"Sit, sit," he commanded, his hand gesturing toward the only empty table in the bakery. "*Un espresso pour la mademoiselle*. And for her friend?"

"The same, thank you," replied Stanton as he held out the chair for Sammi.

"Ahh, a gentleman. You must keep this one," he counseled Sammi with a wink.

Taking a seat, she laid her hand over Stanton's, wrapped over the top of the back of the chair. "Oh, I intend to."

Out of nowhere, a tiny whirling dervish of a girl, about eight years old, swept out from behind Mr. Vouchon, skidded to a stop in front of Sammi, and landed on her lap. A pair of bright, intelligent blue eyes peered over Sammi's shoulder at Stanton. The little girl leaned over and whispered, "Is he your *boy*friend?"

Sammi's laughter rang out and she looped a stray lock behind the girl's ear. "I suppose he is."

"You've never brought anyone here but your brother and Abby," she noted, in a lilting French accent. "And he's holding out a chair for you to sit on so he must be a *boy*friend. Only boyfriends do such things," she declared with a very solemn expression.

Leaning down low, Stanton whispered to her, "I am her boyfriend. My name's Stanton. What is your name?"

The girl inclined her head shyly, and peeking from under lowered lids, murmured back, "My name is Claire."

Mr. Vouchon shooed Claire out of Sammi's lap, despite Sammi's protests. Marveling at her ability to create a family wherever she went, Stanton rounded the table to sit down across from her and petted her hand.

Wrapping a croissant in parchment paper, she handed it to Stanton and said, "Try it. You'll die."

He bit into the crescent-shaped pastry, making the quintessential crackling sound as his teeth penetrated the crisp, flaky crust. Butter oozed onto his tongue and Stanton moaned around the first bite.

Poking his head up, he viewed the empty display case. "Good God, I hope they have more in the back."

Mr. Vouchon flew past, depositing two cups of steaming *café au lait* at a neighboring table before stopping by with a plate holding half a baguette with butter and jam, along with their espressos.

"Enjoy," he said, and disappeared.

"I have to tell my mother about this place. How did you find it?"

"They're still somewhat of a hidden gem, but not for long," she replied proudly, lifting her chin in the direction of the other tables. "They arrived from France a few months ago with dreams of bringing French pastries to America. That, and his sister was able to sponsor Mr. Vouchon to open a *boulangerie*," she stressed the last word. "Apparently, the competition in Toulouse, where they're from, is vicious. On weekends, a good bakery has people lining up outside the door before it opens. You should definitely bring your mom and tell everyone else you know about this place."

"Don't you want to keep it hidden?"

"God, no! I own a business; I know how hard it is to succeed. I've been helping Mr. Vouchon with social media, setting up a website for him and teaching him and Claire how to post. It's easy for her to snap pics on his phone of him baking or schmoozing with the customers. Taught him how to take pics of rows of croissants coming out the oven. That happens too early in the morning for Claire to take. Actually," she took out her phone, "that reminds me. Let me take one of us, post it, and tag the bakery. Smile!"

He groaned but Sammi snapped away.

She showed it to him, and he swiped at her phone to erase the photos of his grumpy-ass face, muttering, "Hell, no, you better get rid of those."

"Then be good and pose like a proper *boy*friend. Otherwise, these will be it," she mock threatened him.

Crossing his arms over his chest, he leaned back and gave her the dirtiest look he could muster, imagining he was sucking on her nipples. It had gone a little too far because his cock twitched like he'd been prodded in the balls.

Sammi snapped a few pictures and then bent her head to look them over.

"Jesus, you look like you're about to eat me alive," she grumbled.

"That's because I am."

She gulped. "I can't post these. They're indecent."

"Post them," he demanded.

"Alright, keep your pants on."

"Easier said than done around you," he griped.

Poking at her cell phone, she muttered, "I'm going to have to use a filter to try to dilute that look. It could get flagged by Facebook as pornographic." She eyed him. "You're a very bad boy."

"You have no idea, little girl."

"Who's a bad boy?"

The question came from a head peeking out from behind a board stand displaying a menu.

"My boyfriend," Sammi quipped. "Sometimes boyfriends

can behave very badly. Then we must punish them and put them in their place."

"Oh." Claire looked down her nose at Stanton. "You must get rid of him if he's being bad. There are *too* many boyfriends a girl can have."

Sammi's laugh rang through the bakery. "Is that the French way, Claire?"

"That is the way in France," she nodded gravely, as if it was the most obvious solution.

Checking over her shoulders, she shoved a paper in Sammi's chest. "I better leave before my father catches me, but I made a drawing for you."

"Oh! That's lovely. Come here, girl!" Sammi cried as she pulled Claire into her, crushing the paper between them. The little girl's shoulders stooped in relief and her arms wrapped around Sammi's waist. Head peacefully resting on Claire's shoulder, Sammi hummed. She looked so goddamn good. Her torso framing the young child's body, dark curls spilling over her back. Like a Mary Cassatt Impressionist painting with feathery brushwork.

Stanton's throat tightened and discomfort roiled in his gut. The woman was *made* to be a mother. Sammi loved her family. Puck, her friends, the club. Her clients. Hell, she even created a mini family at the bakery where she stopped in every day. After losing her own mother, she'd be quick to want to make up for the loss with a family of her own. Could he give her that?

He swallowed around the lump lodged in his throat.

No, he couldn't. He could try to complete her in any way in his power, but not that.

His stomach dropped and bottomed out on the ground. Hell, no. That would be a fucking disaster. He wasn't going to perpetuate the clusterfuck that was his family on a future generation.

Claire slowly detached herself from Sammi and stood up. Glancing at their table, she spotted Stanton's empty espresso cup, whisked it into her hand, and said, "I'll get you another."

Stanton instinctively reached out to ruffle her hair and thanked her before the girl sprinted away.

His terror must have been branded on his face because Sammi angled her head to one side and asked, "What's wrong? Are you still hungry?"

Pushing the plate with the baguette toward him, she urged him, "Eat up. I'm not that hungry."

More proof of her maternal instincts. His appetite was gone, but he picked up the knife to spread butter. Maybe he was overreacting. Sammi was only twenty-one years old, and she was deep into building her business. Plus, there was still Puck. She wouldn't expect him to provide her with a family anytime soon. Time was on his side. For now.

27

SAMMI

Sammi snagged a stray ribbon from the floor and stuffed it into the plastic bag she carried as she cleaned up after Sage's baby shower on a lazy Sunday afternoon. It had been a resounding success. Sage had even cried, which Sammi took as a good sign for a mother-to-be.

After the guests had left, Sammi shooed her into the bedroom to rest while she and Abby went about cleaning and taking down the decorations. Warmth coursed through her veins and she swayed slightly on her feet. She'd had her fair share of drinks.

Checking her cell phone, she smiled to herself. She'd drank enough that the responsible thing to do was to text Stanton to pick her up. The added bonus would be that Stanton loved taking advantage of her tipsy state and she loved to let him do it. She may or may not have had an extra drink, mindful that he'd jump into his car to come get her.

"So, how's the love life?" inquired Abby, as she plucked at a streamer dangling from the ceiling. Peering up at the dozens of taped streamers, she wondered, "Hmm, I think we went a little overboard."

"Hush, girl. There's no such thing as going overboard when it comes time to celebrating a baby."

Abby propped a hand on her hip, the streamer trailing to the floor from her grip. "You know, I recall a certain person rambling on about how she'd never get locked down to a husband or child. How Puck and the club was family enough. Seems *someone* I know has changed their tune."

Sammi ducked her head, embarrassment tinging the apples of her cheeks. "I did say something like that, didn't I? Guess it was before I met a guy that made me rethink everything. You know, in the beginning I thought he'd be like Mr. Big."

"Carrie's billionaire love interest from *Sex and the City*?" One of Abby and Sammi's first bonding moments was over their mutual love of the early-aughts TV show, *Sex and the City*.

Turns out that both had separately watched reruns after the deaths of their moms. Sammi was coasting cable channels one winter afternoon when she stumbled on Carrie and her friends gabbing away at a martini bar. The instant Mr. Big came on screen, her little teen heart fell hard for the fantasy. Never did Sammi think she'd be wooed by a handsome, rich man herself. One that was a hotter, younger version of Mr. Big. Life was funny that way.

"The very one," she confirmed. "I've always loved children. Used to be the go-to babysitter for the club and in my neighborhood as a teen, but I never thought of babies for myself. Being with Stanton has changed that. Completely. I can totally see him cradling a baby in his arms." Sammi winked at Abby. "Who knows, I might join the club sooner than I thought."

Abby clapped her hands together in glee. "A good man is an incredibly powerful motivator."

"A good man who still has a few very bad tendencies," she

confessed. "Seriously, though, I wasn't raised with a father and Puck's not the poster boy for fidelity. He's only had one long-term relationship, and that was before my mother died. He broke up with her right after the accident. To be honest, I kinda worry about him."

"Oh, don't worry about Puck. Before he got arrested, he was living his best life, and when he gets out, he'll go right back to it. If anything, he'll go on a rampage to make up for any loss of time," Abby predicted.

The doorbell rang, and Sammi broke into a wide grin. "My ride."

She thrust the bag of trash toward Abby and hurried to open the door. As usual, her first sighting of Stanton took her breath away. He stood on the doormat, dressed in frayed jeans, a Henley, and his leather jacket.

A frown hovered low on his brows. "You don't check the peephole before you open the door to who the fuck knows who?" he said sternly.

The hairs on her arms stood on end at his scolding.

"Who else would it be if not you?" she threw back.

He gave an exasperated sigh. "That's not the point, little girl."

Lifting to her tiptoes, she brushed her lips over his. His arm wrapped around her waist and tugged her closer.

He rubbed his nose against her throat, sniffed her, and then growled against her ear, "You've been drinking. Better hurry up. You slipped out early to prepare for this shower thing and I didn't get my morning fuck. Just so you know how it's going to go down when we get to the loft. I'm not asking, I'm *taking* what I'm owed."

And there it was. His gravelly tone coursed down her spine, drenching her panties.

Grinding her against his arousal, he said, "Do you fucking

feel the state you left me in? I've been like this for fucking *hours.*"

Oh, she felt him all right. The outline of his cock rubbing against her belly was beyond distracting. Looping her hands around his neck, she sipped at his lips for a moment longer before breaking away and hurrying to find her purse.

Always the gentleman, Stanton greeted Abby from the door. Glancing up from picking up her purse, Sammi looked up to find Abby, rooted to her spot, staring at them, mouth dropped open.

"Sorry about the overly public display of affection," she said.

Abby waved her concern away. "Please, girl, you don't know how happy it makes me."

Giggling, Sammi gave her a quick hug and hustled over to one broody, ill-tempered Stanton. She loved when he was sexually frustrated. It made him bossy and quick to take control. Slipping her hand into Stanton's, she followed him out and softly closed the door behind her.

"Thank fuck that's over with," he grunted, as he pushed her toward his car.

"So impatient," she chided.

He made a disgusted sound at the back of his throat. "Our time together is limited. I can't stand the separation anymore, Sammi. This shit's got to stop."

Her feet halted in their tracks, her hand pulling Stanton to a stop. *Did I hear him right?*

Eyes flaring wide, she whispered, "Are you saying what I think you're saying?"

His jaw pulsed. "You damn well know what I'm saying."

Her head was swimming. It was so soon, but he seemed completely serious. "Spell it out for me."

Dropping her hand, he turned to face her. Cupping her

face in his hands, he said, "It's time you moved into my place. I have more room. We can rearrange the loft for you to have a section for the clothes and shit for clients. It'll be better for your business. I live in a prime location with a doorman. Clients can come over to try on clothes and do whatever else you do with them. It'll cut down on you lugging tons of stuff everywhere you go."

Drawing himself up to his full height, he pulled back and gave her one of his stare-downs, as if daring her to challenge him. "I don't like you sleeping in that house alone. I understand you set the alarm—"

"That's because you text me every night to remind me," she groused.

Secretly, she was flying high as a kite, but she couldn't give in that easily. *Where's the fun in that?*

"See, I knew it! If I didn't remind you, who the fuck knows what you'd do. A sweet little girl like you in that house." He shook his head. "All alone. At night. The fuck knows what could happen to you."

He pinched the bridge of his nose. "Christ, you have no idea how many times I've driven past your house to make sure you're safe. I simply don't have the mental energy for that shit anymore."

Sammi's jaw dropped and she spread her fingers over her breastbone. "Y-you check up on me?"

Stanton's left eye twitched. "What the hell do you think? You're my most prized possession." His tone dropped low. "My little girl. I have to guarantee your safety."

"I'm your possession?" A thrill ran down her spine.

"*Prized* possession," his tone dropped another octave.

He dragged her against his chest, grabbed her ass in his broad hand, and murmured, "Don't you know how perfect you are? Anyone could try to take you away from me. Hide you away and tongue that sugar cunt of yours. Drink the sweet honey from your pussy. Feel it flutter against their tongue."

He swatted her in the buttock.

She yelped, although she secretly loved his display of aggression and possessiveness.

"I'm a jealous, possessive motherfucker, or did you not catch on to that yet?"

"Hmmm," she hummed, lifted to her toes, and nipped his clenched jaw. "Basically, what you're saying is that you can't stand being away from me."

"Basically, yeah," he acquiesced, his muscles loosening as she continued to lick and press kisses along his jaw. "Never hid who I was from you."

"You're pretty bold, I'll give you that. But," she returned to peppering him with kisses, "your possessiveness is a turn-on."

He quirked an eyebrow. "Yeah? You're not angry with me? I can get a little out of hand. Shouldn't have displayed the extent of my greediness for you."

"I like greedy," she confided.

He seized the back of her neck and delved between her lips, attacking her mouth like a starving man. Palming her ass, he pulled his hand back to land a smack on the center of one cheek.

"Get a fucking room," came a bored tone behind them.

Gripping Sammi into his chest, he twisted his head around and glared at Tank. "What in the fuck are you doing here?"

"I was left to guard the house till Kingdom got back. I'm too fucking good at what I do because you didn't notice me for shit, but I can't take you mauling Sammi out in the open like this. Don't know where you live that they let you fuck with clothes on in public, but this is a good neighborhood. They'll be calling the cops on your ass for perverse acts any time now. You're welcome for saving your ass from jail time."

"I'd never expose Sammi in public," snapped Stanton.

"Please, motherfucker. You were minutes away from dry humping her. Church-going people are driving by and covering their children's eyes from your little *public* display so for the love of fucking God, go fuck in private. It's like the Playboy channel up in here."

Sammi stifled a giggle. "Sorry, Tank. Stanton was about to take me home."

Gesturing to Stanton's car, Tank pleaded, "Can't happen soon enough. Fucking go already."

Glaring Tank down, Stanton grumbled about his constitutional right to touch his woman wherever he damn well wanted as he opened the car door for her. Inspecting Tank carefully, he inquired, "What are you doing guarding their house on a Sunday afternoon? Is there a threat?"

Sammi intertwined her fingers with Stanton's and answered to take the heat from Stanton's grilling off Tank. "Kingdom's paranoid when it comes to Sage's safety. Especially after what happened to Abby last year."

"What happened?"

"Oh, you know," she fluttered her hand dismissively, "she was attacked by another biker who wanted revenge on Loki. But he's in prison in Ryker's, securely locked away."

Stanton's facial expression hardened. "Does that happen frequently?"

"Of course not," Sammi replied. "Right, Tank?"

"Threats exist," he replied. "Always."

Sammi pursed her lips together and sighed inwardly. Tank was such an idiot. Stanton's jaw muscle began to twitch away.

Facing Tank, he said, "Puck got on the bad side of a man with a reputation of being violent with his partner."

"That's right," replied Tank simply, locking eyes with Stanton. They stared at each other, having a silent conversation.

If she didn't love the brothers so much, she would've gone stark raving mad with their love of swag. Then she had to go and pick the only rich-boy prosecutor who was crazy protective. The only upside was that after they got past their male posturing, they might end up being friends. At the very least, they'd respect each other. Then again, they might unite forces. If so, she'd lose her damn mind. Come to think of it, perhaps the status quo was for the best.

Sammi planted her hands on her hips. "Oh my God, don't pay attention to Tank. He's as paranoid as Kingdom. Kerri's ex is no threat to Puck or anyone else in the club. No one would dare mess with the Demon Squad. It'd be a death sentence, and he knows that more than anyone."

Directing his question to Tank, Stanton asked, "Where's the fucker now?"

"Around," Tank answered, evasively.

His eyes burned into Tank's. "So the answer is you don't know."

Tank gave a one-nod response. Then he remembered Kingdom asking him about the man Puck attacked.

"You're definitely moving in with me," Stanton declared, urging Sammi into the passenger seat.

She mouthed the words *you're an asshole* to Tank, who let out a guffaw and turned away to resume his post.

28

SAMMI

"Fuck, you feel good on my fingers," Stanton muttered, his forearm on her chest, pinning her against the wall of the elevator as he thrust inside her dripping pussy.

"The cameras," she exhaled as she stared up at him, her vision a little hazy from the pleasure he was currently drawing out of her.

"My back's blocking their view," he stated, adding another finger. She had to widen her stance to accommodate the three. His thumb grazed and flicked over her engorged clit in a maddening rhythm. Delirium was setting in and her head dipped back, knocking against the wall.

"Oh, no you don't," he warned as he withdrew his fingers.

Grabbing his wrist to keep him in place, she begged, "No, don't take them away!"

Clucking, his fingers thrust in rapid succession. His mouth was on hers, swallowing her cries as she bucked against his fingers and came.

An instant later, the elevator dinged, and the doors slid

open. Stanton withdrew his fingers and righted her skirt back in place. He pulled away and she staggered forward on rubbery legs.

Hooking an arm around her waist, he helped her out of the elevator, and asked, "Are you okay? Can you walk?"

She propped herself against the wall of the hallway. "I just had an orgasm. Give me a sec to recuperate."

Laughing low, he assured her, "Sure, babe, but hurry up because seeing you cream on my hand was fucking beautiful." Slipping three fingers into his mouth, he sucked on them, the sound reverberating loudly in the marble-floored hallway. "Delicious. I need that to happen on my cock. Now."

Taking in a bracing breath, she put weight on her feet and found that she was able to stand upright. Holding on to the wall, she walked toward his loft apartment. Stanton had unlocked the door and entered. When he poked his head back out to check on her progress, his shoulders were bare. Damn, he'd already taken off his shirt.

"Hurry the fuck up, little girl, unless you want your ass bright red before I fuck you."

"Stanton, the neighbors," she hissed, casting her eyes left and right as she passed the only two other doors in the long corridor.

"These lofts are too big for them to hear anything from the hallway."

"Not if they're near the door," she argued.

Pausing at the entrance, she had to catch her breath as her gaze trailed up his torso. She licked her lips and stuck out her tongue a little, panting as she imagined kneeling in front of him, using her tongue over the crests of his molded chest.

Shrugging off her coat, her fingers fluttered up to the buttons on her blouse. Slowly, she plucked one button from its hole. Her fingers slid down to the next button and repeated the movement. Once she'd undone the last button, she spread the cloth aside and stroked her emerald-colored satin bra.

Desire raged in his eyes as he palmed his erection. "Fucking hell, you're goddamn gorgeous, you know that?"

She cast off her blouse, kicked the door closed, and sauntered up to him. She dropped her hands on his chest and dragged her nails to his nipple, scratching it to a pebbled point. Then she unclasped her bra and let it drop off her shoulders.

It fluttered to the floor.

Stanton's eyes turned a dangerous shade of blue—the tint of blue that let her know his patience was wearing thin. Heat emanated from his body, penetrating her own skin, and warming her blood. It moved like lava as it meandered through her veins. Her hands returned to the hot, taut skin of his chest, singeing the pads of her fingers.

"I knew red looked good on you. Apparently, green does as well," he noted, appreciation in his tone.

Not bothering to answer, she dipped her head and placed wet openmouthed kisses on his nipple, dragging down the ridges of his ribs.

Then she dropped to her knees.

Grabbing her by the arm, Stanton rumbled, "Not now. I want to feel you pulsing round my cock like you were around my fingers in the elevator."

Pulling her to standing, he bent his knees, tipped her over his shoulder, and stalked to his bed.

Slapping his back, she shouted out, "I can walk!"

"I like the weight of your tight little body against me."

Sammi groaned but let him take her to his bed and gently deposit her back on her feet. Once she was stable again, he divested her of the rest of her clothing and shoved her onto his huge bed. She flopped onto the plush mattress and scooted up to the headboard.

"Brute," she complained as she folded her arms over her chest and crossed one ankle over the other.

In a flash, he was naked. Undaunted by her posture, he placed one knee on the bottom of the bed and crawled up until she was caged beneath him.

"Uncross your arms and legs and wrap them around me."

Throwing him a disgruntled look, Sammi did as he asked. She spread her legs wide, giving him the space to nestle into the juncture of her thighs. His forehead dropped to her shoulder and he made a contented sound against the side of her throat.

"So fucking wet," he murmured as he glided the outer ridge of his cock through her folds.

Wiggling her butt into the mattress, she slathered her juices on the tip of his shaft. Barely a moment later, Stanton notched his cock and thrust inside to the hilt. Thanks to her earlier orgasm, she was more than ready for him. He tangled his hand in her hair and tugged her head back, forcing her to arch, changing the angle of her hips and driving him in deeper. Pausing to give her time to adjust, the shallow puffs of breaths and gritted teeth against her skin told her he was drawing on the last of his reserves of self-control.

"Give me your mouth," he commanded by her ear.

She twisted her head, and his tongue immediately plunged between her lips. His chest hair against her peaked nipples added friction, driving her arousal. He deepened his kiss, each thrust of his tongue mimicking the thrusts of his cock. Spreading her legs wider gave him more space, which he immediately took advantage of, scraping the blunt head of his cock against her magic spot. White hot sparks flashed through her, lighting up her nerves like flickering holiday lights.

"I'm keeping you, Sammi. Once you move in here, don't think you're ever leaving. Hear me? It's not happening. I'm happier than I've ever been and it's only going to get better."

"Yes," she replied hoarsely, tears pricking the back of her eyes.

She'd never thought she'd be this lucky. Lucky to find someone who touched her like Stanton, body and soul. Especially the soul. He was dominant in bed, but more importantly, he had inner strength, honesty, and honor. He'd protect her with his life, put her happiness before his. With those he let into the inner sanctum of his heart, he gave himself completely.

Nimble fingers reached between them and taunted her clit as he pulled out and pumped back in. "I can't wait to wake up every morning with you wrapped in my arms. The scent of your hair in my nostrils. Knowing I just have to lift you and take what I want."

Going in for a hard kiss, his fingers grasped the outside of her thigh. Her flank exposed, his palm came down in a hard swat that had her moaning around his tongue.

He growled into her mouth. Evidently liking the sound and feel of it, he did so again. All the while, his thrusts increased in speed and strength.

Brusquely, he withdrew completely and moved off her. She let out a curse.

He only chuckled and ordered, "If you have nothing to do but complain, finger your pussy for me."

Shifting her to her side, he spooned her, one hand straddling the base of her throat, and sank back in. The sucking sounds of her pussy intermingled with the vibrations of her moans.

Seeking more, she drove back against him, but his hand tightened around her throat, pinning her in place. "Stay still like a good girl and take my cock any way I give it to you."

She tried to shake her head in protest, but found she couldn't move. Frustrated by her impotence, her hips shifted against his groin.

The palm of his hand swatted her pussy, stunning her into immobility.

"Don't. Move," he warned through gritted teeth.

Breathing ragged, she twisted her head a little, snagged the end of the pillow between her teeth, and chewed with vexation.

A satisfied chuckle echoed in her ear. "Do what you need to do, but if you want to come tonight, you better not move another inch."

She was about to throw a curse his way, but he tutted, "No back-talk either. 'Yes, sir' is the only appropriate way to address me."

Her back molars ground against one another as she held back from screaming *fuck me already!*

"Please, sir," she gritted out.

"Please, sir, what?"

She heard the laughter in his voice and wanted to snap her teeth at him.

"Please, sir, fuck me harder."

She almost cried when he finally moved, the long drag of his cock pulling out of her to the tip and then ramming her full of his girth again.

"Like this?" he asked in a hoarse tone.

"Yes, sir," she croaked out, the pleasure of that one movement shuddering through her.

"When little girls follow instructions properly, then little girls get fucked correctly. That's the lesson here." He tapped her clit and she jolted against his body. "I'll let that movement go because your little clit is so damn sensitive, you couldn't help yourself. So responsive to her cock master."

"Cock master. Good one," she scoffed, although it was eerily close to the truth. She was willing to do just about anything for him to consume her.

Fisting her hair, he used his hold on her as a counterbalance and slammed in hard, scooting her closer to the edge of the bed.

"This is what's going to go down when you move in. I'm going to fuck you until you're too sore to take me anymore. But don't worry, I'll still play with that little clit of yours. Make sure it aches for the release only my tongue can give it. I'll be fucking you so damn much that by the end of the first month, your tight cunt will be stretched out to the exact proportions of my cock."

His promises combined with rutting into her pussy and pinching her clit sent her into a frenzy. She lost control of her vocal cords and her limbs, screaming and quaking as she came.

"That's right, babe, milk that cock. Milk that come like you fucking own it," he pressed her as her hips swung back and forth, sucking down on his cock. "Because you do. I fucking love you, Sammi."

His words pulled her into an undertow of ecstasy, her bucking, twitching body tossed under the waves of her climax. With his hard staff buried inside her, and his arms and legs wrapped around her, she could no longer tell where her body ended and his began. Spurts of heat flooded inside her, triggering a round of aftershocks that tossed her about like a rag doll.

Coming back down, all she could do was gasp out, "Me, too."

If that wasn't the definition of claiming, then she didn't know what was.

29

STANTON

After giving himself a moment to recuperate, Stanton rolled off her.

He knew he was heavy, but he needed an extra moment. Only with Sammi did this happen, but tonight he was extra satisfied because she agreed to move in with him. She fought him for a bit, but then Tank unwittingly came to the rescue. Solidifying his win by fucking her into oblivion, everything was going in lockstep with his plan to bind her to him, for good.

Before Tully, he was snorting coke at his desk and avoiding Melanie like the plague. Only a few months later and he found himself lying beside a gorgeous, loving woman, willing to use any tricks to keep her by his side. And, miracle of miracles, she seemed to reciprocate his feelings.

Thinking back on Tank serving as Abby's bodyguard, Stanton confessed, "I don't like the fact that Kingdom hasn't found Kerri's ex. I read the police reports Kerri filed and that bastard's a sadist. If anything were to happen to you, I'd lose my fucking mind."

Sammi cuddled into him, lounging a hand on his chest,

and skating her teeth along the tendon of his throat. She gave him a little nip, and his arm tightened around her. When it came to this woman, he was fucking insatiable. Heat dripped into his veins like he was hooked to an IV of morphine.

"I promise you nothing's going to happen to me. Anyway, I'll be moving in with you."

"How was Sage's party?" he threw out, hoping to distract her hand from edging any closer to his twitching cock. He'd used her pretty hard and she needed a break, but she wasn't going to get one if she kept touching him like that.

On cue, a dreamy smile settled on her face.

"So much fun. We played party games. I had everyone bring baby photos of themselves and we tried to guess who was who. There was a Sage and Kingdom trivia game. I love babies," she sighed as she snuggled back into his shoulder.

Stanton's heart slammed against his breastbone. "You love babies?"

Nestling in deeper, she mumbled, "Of course. Who doesn't?"

The pounding in his eardrums merged with the speed of his accelerated heart rate. "Me."

"What?"

"I said, me," he repeated louder. "I don't want children. Ever."

How was that not obvious? He'd hoped it didn't need spelling out, what with his family history and his own struggles with addiction. Inwardly, he cringed because Sammi had a maternal streak a mile wide. Her declaration wasn't a surprise; he'd just prayed the subject wouldn't come up. Fuck his life, because anytime he tried to avoid a problem, it slammed down like an F5 tornado, ripping into the foundations of his life, and leaving it twisting in the air.

Sammi raised herself up and stared down at him, a

quizzical expression on her face. "You don't *ever* want children?"

"Fuck no," he said vehemently.

Sammi scrambled up and sat cross-legged, her hands hanging off her knees. "But you love Wesley."

"Of course I love Wesley. He's a great kid. I love kids. That's not the issue. The issue is that I'm not fit to be a father. Thought that was obvious as fuck."

Looking baffled, she fired back, "Not obvious, not at all. You're one of the most loyal, protective, and thoughtful men I know. It'd be a tragedy if you *didn't* become a father."

"Christ," he rubbed his five o'clock shadow, "your love humbles me, but look at me. I'm a drug addict, and it's not just me. Addiction runs rampant in my family. I killed the brother I loved and my relationship with my father is fucking hellish. If I had a kid, it'd be a clusterfuck of massive proportions. I'll give you anything you want, Sammi, anything but that."

A vision of his father punching in the wall beside his head echoed in his mind. If he was *absolutely certain* it was *only* his father, that'd be one thing, but the same dark, destructive instinct resided in him. And hadn't his father just cut him off? Hell, he wouldn't risk replicating a relationship like that.

"First of all, you may be an addict, but you're in recovery. I know you. You're the kind of stubborn that will prevent you from falling down that hole again, if only because you don't want to miss work. As for Jax, it was a tragic accident with a drunk driver, Stanton. It wasn't all on you. Okay, so your father sucks, but that doesn't automatically mean you'll be a horrible parent. The opposite could easily be true, especially if you put your mind to it."

"My father disinherited me recently, Sammi. That cut me to the core, the fucking core," he confessed, trying to make her see what he had to deal with. "And it wasn't about the money," he tagged on.

Sammi's eyes widened, and she asked in a small voice, "Was it because of me?"

He grabbed her hand. "It's not the first time he's threatened me with repercussions for not doing exactly what he wants. Technically, it had to do with you, but the friction between us goes much deeper. No money is worth handing my happiness over to that bastard. That's what I'm trying to tell you. My relationship with him is fucked. *Fucked.* And the chances of me messing up are real. It's what I grew up with. It's in my blood. I'm not about to risk bringing human life into this shitshow. At Tully, I made an oath to myself. From now own, I'd do the right thing, even if it fucking kills me."

The stricken look on Sammi's face tore at his heart, but he respected her too much to give her anything but the unvarnished truth.

"B-but," she sputtered, as she pulled her hand away, "you were meant to be a father."

She played with her lips nervously. "I w-want a child. Being with you allowed me to dream that I could have it all."

"Oh, babe, you're breaking my heart," he murmured, taking her hand.

She pulled away, scrambled off the bed, and stood up. "You're breaking *my* heart. I thought anything was possible for us. Anything. And now you're pulling the rug from under my feet."

Sitting up, Stanton balled his hands, his nails digging into the flesh of his palms. It felt like a noose had been hung around his neck, tightening more and more as the conversation wore on. He struggled to breathe through the cinched band around his throat.

Like usual, he was the source of pain.

Yet again, he'd failed to meet the expectations thrust upon him, but he refused to lead her on and kickstart another vicious cycle of living a lie. Experience taught him that it would blow up in his face.

At the same time, he was distraught for letting her down. He wanted to wrap his arms around her, retract everything he'd said, and whisper assurances that he'd do whatever she wanted. The image of holding a fragile little babe in his arms popped in his mind. Perfect and pure, with dark hair like Sammi. Only to be destroyed by his darkness. *No.* He couldn't do it.

Sammi's hands migrated to her hips. She bowed her head and blew out a breath. Her chin jerked up, and she searched his eyes for reassurance. He had none to give her. A flash of hurt crossed her face and her gaze flickered around the room as if she could find the answer somewhere in the dark corners of the room.

Wringing her hands, she said, "I-I have to go. I can't think straight here, and I need time to process what you told me."

Hot anger surged through his veins because he wanted to reach for her so fucking badly. His fingers flexed and twitched at his side. The urge to grab her and blanket her with his body, protect her from everything, rode him hard.

He searched for something to say, but the words died before leaving his lips.

Confronted with his silence, a whimper slipped out from between her lips. She whirled around and scanned the floor for her clothes. Gripping the sheets until his knuckles turned white, he ground down on his back teeth to stop himself from leaping off the bed and hauling her back in.

She needed space. He knew space boded nothing good, but he was powerless. If he loved her, which he did with every fiber of his being, then he needed to let her go.

Knowing he wouldn't let her get into an Uber, Sammi said, "I need a car."

Rising slowly, he went into the kitchen and grabbed his charged cell phone to call the luxury car company he used. By the time he'd swiped to end the call, she was already fully dressed and walking out of his bedroom. He couldn't let her leave without touching her one more time. Striding across the loft floor, he placed his forearms on the door, caging her in before she opened the door. He was still buck naked, but didn't care.

"Babe, I'm so fucking sorry," he implored. "If I could do this for you, I would. I swear it."

"If you want to break up with me, then you say so instead of making shit up about not wanting to be a father," she accused softly. "I'm not saying I want kids now, but I *do* want them." Her tone softened. "And I want them with you."

He buried his nose into her throat, inhaling deeply the sultry whiskey scent of her. Muttering into her warm, sweet-smelling skin, he said, "I fucking love you, Sammi. I swore that I'd be honest with you, no matter what. This is me being honest. A year ago, I wouldn't have faced this head on. I would've strung you along for as long as I could. I'm in love with you and I'm here for you, but I can't be a father."

Grabbing his head, she seared him with a look of desperation and pleaded, "Listen to me, you asshole. Your father has done a number on you. You don't think you're worthy enough to be a father, but you are. I want you to really think about what I said and call me if you change your mind. I have faith in you. In us."

Christ. He wanted to sink to his knees and beg her to stay. Tell her he'd do whatever she wanted. Give her as many babies as she could carry. But he couldn't. It was clear as fucking day to him that he wasn't capable of being a father, but he couldn't keep her from experiencing something she was meant to be. She was a born mother.

Before he could stop himself, his control broke and he seized her by the waist. Cradling the back of her head in his hand, he took her mouth. She tasted so fucking good. They were made for each other. Her fingers clung to his shoulders and he felt her shivering against him. Crushing her against the front door, he pressed as close as humanly possible, surrounding her, inhaling her, devouring her.

One. Last. Time.

Twisting his face to the side, he broke away.

Puffs of her sweet breath wafted over his cheek and he had to tighten every muscle in his body to not take her down to the floor and claim her.

Taking in a harsh inhale, he pushed off the door and stepped away.

"Go," he growled. "Before I take you again, fucking get out of here."

Sammi's warm brown eyes glistened, but she must have seen that he'd reached his breaking point because she whipped around, threw the door open, and tore out of the loft.

✳✳✳

WHAT THE HELL HAPPENED? One moment, everything she ever wanted was nestled in the palms of her hands. The next moment, she was standing outside Abby and Loki's home, empty-handed.

A shiver coursed down her spine. She felt something pass over her as if she was being watched. Checking over her shoulder, the street was empty. She shook off the feeling, rang the doorbell, and waited.

Loki came to the door, took one look at her and said, "Let me grab my gun. Who do I kill?"

Abby reached around him for Sammi, shoved his big frame out of the way, and admonished dryly, "I'm sure your murderous instincts can be put to better use in the kitchen, making us cups of coffee. Now, move out of the way, you big lout."

Tugging Sammi by the hand, Abby drew her into the house, peeled off her coat, and slumped her down on the couch.

Sammi felt numb, like her lungs were being crushed of what little air was left. Dread had curled in her stomach at the idea of going to her empty house, so even though it was late, she'd directed the driver to drop her off at Abby's house. All she knew was that she couldn't go back home. Everything would feel emptier than ever, especially after having expected to move out not an hour earlier. Not only did she not have Puck, but she didn't have Stanton, either.

She had nothing.

Abby took a seat beside her and looked over in concern. "What happened?"

"We broke up," she replied miserably. Even saying the words was like a kick to the gut.

Avoiding Abby's wide-eyed stare, she forged on, "After I left you this afternoon, he asked me to move in with him. Which was great. I was riding on a high like I've never felt in my entire life. We were talking about Sage's baby shower and then he dropped a bombshell. He doesn't want to have kids."

Abby gasped.

She pulled in a heavy breath, and confirmed, "Like, ever."

No more words needed saying. Abby understood

completely. Not only had she always wanted children, but she'd witnessed Sammi's recent hundred-and-eighty-degree reversal on the subject. She knew what it meant to Sammi to enthusiastically embrace the idea of children.

"He's sure?"

"As sure as you've always been about *having* children," she muttered, wretched. Put that way, it was like a guillotine blade severed her dreams forever.

"But ... why? Normally, people don't make such explicit declarations about children."

"He thinks he'll be an awful father because he's an addict. He feels responsible for his brother's death, and his father hates him for it." A sad smile ghosted her lips. "He doesn't want to lead me on. It's his way of being *honest*," she bit out, making air quotes around the last word.

Saying them was like another slap in the face.

Loki came in, holding one glass filled to the rim with wine and one with water, and handed them over. "Thought this would be a better choice," he mentioned.

Crouching down to be at eye-level with Sammi, he said, "If you want me to hurt him, give me a holler. I'll fucking decimate the fucker."

A shaky smile quivered on her lips. "I don't want you to hurt him. I love him. And don't tell anyone at the club. Please, I won't be able to stand the looks. The 'I told you he was trash' looks."

"No one's gonna look at you differently, Sammi," he promised.

Shaking her head, she stammered, "I can't handle it right now, and you know how gossipy the club is."

Patting her lap, he assured her, "Sure, sweetheart, whatever you need. I'm not a big talker anyway. No one will get shit out from me."

Rising to his feet, he caressed Abby's hair. Frowning down on her, he queried, "You okay, babe?"

The adoring way he looked down at Abby widened the cracks of Sammi's precariously intact heart. She'd had that with Stanton just shy of an hour ago. How could life turn on a dime like that? She gave a deep sigh. It was like her mother's death all over again. One moment, life went one way. The next moment, everything veered off course.

Nodding up at him, Abby replied, "Yeah. Do you mind getting the air mattress out? Sammi's staying the night."

Sammi cast her a grateful look.

"Sure thing," he answered, and left quietly.

Sammi took a big gulp of wine and let the alcohol settle in her stomach.

Hanging her head, she let the tears fall. The anger and frustration she'd felt toward Stanton dissipated when he'd kissed her. He'd put it all in that kiss. His love, his desperation, his apology. But also his goodbye, the obstinate bastard.

If he felt that he couldn't do right by a child, then he wasn't going to take the risk of making what he saw as another mistake. Having had similar feelings not so long ago, Sammi couldn't even blame him. Her hands curled into tight balls as tears plopped down on her lap. She was being dramatic, but tell that to her heart, because it was cracking in places she hadn't felt since her mother died.

"I just wrapped my head around the idea that I want to have kids, and I feel like he tore the dream out from underneath me." Looking up at Abby, she continued, "Might not have been such a big deal a year ago, but with you and Sage getting pregnant, these new feelings spilled out of me."

"I know," her friend crooned.

"And just as I was reveling in them, celebrating life and love, he smashed my dream to smithereens. He doesn't want to lead me on and repeat what he did with Sage and Melanie. He'd rather toss me aside," she finished miserably.

"That's going a bit far. What if you stay with him for now? Okay, you know he doesn't want kids, but you're only twenty-one years old. You don't have a timetable of when you want to start a family like I do. You can wait."

Her lower lip trembled at the idea of having a few more years with him—hell, imagine as much as a decade—and then giving him up. If she felt gutted right this instant, what would the future hold for her? She *ached* for him, ached for his scent and his arms around her, like something crucial was missing.

"I could've stayed with him, if I hadn't gone and fallen in love with him. If I stay with him, I'll only get more attached. I can't imagine breaking up with him two or three years down the line. Either I resign myself to never having children, or I suffer worse in the future. Neither of those options look good."

Abby wrapped her arms around Sammi, swaying from side to side as she brushed her hair. Her life was splintering apart. She felt like a little dinghy in the middle of a roiling typhoon, and all she could do was cling to Abby and release the torrent of tears.

30

STANTON

Sitting in the empty dive bar, the neon beer sign flickering in front of him, Stanton swirled the bourbon around and around in the bulbous glass.

The stench of stale beer wafted off the sticky ground around him.

Stupidly, he'd believed that being sober would be enough. Being sober and honest would be enough to keep the worst of life at bay. That was his sponsor's promise. *Stay sober. Keep honest. Everything else will fall into place. Life has a way of working out, I fucking guarantee it, Stanton. It worked for me; it'll work for you.*

What a crock of fucking shit. Turned out Gregory was dead-ass wrong. Might have worked for him because he wasn't struck with terror at the thought of becoming a father.

Stanton had used drugs to run himself ragged working and to avoid his emotions. He thought he'd dealt with the worst during rehab, but there was nothing like an on-the-ground experiment to prove him wrong. His muscles ached like he'd been beaten to a pulp and his chest was so tight it was hard to draw a full breath of air.

Whirling the bourbon for the umpteenth time, he considered it carefully. He'd gotten his two-month NA chip and was working on his third. Although alcohol wasn't his drug of choice, addiction was a slippery slope. It wouldn't take much for him to end up right where he started.

Anyway, he'd committed to ninety days of no substances whatsoever. If he took a sip, he'd be back to ground zero tomorrow. Day One. *If* he made it to tomorrow. Assuming he made it till tomorrow, would he make it through the day? Would he manage to stay clean for an entire twenty-four hours? He'd be right back on the crazy-ass roller coaster that was his life when hooked on coke.

Relapse.

The word started with a hard *rrr* sound but ended in a soft *hisss*, like that hypnotizing snake, Kaa, from *The Jungle Book* he'd watched with Wesley once. He was losing his goddamn mind.

He'd fallen for Sammi and her absence left an ache that made withdrawing from cocaine look like a walk in the park. Despite everything he'd done, the same issue reared its ugly head. He'd never be able to give her what she wanted. Just like he fell short of being Jax, he fell short of fulfilling her needs. Falling short seemed to be the one thing he excelled in. The only way to rectify the situation was to stay the hell away from her. Let her find the picture-perfect biker to give her all the babies she dreamed of having.

Stanton was staring hard at the bottom of the glass when there was a movement to his left.

Cornell.

His friend strode up to him, pulled up a bar stool, and sat down, facing ahead.

The woman tending bar sauntered his way and took his beer order.

Slanting him a side-look, Stanton gave a weary sigh. "How'd you find me?"

"Not that hard. You only go to a few places when you're at your lowest."

"How did you know?"

"Sammi called me."

"Fuck."

"Fuck is right. As in, stop being a fucking pussy. What the hell, Stanton? You broke up with her?"

"It's for the best."

"For the best, my ass," Cornell replied, dragging the stool closer to Stanton.

He swallowed and licked his lips. "I can't give her children."

"Why the fuck not? You're great with Wesley. You're like a blood uncle to him. He adores you and you adore him."

"Yeah, but I don't live with Wesley day in, day out. You're his father and Carl is his dad. I'm a perfect *uncle*. That's the best I can ever be."

"Never saw you as a coward," observed Cornell. "Till now. I found you lying in your own vomit and didn't think less of you. But, this. If you let this stand, then I'll have to rethink my judgment of who you are."

"Fuck you, Cornell, you don't understand."

"Yeah, right. Like I don't understand that this somehow goes back to Jax and your father."

Stanton's stomach rolled and his fist tightened around his untouched drink. "Leave my father out of this."

"Told you the shit with your father would come back and bite you in the ass. Not sure what's going on in your head, but I bet it's something along the line of you never measuring up. I often try to play devil's advocate and stand up for Benjamin, but you aren't Jax and until he gets that through his thick head, nothing's gonna change. As I see it, you've been harboring one of two misconceptions. You either don't believe you deserve love or you're too afraid to open your heart because you're afraid she'll run away screaming if she sees the real you. Which is it?"

"Why choose? Might as well be both."

"So fucking dramatic. Are you for real?"

"Yes, I'm for fucking real," he hissed. "I killed Jax. Killed. Him. I'm not cut out to be a parent. Hell, I'm barely making it as a whole man."

Cornell pulled back, his eyebrows raised high. "Oh, so you're God now? With the power over life and death? Bull*shit*. First off, you did not kill him. It was a tragic accident where you lived and he didn't. I know, I know, you think the wrong kid got killed. The myth your family likes to tout is that he was the golden boy while you were a deadbeat. Nonsense. Time to fucking let it go because I won't allow you to throw away a beautiful relationship out of fear."

Stanton's burning eyes cut to Cornell.

"I'm serious," he continued. "She deserves every happiness in the world, and she won't have it without you. She sees something in you, too. Turns out, I'm not the outlier anymore."

The air left his lungs.

"I hung up on her crying, with the promise to find your ass, and here you are," Cornell's knuckles tapped the top of the bar, "running to your old friend." He leaned over to inspect the glass and mused, "You haven't touched it yet, and the ice has melted. That's a good sign."

His throat closed on him. She was so angry when she left his loft that he hadn't expected her to cry. "She was crying?"

"What did you expect? That she'd dance on your grave. She loves your dumbass."

Stiffening his spine, he slammed his fist on the table. "I'm doing the right thing."

"You're not, though. Not if it includes pushing her away."

He'd come to the bar, looking back to the past, but there was nothing for him there. Not the alcohol nor the winking, flirting bartender who'd hit on him half a dozen times since he sat down. It was Sammi he wanted. Not wanted, *needed.* He needed her to fill the gaping chasm growing wider by the second since she left him.

"Everything you say is true, but I can't go to her. If I beg, she'll take me back and we'll be back to square one. Me, too scared to put a baby in her belly. Her, wanting one with me. If I don't do that, she'll eventually resent me and leave me for a man who'll give her everything her heart desires. As it should be."

Cornell struck the bar top with the flat of his hand. "Dammit, Stanton, you're being a stubborn bastard."

"You don't understand. You have an amazing relationship with both your parents. They're normal, kind people. People like you and Sammi were made to be parents. Not me. I'm not trying to fuck this up, I'm trying to prevent a fuckup. And when I tell you that I can't be a father, I'm telling you the truth."

His head pounded and his stomach churned. He must have looked half-crazed because Cornell laid his hand on top of the hand strangling the glass of bourbon and gently pried it off.

Staring at him with eyes bleeding empathy, he clapped his hand on Stanton's shoulder and whispered, "Okay, buddy. Come on, let's go home."

Standing, he threw a twenty on the bar and pulled Stanton up with a strong grip on his elbow.

"I could do with a long shower and a good night's sleep."

"You'll get them both. At my house. I'm not leaving you alone tonight. You're coming home with me to spend the evening with Carl and Wesley."

Wrapping his arm around Stanton's shoulder, he forced him to turn around and walked him out of the bar.

31

———

STANTON

S tanton shut off the car engine and dropped his head.

It was the third night in a row that he found himself across from Sammi's house. It had started with a drive-by about a week after he ended things with her. At first, he told himself that he was only checking up on her because she lived alone.

Yeah, right, that excuse might've passed the first time around. By the fourth time, he'd given up all pretense and simply parked across the street, a couple of houses down from hers. It was late enough that there weren't even any dog walkers left to notice him. Only the occasional straggler, coming home from the late shift or a bar. It was dead quiet outside, the sounds of scattering raindrops falling on the windshield.

He knocked his head against the headrest of his seat. Unclipping the buckle of his seat belt, he released it, and the woven polyester moved through the metal of the retractor with a slithering sound. The throbbing of his heartbeat mingled with the *plink plink* of the raindrops on the glass.

He saw Sammi's shadow pass by the large bay window of

her living room a few times. Each time he caught sight of her was like having his heart ripped out of his chest cavity, but he couldn't look away. He barely blinked, he was so desperate of any glimpse of her.

Inhaling deeply, Stanton's spine straightened when he saw a flickering shadow below the bay window. Surely he was seeing things.

Squinting, he peered closer and caught the reflection off the metal wristwatch on a bulky form crouched low and moving crab-like along the front of house. It disappeared around the corner of the house. What the fuck?

Fumbling to open the console, he pulled out a military-grade gravity knife and a pair of handcuffs. Tucking them into his jacket pocket, Stanton jumped out of the car, darted across the street, and jogged to Sammi's house.

A loud crashing noise came from inside the house. Skirting the house, he found the back door wide open, clanging against the brick wall. He gripped tightly on the handle of his knife as he glimpsed through the kitchen, down the short hallway straight into the living room.

With a roar, he rushed through the house and pounced on a black-clad figure straddling Sammi, hands wrapped around her trachea. In the blink of an eye, Stanton raised his hand and brought the side of his palm down in a sharp, downward strike on the vagus nerve of the fucker choking her.

Disorientated, the man loosened his grip on her neck. Taking advantage of the man's confusion, Stanton kicked him in the ribs with so much force that he toppled over and crashed to the floor. Jumping on him. Stanton kneed him in the solar plexus.

"Run, get the hell out of here, Sammi!" he thundered, just before the guy regained full consciousness.

Before he had a chance to take out his blade and gut the motherfucker, the giant howled and twisted over, taking Stanton down. Suddenly, Stanton was slammed to the ground, the monstrosity above him, with a forearm to his neck. Wrenching and scratching at skin covering pure muscle, he struggled to gain the upper hand as they both fought for dominance.

A fist flew in his face, knocking his head to the side. Fuck, that stung. Blood gushed in his mouth. The man laid lengthwise above him, using his much heavier weight to pin him down. Wheezing, black dots began to swim in his vision when he heard another crash.

Ceramic splintered everywhere, pelting his face. Sammi had slammed a lamp on top of the man's head.

He slumped down on top of Stanton, knocked out.

Heaving above him was Sammi, eyes wild with fear and trembling from head to foot. There were dark bruises already blooming along her throat. He saw red.

Shoving the heavy weight of the unconscious man off him, he struggled to his feet and lunged for her. His arms couldn't seem to capture enough of her. Mother*fucker*, the bastard was minutes from killing her. His heart restarted once he had her in his arms.

Stroking her hair with a shaky hand, combing out the long length, he said, "Are you okay, babe? Fuck, I-I thought I lost you."

Nodding into his chest, her shudders receded into low-level tremors. "I'm okay. If ... if you hadn't shown up, he w-would've killed me."

"Do you know this motherfucker?"

"Kerri's husband. The guy Puck b-beat up."

"Christ," he breathed out, burrowing his face in her hair, tightening his arms around her. God, she felt so fucking good.

Even though she was shaking like a goddamn leaf, she was alive.

Pushing against him weakly, she stammered, "I have to call Kingdom."

"Kingdom? The police. We need to call the police."

Sammi's head jolted up, eyes bulging. "No police! I want Kingdom. We need to call him." Her voice edged toward hysteria. His nostrils flared, but he locked down his own fury at what just happened.

Continuing his soothing caresses, he assured her, "Go get your phone. I'll put handcuffs on him."

Stepping away with sudden, jerky movements, she stumbled down the hall, holding onto both walls, and into the kitchen. Moments later, he heard her talking on the phone as he rolled the man over and cuffed him. Pressing two fingers on the attacker's pulse, he found a steady heartbeat. Too fucking bad. They had a perfect defense for knocking the fucker out dead.

Sammi came back and he met her halfway down the hall, drawing her back into his arms. Her fingers were clammy and her lips were cold against his throat. He stroked her arms to warm her up. Pulling away, he took off his jacket and draped it around her shoulders. He didn't want her going into shock.

Holding her tightly, he dragged her over to the couch, maneuvered her onto his lap, and pushed her head against his shoulder. He splayed his hand over her chest and rubbed until her breath evened out. Silently, they waited for Kingdom.

The sounds of motorcycle pipes rolling down the street had Sammi tweaking in his lap. Her pulse at the base of her throat accelerated again.

"Shhh," he soothed her. Lifting her off his lap, he brought her to the front door and tucked her into his side. There was no fucking way in hell he was letting her go. He was taking her home with him and that was the end of that.

Peeking through the peephole, he opened the door the instant Kingdom came into sight. The president of the Demon Squad raked Sammi with his eyes from head to toe. He paused midstep when his eyes lit on Sammi's throat. Then, to his credit, he continued his efficient walk to the door, flanked by Cutter and Loki.

Stepping to the side, Stanton threw the door closed and locked it. The slamming sound roused the handcuffed perpetrator on the floor.

"You okay, Sam?" asked Kingdom.

Sammi nodded, eyes on the floor as if ashamed. He went to tuck her chin, but she flinched away from him and cringed into Stanton's side.

Burying her head into his shirt, she sobbed, "I'm sorry."

Backing away, Kingdom murmured, "Not your fault, sweetheart."

"I left the back door open," she screamed into his shirt, beating into Stanton's chest with her small fists.

His already-battered heart cracked in two and fell to pieces at the agony in her voice.

"Baby, shush, baby," he spoke softly, tightening his hold around her like a straightjacket until she couldn't move at all. It seemed to calm her and, eventually, she settled down, although he felt her whimpers against the wet cotton of his shirt.

"It's my fault for leaving you. That's never happening again," he swore.

"Who the fuck is this?" asked Kingdom, his boot coming out to swiftly kick the manacled man in the ribs.

"Kerri's ex. The one that Puck beat up," replied Stanton. "I'm assuming the attack on Sammi was revenge. We need to call the police, Kingdom. I didn't do it earlier because Sammi was so upset and she insisted on calling you first. Time is ticking and the longer we wait, the worse it will be."

"We're not calling anyone," intoned Kingdom, glowering down at the handcuffed man.

"What the fuck are you talking about?" asked Stanton, impatience clawing at his throat. He didn't have time to argue with Kingdom while he had his hands full with Sammi.

Kingdom slanted his head slightly and inspected Stanton carefully. "You want to take Sammi home?"

"Yes, as soon as—"

"Here's your choice, Mr. Prosecutor, and let's see if you make the right one after you broke this girl's heart," Kingdom said with a chin lift toward Sammi. "If we call the police, then Sammi stays with me and Sage until Puck comes home." Sammi stiffened in his arms and her breathing became short. "Or you leave with her and don't ask a damn thing about what's happened here. Just know that I'll take care of it."

Stanton narrowed his eyes. The bastard had him. Kingdom knew he'd choose Sammi over anything else in a heartbeat. Stanton didn't have a choice, but he wasn't going down that easily.

"Why didn't you have someone guarding Sammi like you did Sage? Do you only care about your woman?" he spat out through his teeth.

Kingdom took a step toward them, but halted at Sammi's sharp intake of breath. "Listen, motherfucker. Why don't you first ask yourself why Sammi's here instead of living with you in your loft, like she's supposed to? It was bad enough accepting that you were with her, but then you had the audacity to drop her? What the fuck, man?"

"That's not how it went down, Kingdom," Sammi cut in.

Kingdom pinched the bridge of his nose. "No one knows

how it went down since you won't talk to anyone about it, but that's water under the bridge. As for you," his gaze sliced through Stanton as if he weren't worthy of licking the bottom of Sammi's shoes, "I had a guard on Sammi as well as Sage, but I called everyone off about a week ago. Figured enough time had passed. I now see that this fucker was watching all along. Making sure the coast was clear before he attacked a defenseless woman."

His boot flew out and landed in the center of the man's chest. The miserable fuck yelped like it hurt and threw out a volley of curses until Loki cut him off with a death threat.

"Alright, it seems we both made mistakes," Stanton admitted grudgingly.

"How did you end up here?" Cutter, Kingdom's second-in-command, asked curiously.

"I've been driving by to check on her." Stanton's fingers returned to smoothing out Sammi's curls. "I was parked up the street when I saw this bastard sneaking around to the back of the house. Got here a few minutes later and he had his hands wrapped around her throat."

Kingdom's jaws clenched tight, a grinding noise coming from his molars. "Fuck."

"I didn't see this asshole before tonight, although that doesn't mean that he wasn't around. He clearly knew his way around the house. It was a lucky break that I spotted him sneaking around to the back."

"And my back door was unlocked," added Sammi, in a defeated tone.

An impatient snort escaped Stanton. "Not your fault. You should've been in my bed tonight. I have better-than-average knowledge of how criminals work. I should've known better." He curled his hand around Sammi's nape and pulled her closer into his chest. Staring at Kingdom, he confirmed, "So I get Sammi. You get him. No questions asked. No interference."

Running his fingers through his hair, Kingdom snapped, "I already fucking said that."

"I need a confirmation, because this one," he caressed down the length of her hair, "might want to leave after the shock wears off." He held Kingdom's stare. "That's not happening."

Sammi's head snapped up and whirled in Kingdom's direction. "Kingdom?"

"It's for your own good," he answered her. "You're safer with him than with anyone else. He's good for that much, at least. You'll have to work out your problems with him, Sammi. There's no other way."

"There's nothing to work out," she denied, in a defeated tone.

"Sure about that?" Kingdom asked, giving her a gentle, reassuring smile. "'Cause you haven't let go of him since we arrived, and you flinched when I tried to touch you."

Sammi huffed and tried to pull away from Stanton, but he tightened his grip on her. She was his. He had no fucking idea what was going to happen between them, but, for the moment at least, he wasn't letting her out of his sight.

With that settled, he wanted her out of the house. "We're done here."

"Good, 'cause we have work to do," replied Cutter.

"I have to pack." Her words came out muffled since her face was buried in his shirt.

"Babe, there's no time for that. Kingdom and his men have to take care of things. We'll get anything you need at the drugstore and you'll wear my clothes to sleep in. Tomorrow, we'll come back. Once this scum is gone." He nodded to the man who'd begun writhing on the ground.

Loki hauled him up by the handcuffs, dragged his struggling body halfway down the corridor after a brief tussle, and flung open a door that seemed to go down to the basement.

Shielding her vision, Stanton told her to cover her ears as he led her toward the kitchen. Cutter followed with her cell phone and purse. Handing them to Stanton, Cutter wished him good luck.

Stanton nodded his thanks and guided her out into the quiet of the backyard, grateful that the darkness hid his triumphant expression. As angry as he was at himself for having not shielded her from the attack, at least she was back under his protection. He trusted that Kingdom would take care of the bastard, albeit in his own way. Other than that, Stanton cared about only one thing: Sammi wearing his T-shirt and sleeping in his bed. It was like a breath of fresh air after coming up from the dark dankness of a mine shaft. Despite the cold, he felt like he was inhaling a breath of sweet summer air.

32

STANTON

Sammi was sprawled in his bed, and damn if that wasn't a beautiful sight.

It was past midnight by the time they got to the loft, and she was so exhausted she was dead on her feet. Not able to let her out of his sight for an instant, he helped her out of her clothing and into one of his softest T-shirts. It was a sign of her mental exhaustion that she didn't bat an eye and simply stripped naked in front of him. Sick bastard that he was, it didn't stop him from reveling in the sleek lines of her body and smooth skin. She padded into his bathroom to clean up while he changed into a pair of pajama bottoms.

With a large glass of water waiting for her on his night table, he sat at the edge of the bed, listening to the sounds of her moving around in the bathroom. Soon, she came out and crossed to his bed.

He pointed to the glass, which she dutifully gulped down. Placing the empty glass carefully back on the table, she bent over to pull the duvet and sheet back.

Needing her in his arms, he broke the silence. "Come here."

Without looking at him, she declared, "I don't think we should do anything."

"We're not doing anything. It's been fucking weeks. I want to touch you." He slapped his knee lightly. "Come on my lap."

Straightening, she hesitated for a moment. He held his breath. Lips pursed, she glided over to him and sat primly on one thigh. He stifled the groan rising up his throat. Looping an arm around her waist, he pulled her in closer. She let out a slow breath, as if she'd been holding it in for a while and relaxed against him. Fuck, he missed this. There was nothing in the world like having Sammi in his arms again.

Nuzzling her hair, he rocked her from side to side until there was no more tension left in her muscles. Soon, she gave him all her weight and he cradled her in his arms like she was the most precious thing in his life. He had no idea how, but he had to figure out a way to make this work.

Her lips parted and her breathing came out slower and heavier. She'd nodded off. The fact that she'd felt safe enough to fall asleep in his arms, especially after the horrible ordeal she'd survived, cut him off at the knees. He traced the purple finger marks around her throat.

His head fall back, and he stared up at the ceiling, sending out a prayer of thanks. His heart was in his throat, thick with relief.

Gently, he stood with her in his arms, walked to the side of the bed, and laid her down. She shifted a little, mumbling sounds of disruption. Quickly, he spooned her, and she soon settled again.

Once he was sure she was out, he brought his laptop into the room and made himself comfortable in an upholstered chair by the wall of windows. While doing research on the man who'd attacked her, his gaze wandered over to her repeatedly, confirming that she was there. This wasn't one of the many dreams he'd been waking up to, only to find himself alone with a hard-on.

Eventually, he'd gathered as much information as he could on this fucker and was calm enough that there was a possibility of sleep. Plus, he itched to be back by her side. Shutting the lights off one by one in the loft, he meandered back to the sleeping beauty in his bed.

Moonlight shimmered through the large paned-glass windows, lighting the edges of her curls in crisp relief while leaving her features in soft shadows. Stanton lifted the covers and slid in behind her until their hips were aligned, her smaller one rubbing against the dip in his abdomen just below where his hip began.

The faint scent of her mint and herb shampoo, combined with her own malted sandalwood fragrance, encapsulated him. Inhaling deeply through his nostrils, he breathed in as much of her as he could.

He hooked his arm around her waist and she let out another deep sigh, settling into his chest, as if she sensed his return. Stanton's mind raced, the razor-sharp attorney in him arguing back and forth about what he should do. How he should definitely not fuck her, not even once, while she stayed with him. How he should proceed in guaranteeing her protection. Rationally, he recognized that there was a major roadblock to their relationship but, emotionally speaking, he didn't give a flying fuck. He was keeping her. He didn't know how it was going to go down. Nothing had changed in their circumstances, but after what happened tonight, he couldn't draw his next breath without murmuring to himself, "She's mine. She's mine. She's mine."

He was the dictionary definition of fucked.

❋❋❋

Sammi struggled to open her gritty eyes. A soft snuffle came from the wall of heat at her back and her eyes snapped open.

Stanton.

Glancing over her shoulder, she found his arm locked around her waist, plastering her to his chest. She didn't remember drifting off to sleep. One moment she was on his lap. The next, her head was pillowed by his bicep and her back was up against his chest, which could double as a furnace. Her toes were cold but the rest of her was warm and toasty. Shifting in minuscule movements to test her ability to slip out from under him while avoiding the chance of waking him up, his leg shifted and laid over hers.

Oh, hell, what was she going to do? She couldn't stay here with him. She didn't have the willpower not to touch him, especially with his thick erection prodding her lower back. That was not helping matters one bit.

The hot steel of his rigid flesh, despite the layers of clothing between them, made her want to rub against it like a feline in heat. His leg shifted again and his thigh slipped between hers. The shirt she was wearing rode up her hips, baring her ass.

She squeezed her eyes shut. Oh God, she was getting wet. Last night, she was so exhausted that it hadn't occurred to her to wear panties to bed.

Yeah, that was last night. The bright light of early morning dropped a whole new set of problems on her.

His thick, muscled thigh cradled between hers was like dropping a bloody carcass in a tank of piranhas. Her libido was the tank of piranhas in this situation. His thigh was cradled between hers, but it wasn't nearly close enough to her pussy for her to put any kind of pressure on her clit.

Biting her lower lip, she shimmied her butt, little by little, until her heat was lying right on his quad muscle. She let out a little *hmm* as the little hairs on his thigh tickled her. *Holy shit, that feels good.* Her juices went *drip, drip, drip.* She had to bite back a moan.

Phase one had been implemented, but the modicum of relief she'd felt was instantly replaced by a greater need to massage her slit against the heat of his taut flesh. His quad was so thick and tight she could ride it to high heaven and back. God, but the man was fit. Her hips twitched back and forth a few times.

"Keep rubbing that hot cunt of yours against my thigh and I'm gonna split your sweet pussy open in a heartbeat," a husky voice came from behind her.

Sammi froze, her breaths coming out ragged through parted lips. If she wasn't so aroused, she'd take a shot at feigning embarrassment. *What do I do? What do I do?*

"You're wondering what to do," he stated in a gravelly voice, the low rumble in the curve of her ear.

Her heart skipped a beat. Yes, dammit, she was. Her body was screaming at her to *drag your dripping pussy against the length of his thigh and let him take what he wants.* Either that or roll onto her back, spread her thighs open, and beg him to satisfy her.

"What do you want, Sammi? Whatever you want, I'll give it to you. You want it once, then I'll fuck you this once. You want more? I'll give you that, too," he said, his hot breath in her ear.

Her eyelids fluttered at the sound of his voice. Her monkey brain was hijacking her decision-making functions, and she struggled to remember why it would be a bad idea to give herself over to him. God knows, she'd tried to find a replacement with her fingers, her vibrator, and a few other toys, but it had been hopeless. She could no longer reach an orgasm without him. Her body was striking on her ass and it was downright rude.

"Let me make you feel good, beautiful," he lured her with the rough gravel in his tone. "Doesn't have to mean more than it is."

Sammi inhaled sharply, her nostrils quivering. *What the...?* Heart thrashing against her ribs, she twisted around and scowled. "I see. Might be easy for you to just fuck and move on, but not for me."

The hint of a smile kicked up one side of his mouth. "Who the fuck said it'd be easy?"

"What is this, then? Some sort of pity fuck?" she snipped.

Whatever remained of his fleeting smile vanished. Anger flared in his eyes, turning them a midnight hue. Whenever he got emotional, his eyes tended to go a few shades darker.

"You know me better than that, little girl," he reproved.

"Don't act insulted when you literally just told me it wouldn't mean anything. Maybe you can turn your emotions on and off that easily, but that's not the way I work."

Stanton pulled himself up, bracing himself on his forearm. At the disappearance of his heat, a draft of cool air moved in behind her and she shivered. With her one chance to be close to him gone, she scrabbled to sit up and tossed her chin in the air. Lustful frustration wasn't a good look on her, but anger was boiling up in her soul.

"That's not what I meant, and you know it."

She had difficulty swallowing, and her throat felt sore. Her hand flew to the bruises on her throat. Tears burned the backs of her eyes, but she wasn't going to cry. She wasn't only upset about Stanton; she was shaken from the attack. It was growing into a whirling fireball of emotions in her chest, and she didn't seem to have the ability to control the spillover.

"I don't know anything. I'm not convinced that you didn't make up the child thing to ruin what we had," she lashed out.

Abruptly, he seized her chin. "Don't say things like that," he warned.

She tore herself away from his grip. "Admit it, it is your MO."

"Listen to me, I promised you honesty and that's what I delivered. Sooner or later, this issue would've come up. Was I supposed to drag you along, knowing you'd want something I'd never be able to provide? Because that was the alternative to facing this head-on the instant it came up."

"But, I-I don't understand, Stanton. You're so good with Wesley. You love him."

He clutched his temples. "I can't be a father. We're not rehashing this discussion. If it's not obvious to you what an awful failure I'd be, then I don't know what the hell to say."

✳✳✳

SELF-REVULSION FLOODED STANTON'S MOUTH. He swallowed down the bitterness, although the aftertaste of failure remained on his tongue. He knew he was coming off as an asshole, but there was no way he was having a kid and there was equally no way he was leading her on. She could hate him. Hell, it might be a hell of a lot easier if she did, but he wouldn't stand by and wreak havoc on her life, like he had with others.

Rolling off the bed, he rose to stand. He spun away,

turning his back on Sammi and her sad eyes, although he felt them burning holes in his back. He should be used to disappointing people by now, but it was different with Sammi. That look was never there before.

The difference is that I'm protecting her. Yes, deep disappointment resided in his gut, but it wasn't like with his father, Sage, Melanie, or the countless other women he'd tossed aside through the years. He'd have to be satisfied with the fact that he was doing right by her. The real kick to the teeth was that Stanton knew that Sammi was *the one*. There was no doubt that he'd love her till his dying breath.

At the same time, he had to take whatever measures necessary to keep her close. If she walked out the door, he'd be left tortured by horrific scenarios of her getting hurt. At least until he heard back from Kingdom.

Who was he kidding? Regardless of what Kingdom told him, he'd need her close. The images of her attack replayed in his mind, raiding his headspace. Even if Kingdom assured him that she had a guard on her twenty-four seven, he'd still need to see her, hear her, be in reaching distance of her. At least, for the foreseeable future.

Stanton entered his walk-in closet, tugged on a pair of sweats, and threw on a shirt. Then he padded into the kitchen to make coffee and a good breakfast for her. She was already there, on her tiptoes, reaching for the container of coffee grounds, the hem of his T-shirt lifting almost to her hipbone. Thank fuck she'd donned on a pair of panties. It was the only thing keeping her from getting fucked.

Standing behind her, he said, "Can we table this discussion while you're here?"

She whirled around and clutched her chest.

Fuck, he'd crept up on her and scared the hell out of her. Reaching for her, he brought her into his chest. Hand cupping the back of her head, he murmured, "Sorry, baby girl. Didn't mean to spook you."

She shook her head, but her nails dug into his shirt as she answered, "It's okay."

"Listen, let's try to take this one day at a time and compartmentalize, alright? Today, we deal with chilling out and going back to your house to get your shit, okay?"

Her gaze wandered up to his, her face pale. "Yeah."

She stepped out of his arms, forcing him to release her. Clenching his hands to prevent himself from grabbing at her, he threw open the refrigerator door and peered inside.

Sticking his head deeper into the fridge in a futile attempt to cool off his raging lust, he asked, "Would you like an omelet?"

He felt the heat of her body beside him and bit back a groan. Fuck, it was going to be the worst kind of torture being around her and not touching her.

"Do you have any veggies to put in it? Mushrooms? Scallions?" she asked, her sweet breath glancing over his cheek as she bent over to check for herself. Her forearm grazed his upper arm and he gripped his knees.

"No," he answered tightly. "We can go to a coffeeshop."

Anything was better than staying inside, with her so close. He moved away quickly to put some space between them and left Sammi rummaging around the fridge.

"Nothing," she muttered. "When was the last time you did groceries?"

He shrugged. Hell, he could barely remember his own name with her near him, much less the last time he'd done groceries.

"We'll grab breakfast, stop by your house to get your stuff, and then do groceries," he suggested, impressed with his calm tone, considering how his muscles had bunched up as he waited for a protest.

None came, and he exhaled in relief.

Sammi's shoulders gave out a shudder.

His hand wrapped around her waist. "What is it?"

"Going back to the house. Reminds me of last night." Another shiver coursed through her body.

He brought her in closer, hugging her into his chest.

"I need clothes for certain clients I'm meeting this week," she spoke into his shirt, "or else, I wouldn't step back in there until Puck was back home."

Petting her glossy curls, he murmured, "If you tell me what you need, I can go in and get everything while you stay in the car."

She shook her head. "I have to go through the clothing myself."

"I'm so fucking sorry, babe. If I could do anything to take those memories away, I would." Her head drooped like a wilted flower and he lifted her chin with his forefinger.

"What can I do to make it better?" he asked.

"You've done so much. I don't even want to think of what would've happened if you hadn't been across the street stalking me." She gave him a wobbly smile.

"Fuck, babe, I wish I could've prevented that asshole from touching you at all," he swore.

"I know." She ducked her head. "Are you sure it's okay for me to stay with you? Just a few days until I get over the worst of it."

"More than a few days. I want you here until Puck gets out."

"You know that's impossible—"

"Let's not go there right now. I've been looking into Puck's case and he may be out sooner than you think. I can't get into the details and I don't want to get your hopes up, but I'm personally looking into his case. For right now, let's focus on one week at a time. We'll revisit this discussion on the weekend. How's that?"

"Yeah, okay," she breathed out. "That works." Relief eased the tension in her face, easing the tightness in Stanton's chest.

As he turned her toward the bathroom, he couldn't help but give her bouncy ass a little swat. "Go on, take a shower. We need to get going. We've got a full day."

Then, he went to check his gun. He was going to be ready this time.

33

STANTON

S tanton was getting heated as the young Greek-American waiter at the neighborhood coffeeshop down the street from his place hit on Sammi.

In front of him, no less. The man was shameless and Stanton couldn't do much about it other than glare at the little fucker. Normally, he'd have laid claim to Sammi, but his hands were tied so he had to grin and bear it.

In the end, he broke, moved over to the other side of the booth, and crowded her against the wall when waiter boy came back with their food. He wasn't being subtle, by any means, and she smirked at his display of ownership. He didn't feel an ounce of remorse, especially when her eyelashes batted like butterfly wings after he stretched his arm across the back of the booth or leaned over to pick food off her plate.

He was close enough to see the rapid pulse at the base of her throat or the way she swallowed a few times more than necessary. Teasing her, he made certain to brush against her breasts when he reached over to grab the saltshaker. And then again with the pepper shaker. He didn't give a fuck. There was no way he was letting some twenty-year-old little twerp hit on his woman in front of him. Not happening.

During their meal, he called Kingdom and learned that the house was empty. The men had cleaned up, and *everything was taken care of*. As per their arrangement, he didn't ask any follow-up questions and Kingdom didn't offer any details. He was skating the edge of his moral boundaries, but there it was. Sammi was the priority.

At her house, Stanton did a quick check before allowing her to step inside. Kingdom told him that Kerri's ex had acted on his own, but he wasn't taking any chances. Not a shard of the broken lamp was left on the ground. He'd brought his Land Rover to transport the clothing, and other various bags and suitcases Sammi would likely bring along. In his view, the more, the better.

After food shopping, they went back to his loft. It was barely past six o'clock, but dusk was falling. Sammi looked wiped out, so he started a fire in the fireplace while she went to change. They'd fallen into a place where they didn't mention the big problems of their relationship but focused on the details of getting through the day together. They'd always worked well as a team.

Returning in a red sweaterdress with a thick black belt emphasizing the tuck of her waist and the curve of her hips, his dick definitely took notice. And it stiffened further as she bent over to arrange pillows on his couch before sitting down and folding one shapely leg over the other. She'd brought her laptop with her, but soon abandoned it for flipping through the pages of a fashion magazine. A curly raven-colored lock escaped the pencil holding up a chignon at the back of her head. The fugitive curl sprang forward as she dipped her head, concentrating on whatever she was reading, a cute little frown notched between the fine lines of her winged brows.

Poking the fire, he couldn't help but ask, "What is it?"

Sammi canted her head to one side, flapped the magazine taut, and turned it on its side. "Looking at the red-carpet Oscar dresses. Or, in Billy Eilish's case, her oversized Chanel suit. Not sure I'm into it," she mused.

Stanton snorted softly. He didn't care what anyone other than his woman was wearing. Dammit, he cursed inwardly. *Not my woman, not my woman, not my woman.* It was hard to convince himself of that when she sat on his leather couch, looking so fucking sexy in that curve-hugging red dress and a belt matching her hair.

"Hmmm," he replied neutrally. He barely knew what Billy Eilish looked like.

Sammi held up the spread magazine and a dark-haired woman with neon-green highlights floated into his vision.

"Not hotter than you," he mentioned. That was all he saw.

Sammi bit down on her plump bottom lip to stop from laughing at him.

Whatever. He didn't notice that kind of shit outside of Sammi.

"Is that really all you see? You didn't notice her suit? Shoes? Hairstyle? *Anything* else?"

"Oh, yeah, now that you mention it," he replied. "She is *not* wearing a dress."

She rolled her eyes. "Ugh. So hopeless."

"I notice what you wear," he said, with an edge of defensiveness.

An adorable flush crept up her cheeks and she lifted the magazine to hide behind it, with a little, pleased *hmm* sound.

The energy between them ebbed and flowed. Right now, it was easy and relaxed. Other times, it crackled like a live wire, jumping and skipping in the air.

Stanton crouched by the fire for a few more minutes, stirring the logs and kindling until there was a solid blaze going. Either way, he had to stay present and aware so that he could help her as much as possible. Thank Christ he hadn't picked up the bourbon in that dive bar before Cornell showed up. He would've slashed his wrists if he'd been high and partying while she was getting beaten to death.

From the edge of his vision, he saw Sammi kick off her black heels, tuck them under her bottom, and rub her feet together. His fingers clenched tightly around the poker. His skin was on fire, his Henley feeling tight around his arms and scratchy on his skin.

What he'd give to be able to reach over and take her dainty little foot in his hands, knead into the arch. Have her throw her head back and let out a groan of pleasure. He'd trail kisses along the curve of her supple calf. Work his hands up her thigh and massage the pliable flesh until he reached the sweet spot he was looking for.

He must have been staring at her because Sammi's magazine slipped from her fingers, her eyes glazed over, and her glossy lips puffed out small breaths.

Jesus Christ.

Clearing his throat, he rose to his feet and snagged a chenille throw off the love seat and dropped it on her feet. "Your feet seem cold."

"Thanks," she uttered back in a hushed whisper.

He rushed into his bedroom, ostensibly to get his laptop and files, but really to put distance between them before he knelt in front of her, spread her thighs open, and licked into her cunt the way he wanted to.

He grabbed what he needed, although the chances of him getting any work done were slim to none. Maybe it was better to take a cold shower. Anything to douse the inferno building inside him. Stalking to the closet, he grabbed a fresh towel and entered his bathroom to strip off his clothes.

This situation is heaven and hell wrapped into one.

34

SAMMI

After a week of living with Stanton, Sammi was beginning to unravel.

They woke up every morning, legs entwined, rubbing up on each other. The only solution was to sleep separately, but neither of them were willing to even bring it up as a suggestion.

She certainly wasn't going to do it.

Every evening, she waited impatiently to get ready for sleep. Each took their respective sides of the bed, knowing that they'd migrate toward one another at some point in the night.

Kingdom had told her that the attacker had been taken care of and she had nothing to worry about, but she was suffering from the jitters. She jumped at the slightest sounds. She constantly looked over her shoulder. She could still feel the bastard's fingers wrapped around her windpipe, squeezing as she tore at his hands and face to dislodge him.

No way was she ready to surrender the little bit of comfort she had with Stanton. She dreaded the moment he told her to return home, but she couldn't afford to think that far ahead. If she did, her breathing immediately became short and jagged.

Stanton seemed to be getting off work earlier than usual, and they'd end up at his loft. Most evenings, he'd pour her a glass of red wine and start a fire. Nights in Poughkeepsie had a bite to them that the fire chased away. Okay, the fact that Stanton rolled the sleeves of his dress shirt up—displaying honed forearm muscles that bunched and flexed as he stirred the fire, which also happened to increase her body temperature to a fever pitch—might have contributed to chasing away the cold.

Sammi propped her laptop on her folded knees and caught up on billing while Stanton poked at the logs in the fireplace. His cell phone rang. Sammi jumped at the sound but tried to cover her reaction by hurrying to get it off the kitchen counter and speed over to hand it to him. He looked at her as if he hadn't missed her reaction one bit, and checked the number.

Swiping it open, he held it to his ear and said, "What's up?"

Stanton pulled the phone away from his ear and Sammi heard a hacking cough shudder through the phone.

Putting it on speakerphone, he said, "You sound like shit, man. What's wrong with you?"

"Stanton," Cornell croaked out, "we have the flu. Both of us. Carl is laid up in bed, shivering, and I just checked my temperature. I'm at a hundred and one. If it's anything like Carl, this is the just the beginning. I hate to ask, but can you take Wesley for a few days? He's not showing any symptoms and he's been in front of the TV for the past three hours. He was vaccinated for the flu months ago, but we don't want to take any chances."

Stanton's gaze lifted to Sammi, and she nodded swiftly in assent. "Yeah, of course. I'll swing by and get him now."

"Great. I'll have his things packed and by the door. I don't want you in the house to get this from us."

"I don't get sick, Cornell." His tone was slightly insulted.

"Thanks, man. Appreciate it," Cornell replied, and then another coughing fit took hold of him.

Stanton hung up and said, "You're sure about this? We could end up having him for days."

"Of course, I'm sure. You heard Cornell. They just parked him in front of the TV. That means things are bad. He's much better off here." Standing up, she asked, "Do you want me to come with you?"

"No, stay here and get one of the spare bedrooms ready. I think we have pasta."

"I'll make macaroni and cheese if we have the ingredients."

Stanton looked on her with an expression of relief. "Thanks, Sammi."

"It'll be fun." Clapping her hands together, she exclaimed, "We have Wesley for a few days. I hope he'll be okay here."

"He's a trooper. He'll be going to camp next summer so I'll tell him this is a test to see how he likes it," Stanton explained, as he shrugged on his coat and grabbed his keys.

Sammi followed him to the door and on instinct, he curled his hand around her nape and pressed a kiss on her lips. God, she missed the taste of him.

"Thanks, babe, you don't know what this means to me. I've babysat at their home before, but it's the first time they've asked me for something this big. They must be wrecked if they're calling me."

Wrapping her fingers around his wrist, she asked, "Will it be okay that I'm here?"

"Cornell knows already, but I'll text him on the way and ask, to be on the safe side."

"Drive safe," she called out before closing the door. She noticed that he waited until he heard all the locks engage before setting off down the corridor.

⁂

"I GOT CAUGHT up on the last three episodes of *The Wild Kratts*," Wesley rattled off, jumping up and down in the elevator of Stanton's building.

"Is that right? That's the cartoon with the two brothers who travel around the world and save different animals," confirmed Stanton.

"You remember," Wesley said proudly, holding up his palm for a high five.

"Of course I remember. Like I was telling you on the way over, my friend Sammi is staying with me, too."

"Yay! My first sleepover. Do his parents have the flu, too?"

"Sammi's a woman. Her real name is Samantha, but everyone calls her Sammi, and she's an adult like me."

"She your girlfriend, Uncle Stanton?"

"I wish," he muttered.

"Whatcha say?"

"I said just friends. We're friends," he replied between gritted teeth.

"Like me and Caitlyn who lives across the street."

"Not quite like that, but yes, she's special to me," he confided.

"Can't wait to meet her," finished Wesley, as the elevator reached his floor.

Dragging a carry-on filled with Wesley's clothes and toys, Stanton tried to keep up with the kid, who'd jetted down the hallway the instant the elevator doors slid open. Wesley hadn't finished pressing the ringer when the front door flung open. Stanton smiled to himself. Sammi had definitely been waiting by the door for them to arrive. She helped Wesley take his coat off as she introduced herself and answered his battery of questions.

The scent of baked macaroni and cheese drifted through the air. His stomach grumbled, although no one heard it. He didn't mind since two of his favorite people were fully engrossed in each other.

"Is that right? A pair of brothers? Who's your favorite?" Stanton overheard Sammi asking Wesley.

"Martin because he's funnier than Chris. I think he's the older one. I want to have a younger brother, but my dads told me that I can't have one, even though I put him first place on my Christmas list for the past *two* years."

"Two years!" she exclaimed in shock.

"Yep," Wesley nodded proudly. "But my dads told me that it's not something Santa can give you. Only parents can give you a brother. I said that it wouldn't *hurt* to put it on my Christmas list and they agreed that it wouldn't *hurt*. And if it doesn't hurt, then maybe it could *help*, and I need all the help I can get because they're tough, those two," he finished, out of breath.

Stanton left Wesley's bag by the door and stripped off his puffy jacket. It was past seven o'clock and Wesley hadn't had dinner yet, so he knew the kid was starving. Sammi hustled over to take the carry-on into the spare bedroom, but he waved her off.

"Why don't you serve the food. It's an hour after his dinnertime and he hasn't eaten yet. He's famished, and it smells delicious in here."

She flashed him a quick smile and brought Wesley into the kitchen area of the open-concept loft. Boosting him onto a stool, she pulled the dish of macaroni and cheese out of the oven and began dividing it into squares. Returning from the spare room, Stanton set out plates for Sammi to dish out the food. He placed one in front of Wesley with a command to dig in and grabbed milk from the fridge for the boy.

Moments later, they were settled around the kitchen counter and enjoying the best meal he'd eaten in a long time. He couldn't remember the last time he'd tasted macaroni and cheese, but it brought back memories of him and his siblings huddled around the kitchen table for an early supper, his mother slapping his hand as he tried to swipe a forkful of macaroni from the ceramic baking dish.

"I hope you like apple crumble because I whipped some up. It should be ready in about ten minutes."

"I love crumble! Cinnamon is the best," insisted Wesley.

"We have some vanilla ice cream to put on top of it."

Stanton arched an eyebrow. "We do? We didn't buy any when we did groceries."

"Oh," Sammi shrugged lightly, "I went down the street and the small market was open. Popped in and bought a quart."

He simply arched a brow, but internally he was seething. "Alone?"

Avoiding his piercing gaze, she rattled on, "Oh, you know the streets aren't empty yet. Plenty of people coming home from work."

Sitting beside her at the counter, with Wesley on the other side of Sammi, he leaned in close and murmured low for her alone to hear, "If you think that weak-ass argument is going to save your behind from the punishment that's coming, then you're sorely mistaken."

A heated gaze cut sideways to him. "Promises, promises."

She thought he was joking, but he wasn't. Of course, he wouldn't hurt her, but he'd damn well make sure she understood where he stood on the subject by the time they were done.

Pinning her with a glare, he warned her, "Don't test me, little girl."

She surveyed him with a languid once-over but, instead of answering, turned to Wesley and engaged him in a conversation about his school. Her doubt was legitimate since each time they woke up, entangled in each other's limbs, he let her slip out of the bed. She always waited him out, but when he didn't engage, she'd extricate herself from his embrace and they'd go about their day as if they hadn't been a moment away from fucking.

He was *trying* to be good, dammit.

Trying to do the right thing.

Her certainty that he wouldn't engage grated on him. Did she think he didn't want her? Did she think he wasn't going to reprimand her for compromising her safety and practically giving him a heart attack? Nothing could be further from the truth.

Daytime was one thing, but she was in need of a serious lesson if she thought popping out to a store at night was acceptable. Early evening during winter in Poughkeepsie was like midnight in Miami. Streetlamps be damned. Anyone could've snatched her outside.

Stanton slowed down his breathing because the flare of dread that flashed inside his chest thrust him back to the night of her attack. Air seized in his lungs and his throat closed. Tapping his foot on the lowest bar of the stool, he pulled in a slow breath.

Wesley's head poked out from the other side of Sammi, and he asked, "Can we play *Minecraft* tonight, Uncle Stanton?"

"Did you finish your homework?"

"I didn't have homework today?"

"Why did you answer in the form of a question? Today's a Tuesday. Do you not normally have homework assigned on Tuesdays?"

"Aww," Wesley moaned.

"I was a kid once, too. Had homework every night, and I'm sure your dads were too sick this afternoon to help you with it or to look it over," he deduced.

"After I finish?" Wesley asked, a hopeful expression on his face.

"How much do you have?"

"Only spelling."

"Alright, how about you show me your schoolwork and, if there's time, we'll play for thirty minutes. But remember, you have to take a shower and get a good night's sleep. It's lights out by nine-thirty, hear me?"

Wesley nodded enthusiastically and started shoveling food into his mouth.

"Eating faster doesn't mean we'll be done faster. Sammi took the time to make this meal for us and I intend to savor it."

Sammi's head snapped back and forth as she followed their conversation.

Wesley duly slowed down his eating. "Sorry, Sammi."

Sammi smiled down on him. "I'll make sure you have enough time to play with Stanton. What's *Minecraft*, anyway?" she asked, her eyes innocently wide, although he had his suspicions she knew exactly what *Minecraft* was. A few of the boys at the club party he'd attended were about Wesley's age.

He sat back as Wesley launched into the reasons as to why it was the best video game in the world. Even better than *Fortnite*, apparently.

Upon Sammi's insistence, Stanton looked over Wesley's homework while they ate dessert. He quizzed Wesley until he was satisfied. Then they played *Minecraft*, and he even let Wesley finagle another ten minutes out of him.

"Time for a shower, buddy," Stanton stated, clapping a hand on the boy's narrow shoulder.

He walked Wesley to the guest room and saw that Sammi had already laid out his clothes in the drawers and a clean towel on the bed. Wesley's camel lovie took center stage in the middle of the pillows on the bed, which had already been turned down. They called his fathers, who both sounded horrible, and wished them a good night.

Then Stanton asked, "Need anything?"

Wesley shook his head.

"Give me a shout when you're ready for me to read to you."

"I'd like Sammi to read to me tonight," piped up Wesley.

Stanton's breath caught. He swallowed around his clogged throat and replied, "Sure thing, bud."

Shutting the door softly behind him, he returned to the kitchen and came up behind Sammi, who was setting the dishwasher. He couldn't stop himself. His hands landed on her trim waist. Nuzzling into her throat, he gave her a small nip. Sammi stifled a yelp.

"You were very bad earlier," he began.

"Is that right?" she asked in a breathy voice that almost had him salivating.

She was so fucking in tune to him. After a week, the sexual tension between them was like a living, breathing thing. He might have been able to hold out longer, but her admission that she'd walked the dark streets alone triggered his protective instincts, and they'd come roaring out. That, and Wesley had taken to her so quickly. The combination of those two things layered on top of the past week, and he couldn't stand it any longer.

His hands inched up her rib cage and cupped her heavy tits. Thumbing her erect nipples, he warned, "Fuck, woman. You're seriously testing me. I don't know if I can wait. What if I yank up this red dress and give you a quickie while Wesley's in the shower?"

Her breathing grew ragged, her tits pressing into his palms at her deep inhalations. "Are you seriously asking for an answer to that question?"

"He wants you to read to him after he's done."

She went weak against his chest. "He's such a sweet little guy."

"Listen to me carefully. You read to him. Then it's lights out. We'll wait until he's asleep. Once I check on him and make sure that he's asleep, you go to my bedroom, strip, and lay down on your belly over the covers. Ass up."

"It's cold."

"You won't be waiting long, believe me," he promised darkly. "I'm going to spank that ass bright red for pissing me off. That'll warm you up real fast."

"Doesn't sound like much of a threat," she drawled.

Stanton trained his eyes to the ceiling. She wasn't scared. Not at all.

They were hidden behind a column, should Wesley come bounding out of the guest room without announcing himself first. Pressing his chest against her back until she was bent over the counter, he dipped his head and hissed in her ear, "How about I lick your pussy now. Take you to the edge and then cut you off?"

Her cheek lay against the marble counter and her breath came out in quick pants.

"You mean, like how you've been teasing me all week without touching me once?"

Palming her backside, he ground his erection in the dip between her ass cheeks. "You want to play tonight, little girl? Prepare to play hard 'cause I'm not in a patient mood. If the boy wasn't here, I'd be fucking into you, rougher than you've ever had it before. My cock's been hard as a rock since the last time I pounded into this tight pussy."

"Why didn't you do anything before now?" she gasped out as he yanked up her dress enough to expose her outer thigh and gave it a sharp slap.

"I was trying to be good. Doesn't come easy to me, let me tell you," he growled, his fingers clenched firmly around her thigh.

Writhing against his hand, she replied in a husky tone, "Maybe you shouldn't be so good. I like you at your worst."

"Fuck, little girl—"

His ears picked up far-off sounds in the guest bedroom. Relinquishing his hold on Sammi, he smoothed his hand over her ass and groaned as his fingers stumbled over the thong nestled between her ass cheeks. Gripping the slip of satin, he was about to pull them down when he heard a noise.

Inhaling noisily, he efficiently rearranged her dress and pulled her up to standing just in the nick of time.

"Hey, I'm done," Wesley called out, bounding down the hall. Stanton circled around and pretended to busy himself with the silverware drawer to hide his arousal.

Over his shoulder, he said, "Sammi's ready for you. Aren't you?"

He glanced over at her. She'd pulled herself together

remarkably well for a woman who'd just been bent over the counter and smacked in the ass.

"I'll come in to wish you a good night once Sammi's done."

He'd be back to normal by then. Sammi ruffled Wesley's wet hair and walked with him down to the bedroom. She was so beautiful, nodding attentively to whatever Wesley was saying to her. It ached to look at her. But it wouldn't be long before he had her exactly where he wanted her.

35

SAMMI

Wesley was nodding off by the time she was halfway through the *Magic Treehouse* book he'd picked for her to read.

Closing the book and setting it on the nightstand, she whispered a goodnight to him as she petted damp bangs off his forehead. She plugged the night-light she'd found in his carry-on into the wall by the nightstand and flicked it on.

As she came out of the room, she found Stanton staring at her keenly from across the open space. He slowly uncoiled his body from the couch and prowled toward her like a lethal predator.

With a chin lift in the direction of his bedroom, he dipped his head and murmured, "I want you naked and in position." His voice was a low growl by the time he finished giving his command, more animal than man.

Sammi dropped her eyes and moved past him to his bedroom.

A tension vibrated off him that she wasn't familiar with. They'd never been forced to restrain themselves before, and in the past week, Stanton displayed an edge she'd never felt before. Sure, he had a dominant personality. It came along with his intense charisma, but there was an underlying rawness that was unusual. Even for him.

Tonight was also the first time she'd ever done something really wrong. He was genuinely upset with her for going out alone earlier. Not that he'd take his frustration out on her. He was too controlled for that, but he wasn't playing around either.

Beneath the fluttery nervousness of being in the wrong, heat slithered down to pool in her core. The fact that he'd made the decision to break his unspoken rule and touch her for the sole reason of punishing her was telling.

In his bedroom, she unbuckled her belt and pulled it off. Her fingers caressed the pliable leather before letting it drop to the floor. Might give him an idea of how to punish her, although he'd never hit her with anything but his hand before. And those had been love slaps while he fucked her, nothing like an honest-to-god punishment.

Lifting the hem of her dress, she stripped it off and unclasped her bra. That left her in her red satin thong. She wanted to change but, tugging at the band, she peeked down and found a wet spot seeping through the gusset of her panties. Lying on her belly with her legs spread wide and ass up, it'd be one of the first things he'd see as he entered the room. Anticipation rippled over her skin. That cinched it: the thong stayed.

She crawled up on the mattress and was just about to get into position when she remembered the pair of red-bottomed heels that matched her panties. *Oh, hell yes.* Scurrying off the bed, she almost tripped on her way to the closet. Bracing her hand on the closet door, she put them on and then rushed back to bed.

Sammi wasn't sure how long she waited, but she heard the

unmistakable *swish* of the door followed by a sharp inhale of breath that made her lips curve upward. Cheek against the duvet, Sammi cocked her head a little to the side to get Stanton in her line of sight. And what a sight he was. Shoulders leaning back against the door, his chest rose and fell as he engaged the lock behind him.

"He's asleep," he declared in a no-nonsense tone. Nodding toward the floor, he said, "I see you left the belt on the floor as a suggestion. Unfortunately, darling, we can't afford to have you screaming and waking up the boy. He may be a child, but he's not totally impervious to sound."

He picked up the leather belt. The sound of leather smacking against his palm echoed from the high ceiling of the room. "But I'll keep it in mind for the future."

"Future?" she squeaked. Wasn't this a specific punishment? Maybe with the added bonus of getting their sexual frustration out of their systems?

"I can't do this shit any longer, Sammi. Sleeping in bed with you. Having you rub that hot cunt against me all fucking night. I haven't had a good night's sleep in forever, and I walk around with the equivalent of a steel pipe in my pants. Not surprising since you do everything in your power to keep me hard."

Her head popped off the bed, a denial about to fly out of her mouth, but he put up his palm up and ordered, "Don't deny it. Put your head back down. I didn't give you an order to move."

Narrowing her eyes, she tossed her head in a silent *whatever* before she plopped her head back on the mattress with a little bounce.

"The chances of this being a one-off is slim to fucking none. I can't concentrate and I don't have the kind of job where I can fuck around or take a break to rub one off in the middle of the workday. Stephanie is the longest-lasting paralegal I've had, and she's threatened to quit and become a stay-at-home mom if I don't stop snapping at her. Apparently, I've been more irritable of late. I may not know the details of how this is going to go down but there are two things I'm sure of. You're staying here until I get Puck's ass out of jail, and we're fucking every single night. Everything else is up for negotiation."

"Everything?" she piped up.

What does he mean? Are we getting back together? Is the discussion of children up for discussion? Her own thoughts had changed somewhat on the subject. She wanted children, for sure, but being without Stanton was a day-to-day agony. She couldn't relinquish the ultimate decision, but she decided she could give him more time to work through his issues. Of course, with the tension sitting heavy between them, she didn't have the courage to reintroduce the touchy topic again.

"Everything," he swore. "But first things first. Let's focus on why you're here, with your ass up in the air."

The mattress dipped beside her and warm fingers encircled her ankle. She could feel his eyes grazing down her back and ass to her shoes.

"I appreciate the attempt at matching."

Sammi flipped her head to her other side and stared at him. "What exactly do you mean by *attempt*? I *am* matching."

His eyes drifted from the red bottoms of her heels to her ass and back. "Ahh, so you are. My bad."

"Humph, you need to get your eyes checked. Maybe you're colorblind. I hear that afflicts men more often than women."

His hand landed on her ass with a sharp swat. "Settle down, feisty one."

Sammi bit down on her cheek to stop from moaning. *Keep quiet.* This was a good lesson of what it would be like to have a child, because this had to be quiet sex. His hand kneading her butt cheek was causing her entire spread pussy to pulse with need.

Stanton widened his legs, his hand slowly stroking the cock pressing against his zipper and tenting his pants. The hand on her ass slipped between the back of her thighs and a knuckle pressed wet satin between her folds.

"I like this color here. It's an exact match with the shoes. Or is that my color blindness acting up again?" he teased.

Heart hammering against her ribs, she squirmed against the pressure at her entrance. "Oh, God," she moaned.

"Yeah, the next time you scream *oh god*, it's going to be while you're coming on my cock."

"Dammit, Stanton, how long are you going to torture me?" she cried out.

"Depends on what you consider torture," he remarked. "Sit up. Hands on your knees."

She rushed to the position he demanded, feet tucked underneath her, palms on knees.

His eyes roved over her chest greedily. "Christ, those tits."

He leaned in and lapped at a peak. She jerked against the rasp of his tongue. Curving his fingers around her breast, he fed on more of it and sucked her nipple to the roof of his mouth. His other hand dipped under the band of her panties, where he caressed her hypersensitive skin. She grabbed his head and pressed his mouth closer, but he broke from her grip.

"Hands on your knees. No touching. No moving unless I tell you exactly what to do." Shaking his head, he asked, "How have you survived these past ten days without my cock?"

"Just peachy. I'm not like you. I can handle my bodily needs."

"Is that right?" His head canted to the side. "So all those

times I caught you squirming that tight ass of yours on my couch, you were just getting comfy?"

She gritted out the lie. "Yes."

He leaned in close. His tongue flicked out and traced the tendon leading up her throat to her ear, where he whispered, "So why did I find a wet spot when I sat down on the leather couch after you left to get ready for bed the other night?" He rubbed his thumb and two fingers in front of her face. "So wet from your ripe pussy leaking all over my couch. Not been wearing panties, naughty girl?"

"That could have been anything," she fired back.

"Could have. Only I swiped as much of the juices as I could on these fingers," he waved them in front of her, "and put them in my mouth. They tasted of *you*, and God knows I've tongue-fucked you enough to know exactly what you taste like."

The breath in her lungs stuttered.

"Busted," he said.

Oh God. She felt the heat rush to her cheeks and lips. They felt swollen and inflamed. She licked them and swallowed around her dry throat. Sammi curled her upper lip.

"That's fucking disgusting." *No it's not. It's hot as fuck, I wish I'd been there to see it.*

"Really, I can't believe you'd do something like that." *I so believe it. I'm only sad I missed it.*

"Mmm," was his only answer. "Desperate times call for desperate measures, and I was fucking desperate to taste you again." The back of his fingers brushed against her flushed cheeks. "You shouldn't have been out by yourself tonight," he murmured soberly.

"I just ran to the store and back. I was fine," she argued.

Ignoring her excuse, he shook his head. "That was a big

no-no. After what happened, you know better than to go walking around by yourself after dark."

She turned her pleading eyes on him. "It was for Wesley."

"That's why you're going to make a fantastic mother. Because you'll go to any length for a child. But I *need* you to be safe. For my sanity."

"Fine, I won't do it again. You don't need to give me a spanking."

The word *spanking* hovered in the air, and she pressed her thighs together as liquid heat gushed from her core. Okay, she was totally lying. Embarrassment tinged the tips of her ears. The idea turned her on beyond anything, but she had to fight him on it. She wriggled a little and he gave her a knowing look.

"Words won't make the same impact as my hand will. If you don't hear it, you're going to feel it."

Catching the corner of a pillow, he grabbed it and dropped it on her arms. "You'll need that to scream into. We wouldn't want to wake up Wesley, would we?"

He patted his lap. "Now, be a good girl and come here."

She eyed his lap warily.

Stanton leaned back on his outstretched arm, staring her down. Her gaze wandered over his face, gauging his expression.

Watching her sharply, he waited her out. Blowing out a large gust of air, she lifted onto her knees, shuffled over to him, and flopped over his lap. His hard cock prodded her, and the muscles of her belly bunched in reaction. He placed his hand on the small of her back and adjusted her position.

At first, he teased the lace trim of her panties. Then suddenly, he tore them down her thighs. Sammi clutched the duvet cover and let out a surprised wheeze.

Stanton splayed his large hand over her buttocks, covering

them almost entirely. She peeked up at him and found his eyes riveted on her ass.

He smacked it lightly. "So fucking pretty. It's going to look even better a shade of hot pink."

Sammi's eyes fluttered shut and her breathing became shallow.

"The pillow," he reminded her.

She reached forward, grabbed hold of the pillow, and brought it to her mouth. Her fingers gripping it tingled and she bit nervously on her bottom lip as she anticipated the first smack.

"We'll start easy. Count off ten to start."

Her head wobbled in a caricature of an overeager nod, but she didn't have much time to think before his hand landed on her ass, catching both of her cheeks. The smack was sharp, but it wasn't so bad.

"Concentrate, Sammi. What number was that?"

What number what? Oh, yeah, count off. "One."

"Keep your focus, baby girl. Otherwise, I turn you over and use your pussy for this lesson."

Another rained down, and then one more on top of it. She pushed out a *two* and *three* from between her lips. After the initial shock, a burn settled in, but before she could get comfortable, another four smacks came down in rapid succession.

Stanton paused, waiting for her to catch up, and that brought them up to seven. Sammi squirmed in his lap until his hot palm kneaded the sharpness away, leaving a hot tingling sensation behind.

"You're doing so well, sweetness. Let me check your pussy," Stanton said, as he dipped two fingers between her thighs. "Fuck, baby."

The fingers slipped in easily and she twisted on his lap to push them in farther.

He withdrew them and she mewled at the loss. "Five more on each cheek, yeah?"

Sammi's head flung up, arching her back. "That's more than ten."

"You can take more," he replied patiently. "And I'm going to make them count."

She grumbled under her breath, but lowered her head to comply. He had a point because his smacks were no hardship. They'd done nothing but excite her.

"Pillow, Sammi," was the only warning he gave her before the flat of his palm landed down hard, twice, with whacking sounds.

"Ah!" she cried out, burying her face in the pillow to catch the rest of her scream. Those last two were scorchers.

"Call them out," Stanton ordered.

"Eight, nine," she gritted out between clenched teeth. He peppered her ass with two more blows. "*Ten*, eleven." She spat out the ten because it was supposed to have stopped there before he changed his mind.

"Why are you getting these swats on your fine ass?"

"Because I went out walking alone at night," she snapped.

Sammi flinched in anticipation as she felt the whoosh of air on her seared skin an instant before his hand came crashing down.

Smack. "Twelve."

Smack. "Thirteen."

Sammi screeched into her pillow as he delivered the remaining blows. Once done, she listened for sounds of Wesley, but all was quiet outside of her heavy breathing. Abruptly, she twisted onto his lap, hissing as the rough denim of his jeans scratched against her scalding ass.

"Dammit, Stanton, that hurt!" she complained, in a high-pitched voice.

"It's supposed to hurt," he replied solemnly. "Good to know you enjoyed the earlier smacks, but I wanted you to feel a fraction of the pain I felt when you told me that you roamed around outside without protection. Especially, after your recent attack."

She glared up at him, but he gathered her into an embrace, shifting her to lean against his chest and take pressure off her buttocks. Although the pain had dulled, Sammi sulked against the taut outline of his chest.

Caressing her abused flesh, he nuzzled close. "You did so well, gorgeous, I'm giving you a little reward."

36

SAMMI

"What reward?" Sammi pouted, her eyes hovering at half-mast at the thought of his mouth or fingers on her.

Finally, a reward because he put more force into those slaps than he'd ever done before. He must've been seriously. The thought melted her heart.

Stanton caught her jaw and held her in place for his invasion, his tongue thrusting inside her mouth. She moaned against the incredible feeling of being controlled by this man. Whatever he did to her was always exactly right. He knew how to kiss her, touch her, and fuck her within an inch of her life.

Carefully bringing her down to the bed, he moved on top of her, kissing her collarbone and down one breast, teasing and biting her nipple before switching to the other. Sammi yanked at his shirt in a silent plea for him to undress.

Rising to his knees, he grabbed the back of his shirt and whipped it off in one graceful move, revealing his sculpted chest lightly sprinkled with hair. He heaved a few breaths and was on her once more. He suctioned his lips around her nipple while his fingers tweaked the other. Then he popped off the nipple and rotated between pinching and thumbing it until she was panting. She squirmed under the back-and-forth volley between pain and relief, but whatever he did, it directly shot down to her clit.

He moved his open mouth over her ribs and down her belly. Sammi's knees dropped open and Stanton made himself comfortable, pushing them farther apart with his broad shoulders. The visual of his dark blond hair and broad shoulders, flexing as they nudged her thighs wider, was almost enough to make her come.

Sammi's eyes flicked up to the ceiling, silently anticipating the moment he tasted her. Instead of wet roughness, however, she got a hot breath across her pussy. Her clit twitched and quivered.

He nipped her inner thigh and she stifled a yelp; her head popped up and eyes raced to the door. Was that noise from Wesley? No, it was nothing.

Collapsing back down, she grabbed hold of his hair to place his mouth where she wanted it.

Yeah, I'm so not ready for quiet sex.

"So demanding," he mumbled, when her grip tightened harshly on his locks. He chuckled against her sensitive flesh and she wanted to scream in frustration.

"Please Stanton," she pleaded, yanking harder.

"The harder you pull my hair, the longer you'll wait."

His tone was stern.

Scoring her nails down his skull, she released her grip and let her arms flop to her sides.

"Fine," she ground out. "Have it your way."

"Good girl, be patient and let me feast on your pussy."

A low moan slipped out as he finally buried his head between her legs. His tongue darted between her wet folds and she bolted off the bed. Wrapping his hands around her knees, he went in deeper, stiffening his tongue and stabbing inside with a precision that had her thrashing her head from side to side. He added his fingers, which danced over her clit. It wasn't long before she was bucking into his face, seeking more and more pressure. Whimpers escaped her in place of the screams she worked to muffle.

Slicking over her clit one last time, he said, "Fuck, I need to feel that tight flesh around my cock."

He chucked off the rest of his clothing and climbed on top of her. She welcomed his with open arms, the feeling of his hot, smooth skin against hers was the absolute best.

She'd never get enough of him. He'd ruined her for other men. She scraped her nails down his flanks, took hold of his hips, and pressed closer, rocking up into him as he entered her with one long, deep thrust.

"Hold on to the headboard. If you let go, I'll pull out and lash your wrists to the posts," he warned.

Stanton took each of her feet, straightened her legs, and propped them on his shoulders. Grasping her ankles, he leaned forward and slid in until she felt his balls connect with her ass. She sighed. This was the meaning of being balls deep. She pivoted her hips as he pulled out so when he pushed back in, he hit her G-spot.

She clenched her pussy, clasping around his cock to prevent him from withdrawing. Withdraw he did but, thank God, only to impale her again with a rough thrust. Her pussy throbbed around the hot steel rod of flesh that filled her to the brim. Sammi writhed her hips to create more friction.

"Damn, baby, you're the most beautiful thing I've ever set eyes on. With the tightest, hottest little pussy I've had the privilege to fuck."

His pace increased, brutal, just the way she craved. Desire coiled tighter and tighter as his magic cock hit the same spot, sparks of white-hot pleasure shooting through her body. He flicked her clit, followed by a series of light, rhythmic smacks. He punched his hips forward, his balls spanking her lightly. A wave of desire rolled over her.

Her eyes rolled back, and she went flying, spasming around his battering cock. Losing all control, she thrashed around, only aware enough to bite her tongue to stop from crying out. Her mouth flooded with blood, but she barely registered the iron tang through the intensity of her climax.

Stanton's movements turned erratic. Moments later, he froze as his body tightened. A single low growl vibrated through the room as he came inside her wet heat. The sound shook through her, sparking aftershocks that almost made her orgasm again.

Stanton swooped down for a kiss and half shouted, "What the fuck? You're bleeding."

His eyes were wild with fright. He popped her mouth open and bloodied saliva dribbled out. She swallowed as he pulled out of her, dragged her to the edge of the bed, he helped her to the bathroom. She bent over the sink, spit, and washed out her mouth.

"I bit my tongue to hold in my scream. I must have gone down too hard. Mouths bleed a lot," she explained, wiping her mouth on the hand towel he had waiting in his hand for her.

He fisted her hair, held it back, and bit into the side of her neck hard enough to leave a mark. "Christ, woman, you scared the hell out of me."

She attempted to shy away from him, but he tightened his grip. "Hey, stop it. There's nothing to be ashamed about. We're not used to sharing our space with a child, and it's better to be safe than disturb Prince Wesley."

Sammi's lips twisted into a reluctant smile. "He is precious."

Stanton cupped her cheek and turned her to face him. "I fucking love you. You know that, right?" His eyes bled sorrow. "Whatever happens, I need you to know that."

"I know," she murmured softly, that knowledge seeping into the marrow of her bones. The second time hearing it wasn't any easier. Her heart was both elated and breaking, at the same time. She felt the last of the barriers she'd erected to protect herself splinter apart and crumble, leaving her defenseless. She never doubted that he cared for her, but to hear it wrung her heart to hear his declaration because nothing had changed between them.

In a scratchy voice, he ordered, "Come on, back to bed."

Sammi followed him meekly, head down. He fluffed up the pillows before prodding her to get in and joined her. He dragged her into his arms, her back flush against his chest. She focused on the steady thumping of his heart on her bare back. Breathing in and out, she slowed her breathing until it matched his pace.

Cushioned against him, with nothing of the outside world intruding, she wanted to remain like this forever. Outside, the sound of snow crystals striking the windowpane merged with the symphony of his heartbeat and their mutual breaths until she fell sleep within the cocoon of his arms.

37

STANTON

Stanton rushed down the dark corridor of the cramped offices of the District Attorney at the courthouse.

He'd had barely slept a wink, yet again. He'd thought fucking Sammi would knock him out, and it would have if he'd allowed it, but he was unwilling to miss a moment of holding her in his arms. That had been one motherfucking intense bout of lovemaking. He didn't know if it was the weeks of abstention, his punishment, or his declaration of love, but he felt torn open and raw. That, and also desperate to figure out a way to keep her.

Impossible, I know.

Cornell's ringtone emanated from his pocket. Fishing out his phone, he waited for facial recognition, which took a bit longer in the dusky lighting of the hallway.

CORNELL: School called. Wesley's sick. Can you pick him up?

Fuck. Court started in less than half an hour. He dialed Cornell immediately.

"Yes, I know he got the flu vaccine, but that doesn't make

you impervious from getting it," Cornell answered the question before it left Stanton's lips.

"What the fuck is it good for then?" he asked.

"He caught it, but it'll be much milder. Unfortunately, he can't stay in school and infect his classmates. He's currently waiting for you at the nurse's office."

"I've got court in thirty minutes."

"Oh, no," groaned Cornell.

Stanton thought fast. Amy was in New York. His mom was at a silent meditation retreat before the next wave of campaigning. *Sammi.* "I'm going to call Sammi to pick him up. Can you call the school and tell them to hand Wesley over to her?"

"No problem. You sure she can do this? I'd go, but I can't drive with the way I feel, and I don't want to expose a poor Uber driver to this hellish flu."

"Call the school to tell them that either Sammi or I will come. If I can't get her, then I'll go. I'll text you either way. There's no way you or Carl are going out."

"Thanks, man. You don't know what this means to me."

"No worries, bro."

He hung up and texted Sammi. Thankfully, she texted right back. Shouldering open the door of his office, he googled the address of Wesley's school and sent it to her. He dropped his briefcase on his desk, and then dialed her.

His teeth raked his bottom lip her sultry voice came through the phone. "I'm so fucking sorry to do this to you," he said.

Her beautiful laugh rang out. "Please don't worry about it. If he's sick, he needs to be home, not waiting in some dreary nurse's office."

"I'm sure the office is painted in primary colors with animals on the wall. It's school, not prison."

"Says the teacher's pet," she teased. "For the rest of us, it was prison*esque*. Seriously though, I can reschedule my appointment. I only had one this morning and she's a mother, so she'll understand. That's the beauty of working for yourself."

"You're my savior," he breathed out. It was the absolute truth.

Another adorable giggle. "See you tonight."

"I'm ducking out early. No way I'm leaving you alone with Wesley all day."

"We'll be fine," she reassured him.

"Text me when you get home," he demanded. "Let me know if I should get anything from the pharmacy. I going to order Mexican before leaving so I'll have to stop off and pick it up on my way home. Anything else you want?"

"I'm good, Stanton. Focus on court and I'll see you tonight."

"Okay." He paused and then pushed out what he couldn't fight to hold in any longer, "Love you."

He heard her quick intake of breath, and it made his heart ache that it still elicited that kind of reaction out of her.

"Love you, too," she replied and hung up.

✳✳✳

"ALL RISE," boomed out the guard.

Stanton rose to his feet as Judge Matthias entered the courtroom. His phone vibrated in his pants pocket. Motherfucker. He glanced up to see the judge taking her seat, dropped to his seat, pried the cell phone out of his pocket, and furtively peeked at the screen.

"Since when do we check our phones as a trial is about to commence, Mr. Prescott?" came an imposing voice.

Shit.

Dropping the cell phone on his lap, he lifted his gaze to the face of the older woman. She was smoothing the front of her robe with her hand and staring at him with an arched eyebrow. He'd committed a serious no-no, but he couldn't go through another hour and a half without knowing if Sammi and Wesley were okay.

"It's my son, Judge. I just got a call he's got the flu and I'm having my girlfriend pick him up. I need to check if everything's fine."

Once upon a time, he'd have shot himself in the head before disclosing anything so personal to a judge, but he had zero hesitation in claiming Wesley and Sammi as his.

"Son?" chirped Jessica Ramirez, the opposing counsel across the aisle from him, her eyes busting out of their sockets. "Since when do you have a son?"

Stanton narrowed his eyes at Jessica. The problem with having a well-known family was that everyone in this town knew his fucking business. Not one small white lie went under the radar.

"Not my own flesh and blood, but he's like a son to me, and he's currently under my custody," he snapped. Not *legal* custody, but whatever.

"I see," Judge Mathias pondered aloud.

The judge wasn't a stickler for formality, outside of a few pet peeves.

"By all means, check your text and get it out of the way because we have a lot to get through within the next ninety minutes."

Stanton released an audible sigh and quickly looked at his phone. Sammi had picked up Wesley. She attached a photo of him in the back seat of her car, a big grin and two thumbs up. He huffed out a laugh. *Okay, someone's happy.*

A rush of relief flooded through him and he slumped slightly forward before firing off a quick text thanking her, telling her he'd be out of communication for the next hour and a half, and that he loved her. The floodgates were open and he couldn't hold back every time the feeling came over him to declare his love for her.

Turning the ringer to silent, he left it face up next to his folder. That instrument of communication with Sammi and Wesley, beside him while he worked, gave him a sense of comfort, a tether to the people he loved, and it grounded him.

"Done," Stanton pronounced, and thanked the judge for her patience.

"In my day, men weren't as involved as they are now. It's good to see how couples work together in child-rearing. Gives me hope for these next generations," concluded the judge before turning to procedural matters.

Stanton's eyes roamed a few times to his cell phone. He felt a deeper bond to Sammi, with the responsibility of Wesley shared between them. Stanton never believed he could be a father, or more specifically a *good* father, and he was terrified that he'd be a horrible one, but a revolutionary thought crossed his mind.

He might be able to do it. Not alone, but with Sammi.

His mind tripped over the idea, but once it lodged inside his brain, he couldn't shake it off.

38

STANTON

S tanton rang the doorbell with his elbow, using his briefcase to leverage the take-out bags slipping out of his grasp back into the crook of his arm.

He heard the quick click-clack of heels trotting toward the door and then it swung open to Sammi, dark curls tumbling over her shoulders.

With a soft *hey, baby* that made his cock twitch, she grabbed the large paper bags from his arms and strode toward the kitchen. He stood stock still for a moment, drinking her in. Then, it dawned on him that she'd answered the door without checking the peephole first. His gaze narrowed on her dangerously.

Coming in behind her, he was momentarily distracted by the swing of her hips and her plump ass wrapped in a fitted leather skirt the color of butter. He didn't think he'd ever get tired of following her hips around, but tonight, he definitely planned to use her earlier infraction of not verifying the peephole to get his hands all over her plum-shaped ass.

She gave him a knowing smirk when she turned around and caught his gaze lingering on her rear.

He made sure to give her a distinctly unapologetic grin in return.

"Wesley's fever came down after I gave him Tylenol and he's been resting in the guest bedroom. I may or may not have played *Minecraft* with him. That's a secret I'll take to the grave, and no amount of torture will break me," she finished.

"Is that a challenge?" he asked, getting into her space. "You do know how competitive I am, don't you?"

He dropped his briefcase to the floor and placed the last bag on the kitchen counter. Shedding his coat and suit jacket, he threw them over the back of one of the high stools and corralled her against the sink. He caged her in and took a taste of her lips. "Been waiting all fucking day to do this."

Sammi linked her hands behind his nape, rubbing the soft mounds of her breasts against his chest, and he moaned against her mouth.

Tearing her head away, she panted lightly. "He's coming."

The woman had a keen sense of hearing, he'd give her that. Stepping away, she began tearing open the bags of takeout just as Wesley rounded the corner of the hallway.

"Hey, buddy, how are you doing?" he asked the little guy.

"Better," he replied, yawning as he rubbed his eyes. "Sammi stayed with me today. She read to me and we watched TV."

Ruffling Wesley's hair, Stanton dropped to his haunches and hugged the boy. "Are you coughing? Nose bothering you? You were sleeping when I called to check up on you earlier."

"Nope. My body hurt," he said, demonstrating by grabbing at his arms and legs. "I felt hot in school and my head hurt too, so I told my teacher. It went away after Sammi gave me the candy-tasting medicine. I like that medicine. I talked to my dads and they think I can go home tomorrow, but I told them I wanted to stay here."

"We can talk to them and see if they'll give us one more day together. I'm taking the day off tomorrow. Sick day."

"You're not sick."

"Turns out you can take a sick day if your child gets sick. Told my boss I was in charge of my nephew and that I had to stay home with him tomorrow." Stanton spoke to Sammi over his shoulder. "It's a thing, did you know that? Family sick leave."

Sammi paused in taking out dishes from the cupboard and pursed her lips together to keep them from twitching. "I've heard of it."

"Is that right, Ms. Know-It-All?" he huffed peevishly, fixing her with a look promising retribution. Turning his attention back to Wesley, he said, "I bought fajitas. Think you can eat something?"

"Yeah," he replied with a shrug. "Did you get the flan from El Sombrero?"

"Did I get the flan, he asks?" Stanton clucked his tongue. "How could I go there and not get the flan? That's the whole purpose. If you try to eat some rice and beans with the fajitas, you may have some flan."

Wesley bounced on the balls of his feet and cried out, "Yes!"

Hurrying to the kitchen, he jumped in to help Sammi set the table for dinner.

After dinner and the famous El Sombrero flan, which Wesley exclaimed tasted better since he got to have dessert in the middle of the week, Stanton poured an after-dinner glass of cognac for Sammi as she caught up on work and he went with Wesley to get him ready for bed. Since he'd dozed off earlier in the day, it was past ten o'clock by the time he fell asleep.

Roving around the dining area and kitchen, Stanton tidied

up for a good half hour before he joined Sammi on the couch. She glanced up from her typing and sent him a sexy little smile that made his cock take notice. What that woman could do with just a smile was criminal.

Speaking of criminals, he stated, "Puck's case is going to get dropped."

Sammi's fingers froze and she blinked rapidly at him. "W-what are you saying, Stanton?"

"I'm saying that the District Attorney will not go forward with his case." Taking her hand in his, he gazed down at his fingers playing with hers.

"What did you do?" she asked in a hushed voice.

"Puck said something during his arraignment—in the middle of arguing with you—about the cops that sounded off to me. I made a few calls and got access to the police car dash cam of the arresting officers. Turns out there was some improper behavior prior to his confession."

Needless to say, he didn't reveal to anyone but his boss that the arresting officer was a blood relation of Judge Korman.

"I can't go into further detail, but I brought this to Sage's attention. She filed for a FOIA—"

"A what? Speak non-legalese English, please."

"Freedom of Information Act. It's a request Sage can file that will allow her to see the dash cam. I already alerted the police commissioner to make certain that it's accessible in a timely manner. Gave my boss a heads-up. Let's face it, it's an election year and he is not a man who likes to lose. Meaning, no scandals. The media would eat this kind of shit up right now, and his seat is contested. I expect it to be resolved quickly."

"Oh my God, Stanton," she sniffed, flinging her arms around his neck. His arms naturally circled her and pulled her in closer. Burrowing into her throat, he inhaled her sweet, sultry scent intertwined with the faint traces of the spicy floral fragrance she wore.

Face muffled in his shirt collar, she said, "I know you did this for me, and I'm forever grateful."

"Yeah, and how are you going to show me this so-called gratitude?" he joked.

Her hand immediately ran down his shirt, popping each button open along the way as she murmured in a husky voice, "Oh, baby, any way you want. You just have to ask." Her eyes flew to his. "You know this has nothing to do with Puck, right?" She paused at tugging out his dress shirt.

"Of course I know. I know you fucking love me, Sammi."

Her gorgeous chocolate eyes shimmered. She dropped her eyes to focus on his shirt again. He placed his hand over hers and said, "I'll have to marry you and breed you before your brother gets out of jail. It's the only way to prevent him from taking you away from me."

Her eyes bolted up and drilled into his. "What the hell are you talking about?"

"I'm talking about putting a fucking ring on you, little girl, and putting a baby in your belly."

She placed the back of her hand against his forehead, her brows puckered in concentration as she felt for flushed skin. "*Ohmygod*, you have the flu. You're delirious, surely."

Plucking her hand off, he said, "I'm not sick, Sammi, I'm serious. Today taught me an important lesson. It took a while for me to realize that you were right about parenthood and seeing us in action today cinched it for me. You're my other half, and I understood that I can be a father with *you*. I can be a father if *you're* the mother of my child. I wouldn't risk that shit with any other woman, but I trust you to hold my hand through the process and safeguard me from fucking up too badly." He hesitated. "If that's still something you want."

Tears gathered at the corners of her eyes and toppled down her cheeks.

Framing his face with her hands, she breathed out, "Stanton, you're killing me. You may not believe it yet, but I *know* in my soul that you will make an incredible father. With or without me. You want to have a child with me, then I'm game, but you'd make a wonderful father regardless. You have self-awareness, you love hard, and you protect even harder. Many men start with far less and do a decent job. You'll be phenomenal. I promise you."

"I'll hold you to that promise, little girl," he swore.

Her hands dropped away, and he instantly felt the loss of her warmth. Her eyes darted away, and a stab of fear struck Stanton in the chest. "What's wrong?"

"Nothing," she said with a small shrug, but her eyes stayed glued to the rug.

"Come on, Sammi. Something's going on. You don't want to have a kid with me. That's it, right?"

"No, that's not it at all." Her fingers fiddled with the slim leather belt of her skirt. "It's that, well … I've also come to a realization. I definitely want a family with you, but I want to wait a bit. I mean, I love having Wesley with us, but I think I was taken up in the whirlwind of Sage's and Abby's pregnancies. But Sage is older than me and Abby always wanted to start a family young. With our busy careers, we barely have time to enjoy ourselves. I want to travel, and have loud sex whenever we feel like it. Walk around half-clothed if we want."

"You don't want a baby right now?"

She shook her head. "I know, I know, I decide this after the discussion that led to us breaking up. But I still believe it was an issue that needed to be dealt with because I do *eventually* want a family, but not right starting tomorrow."

He placed a hand over her belly. "Not gonna lie, I was

warming up to the idea of filling you with my come again and again until I breed you, but I can hold off until you're ready. That still leaves one last problem unresolved. You need to be mine before Puck comes out of jail. Pregnancy is by far the best proposal, but we must be married, at the very least."

He could get behind marriage for a cause. Keeping his head attached to his neck and Sammi in his life were two very good reasons. If nothing else, he was pragmatic. Thank fuck he had the wherewithal not to spout that bullshit out loud. Truth was, he was a possessive mofo when it came to her.

"I must say, I'm starting to see the appeal of having a tat with the words Property of Stanton slapped on your ass."

Peals of laughter escaped her. "For a rich man, you're such a savage."

He shrugged. "Nothing new there."

Shaking her head with pity, she said, "My brother won't ever separate us. If you're good to me, he'll learn to accept our relationship. The only thing that man cares about is my happiness."

Giving her a deadpan expression, he stated, "Sammi, he was pissed off every time he looked at me in court. Can't imagine he'll be pleased to hear that you're with the man who attempted to lock him up."

"You're also the man who got him out of jail. Puck didn't expect to get out free. Confession or not, I know that man, and he pistol-whipped Kerri's ex." A shiver coursed down her spine at the mention of him, and Stanton clutched her hand.

"Puck was taking out his anger on you. He also knew of your past with Sage," she added.

His past again coming to bite him in the ass. "There you go."

"But he'll get over it. Sage and Kingdom are over it. He's not going to hold a grudge longer than they will. Puck's a simple guy. He doesn't complicate his life. Once he gets to know you and sees how protective you are of me, he'll be relieved of the responsibility of taking care of me."

Stanton's fingers caressed her arm. "Just as I was getting excited with the idea, you tell me you're not ready for children."

Sammi scooted closer to him and cuddled into his chest. "It really hurt when I bit my tongue last night. It made me think, do I really want to wake up in the middle of the night to feed the baby and change diapers? I'm twenty-one years old. You're in a different place in your life, old man, that's why the thought appeals to you."

"Very funny, but I'm good. I'd like a couple years of sobriety under my belt before we try. That, and getting practice so that when the time comes, I'll up to the task of breeding you," he said, grazing his hand over her breast and squeezing the firm, plum flesh.

Sammi kissed along his jaw line. "Babe, you'll be a wonderful father. There's nothing written in the stars saying you'll repeat your relationship with your father. You will make your own destiny."

Toying with her fingers, Stanton replied, "Hopefully, the first child will be a girl. Ease me into parenthood with a child of the opposite sex. Much less tension."

Sammi snorted. "Until she starts dating. Then all hell will break loose."

"Not with my baby girl, it won't. She's going to be a daddy's girl, through and through."

"Famous last words," Sammi replied. "Anyway, I can't wait for Puck to be released. We're going to have a huge party at the clubhouse. It's gonna be poppin'. True madness. All because of you." She fluttered her eyelashes at him, and he groaned.

His insides turned to gelatin when she got flirtatious on

him. "You're asking to get fucked right on this couch if you keep looking at me like that."

"Is that right?" Her hands slipped underneath his open shirt. She curled her fingers, pressing her nails into his skin, and scraped them down his pecs, leaving light red claw marks. Fuck, that got his cockstand up in under a second.

"That was very naughty of you," he murmured against her lips. "I think you did it on purpose to garner a punishment."

"I'll never confess to a single thing, counselor."

"Well, I happen to have a set of skills to make naughty little girls like you admit to their crimes. You know you want to unburden yourself," he crooned, his hands attacking the leather tie around her skirt, "and confessing your sins will set you free. Punishment will do that, as well."

"You don't say? I could be innocent of all wrongdoing," she suggested, tilting her head to expose her throat to his kisses.

"Somehow, I find that doubtful," he murmured against her skin. "You have a stubborn streak and a past pattern of insubordination. A brat is what you are."

"Hmm, would a brat confess?"

"A brat might, but only because she thinks she'll get out of her punishment and I won't pass up a chance to discipline that bubble ass of yours. It's a dirty job for a dirty girl, but I'm the man for the job. Anyway, you need to be reminded of your place."

"What place is that?" Sammi panted out.

"Over my knee," he rumbled. Standing, he scooped her into his arms and stalked into the bedroom to teach her another sensual lesson in obedience.

39

STANTON

Another sign that Stanton was madly in love with his woman was the fact that he was standing in the middle of another raging clubhouse party, fighting off men who were coming on to Sammi despite the fact that he was standing right beside her.

What in the fuck was wrong with these people?

She'd gone to get a drink, which he'd resigned himself to allowing in this hellhole. The moment she was gone, Tank began spouting off the rules of the club, making him itch to sucker punch the asshole.

"If you don't make her your property, she's free pussy. Those are the rules. You can't have it both ways," the big man boomed out.

Both ways? Did these idiots think *he* didn't want to put a ring on her finger? *She's been pulling an Abby on me*, he wanted to holler in their faces. Truly, the only man he had pity for was Loki.

Puck cut in, "You've got to put a tramp stamp on her ass with those words on it or it won't be legit. Just sayin' that's how it is if you want to keep the men off her. You should go to her now. Demand she gets your name tatted on her ass. Go on," he prodded Stanton.

Stanton narrowed his eyes. Did her brother think he was an idiot? He could smell a setup by a mile, but he had to take a breather from these dumbasses because they were doing everything in their power to fuck with him. After Sammi's attack, the brothers had toned it down for a while. Unfortunately, Puck's release seemed to have riled them up again.

"Alright, I'll do it," he lied. *Hard pass, motherfuckers.* It gave him an excuse to take a break before he decked one of them. Oh, and to get Sammi away from the men swarming around her.

Puck clapped him on the shoulder with a chuckle. "You do that, man. She'll appreciate it. It's like you're saying you *love* her."

Side-eyeing him, Stanton witnessed him almost gagging on the word.

He stalked over to Sammi by the pool table, surrounded by half a dozen men, and growled, "Get up. We're leaving."

Taken by surprise, she didn't move, so he yanked her by the arm. Her gaze shot wide. He gripped harder, hard enough to leave marks, but was she scared or angry? Not his Sammi. Her breathing deepened and the corners of her lips curved up in a Cheshire Cat smile. She saw him. Saw that he was jonsing to be inside her every hour of every day. Not just to fuck. No, he wanted to own her. Bury himself inside her sweet pussy and claim her as his own.

He plucked the pool stick out of her grip and handed it off to the nearest man.

"Where are we going?"

He heard the thread of excitement in the question. Leaning into her, he cupped his mouth into her ear, and said, "Somewhere where you can scream to your heart's content."

She shivered, her shoulders shaking slightly.

"You should be scared," he warned, "because you're going to drown in the come I have stored up for you. I'm going to put my dick so far down your throat you're going to choke on my cock."

Grabbing her ass in front of an array of bikers and bitches, he asked, "Which way?"

He heard her low moan, despite the pounding music booming through speakers hanging from the walls. She nodded in anticipation and pointed to an exit at the back of the club. Christ, this woman wanted to kill him. Slay him. Grind him to dust.

He was going to take her up against the nearest wall. If some asshole came outside and caught them, so be it. Might just be the thing to appease the beast raging inside him, the one that'd been provoked up by these fuckers.

Stanton grabbed her hand and hauled her behind him as he maneuvered around groups of people partying and threw the door open. Slamming it closed, he saw they were in the alleyway on the side of the clubhouse building. It was quiet enough. The spring air still had a tiny bite to it and Sammi rubbed her arms. Crowding her against the brick wall, he covered her body with his own.

"You cold, baby?"

"A little," she replied with a coy look. Her pink tongue came out and, slow as fuck, she licked her bottom and then her top lip. Lust pumped in his veins and thickened his cock behind his worn jeans.

Lungs straining in his chest, his breath came out unevenly. "I see behind your games, little girl, but this is not the moment to test my control. I'm close to fucking you up against this wall."

"Wouldn't be the first time," she reminded him, smoothly.

He blew out a breath, his fingers digging in around her hips. "You have an exhibitionist streak, girl? Fuck me."

"No, fuck *me*," she asserted.

His forehead touched hers. "There's something I have to do first before those bastards in there drive me insane. They were trying to convince me that the only way I can prove my ownership is to have you tramp stamp my name across your ass."

"Hmm," she considered, "I don't have an issue with your name inked on me, but I think we can find a classier location. Here." Her finger hooked onto the neckline of her shirt and dipped it down to expose her breast. "Or here." She dragged it to where her hip curved to her abdomen.

"I've got a better idea."

Her eyes lit up. "Yeah?"

Stanton went down on one knee and she squirmed in his hands. Nuzzling her mound, he reached into his jeans and pulled out a small black velvet box.

Sammi's hand flew to her mouth. "No!"

Snapping the box open, he said, "Yes. Your only answer is yes."

Fixated on the diamond, her eyes were as wide as saucers. He'd gotten the biggest damn rock he could find. It was a retro Cartier cushion-style ring with diamonds around the band. Angling his head to the side, he asked, "Is it too much?"

"Of course not," she replied, plucking the ring out with trembling fingers. "It's beautiful and it's vintage and I love it," she said with a smile.

Standing, he slid it on her finger. "It reminded me of the outfit you wore when I first laid eyes on you in court. The one with the little pincushion hat and lace veil."

Sammi's eyes softened. "You remember that?"

He furrowed his brow. "Never forget that outfit. I considered a black diamond for that reason, but the man at the Cartier store persuaded me to go with a classic diamond."

"You can get it for our first-year anniversary," she suggested.

"So that's a yes?"

"Did you give me a choice? I don't believe you asked me."

"No," he growled, "I fucking didn't give you a choice. I suppose I can ask," he conceded gruffly, "but it'd merely be for the sake of formality."

He picked out a curl and focused on the silky hair twirling around his finger. "I love you so damn much, sometimes it's hard to breathe. The moment I saw you in that courtroom, my heart began beating so hard I got dizzy. Since Jax died, I was half a man. Until you."

He heard her breath stutter.

"You complete me, Sammi. I don't feel the need to crush my father, don't feel the need to rebel or turn to drugs. Not saying I'm perfect, but you're my other half. So, no, you don't have much of a choice because I couldn't go on living without you."

He glanced up and found tears running down her cheeks. "Babe, don't cry."

"I love you," she cried and then her lips were crushed against his. Moaning against her lips, he took the kiss she offered and then gave her so much more.

EPILOGUE
STANTON

"That is so cute!" exclaimed Sammi, as she held up the pink baby bib with the words "Future Best Jurist of the Year" stitched in cursive.

There was a chorus of *oohs* and *ahhs* around the table over the bib his father had bought for little Jacey.

Cornell applauded with an extra *bravo*. Not surprising, he and Benjamin had always gotten along like two peas in a pod. Frankly their bromance continued to be downright annoying. Wesley sat on the other side of Cornell, between him and Carl at Sunday brunch, which had doubled in size over the past year.

"Oh brother," grumbled Stanton.

His wife's eyes narrowed in warning, but seriously, his father went overboard. He'd seamlessly moved on to the next generation without skipping a beat.

"It's not like in my time, when women only started breaking the barriers. Nowadays, women comprise thirty-seven percent of jurists in New York," his father declared proudly.

Stanton barely controlled the eye roll that was itching to be set free.

Benjamin began accepting Sammi after their engagement, but he'd noticeably relaxed once they had gotten married. Considering Stanton's checkered past regarding failed engagements, he couldn't fault his father on that one point.

Sammi solidified her placement as one of Benjamin's favorites when she made the cover of the *Hudson Valley Magazine* with her body-and-sex-positive styling business. Stanton wasn't surprised whatsoever that his wife crushed it in her career. After that article, Benjamin's poll rankings had a swift uptick among the millennial voters that he'd coveted for years. His father's connection with Sammi was able to do what Amy's high-end fashion house had never accomplished. Youthful and down-to-earth, Sammi injected new blood into his campaign. Ever since, he'd been *extra* about feminist issues.

Stanton admitted that Sammi, and later Jacey, also infused his father with a new leniency. Sammi chose Jace, nicknamed Jacey, as their daughter's name because it sounded like Jax. That had cinched his father's approval. It also meant "healer" in Greek, which made Sammi mist up when she found it on a baby-name website. And Jacey was a healer; it was almost comical how she'd changed Benjamin from a classic asshole into a mellowed-out grandfather. Knowing better than to attempt to return his inheritance back to Stanton, according to his mother, Benjamin had simply given his half to Jacey and any future children.

Stanton watched as his father stood up to attach the custom-made bib on little Jacey.

"Bab-bab!" she cooed, as her chubby little fingers clutched onto his big pointer finger and tried to stuff the tip in her mouth. Benjamin shook his finger away and she twisted her lips like she was about to cry. He made raspberries into her neck until she giggled and pulled on his hair.

Lifting her arms up to be held, she cried out, "Bab-bab! Bab-bab!"

"Okay, just this one time." Benjamin smiled as he picked up the baby and hugged her close to his chest.

Pulling his tie, she repeated, "Bab-bab."

Wesley leaned over and tickled Jacey's chin. "I think she said her first word. Grandpa. Bab-bab."

As if concurring with him, Jacey bounced on her grandfather's chest, chanting, "Bab-bab."

Marie turned awed eyes toward her husband and granddaughter. "I think you're right. They have such a special connection, the two of them."

Stanton witnessed his father raising a shaky finger to the corner of his eye.

Shifting in his seat, he stared up at the ceiling and sighed. That was it. He gave up. His own father was tearing up because his daughter's first words were a bastardized form of *grandpa*. He didn't think he could hold on to his grudge for much longer.

Reaching over, he placed a hand on his father's shoulder, which was still broad in his mid-sixties, and gave it a squeeze.

Benjamin turned his head slightly in Stanton's direction and said, "Thanks, son. After your mother, you gave me the most precious people in my life."

Christ.

Stanton swallowed the lump lodged in his throat. Couldn't remember the last time his father thanked him. He didn't know if their relationship would ever be resolved, but there was no denying it any longer. The man was changing.

Sammi's eyes widened at Benjamin's comment.

Leaning over, he murmured into Sammi's ear, "It's because of you."

She gave him a sidelong look, and her hand found his underneath the table.

"Because of you," he went on, "I became a husband and father, making me the luckiest man alive. Because of you, he became a grandfather." He tilted his chin in Benjamin's direction. "Making him the second-luckiest man alive."

"I love you, babe," she mouthed.

He lifted her hand and turned it over, kissing over his name inked on the skin of her inner wrist. Then he did the same with her other wrist, etched with Jace's name.

"There's no fucking words for how much I love you," he whispered, his chest teeming with a sense of completeness. Despite his sins. Despite the wreckage of his past, he'd been given a second chance. With a heart full of gratitude, he lapped up every damn second of it.

THANK you for reading Stanton's Sins! I hope you loved meeting Stanton and Sammi. The next book in the series is Sammi's older brother, Puck. Puck's Property is a scorching-hot second chance romance.

A LONELY SOCIAL WORKER.

A biker behind bars.

Can their red-hot passion set them free?

WHAT IF YOUR **first love was your one true love? Eight years ago, Puck broke Ava's heart. She picked up the pieces, patched them together, and kept going. Yet she never forgot** him. When Puck sauntered through her office, she was shocked to find a brawny, tatted-up biker dressed in an orange jumpsuit with the word INMATE stamped on the back.

CLICK HERE TO READ PUCK'S PROPERTY >>

WANT A TASTE NOW?

A CO PULLED Puck out of the hole, snapped cuffs on him, and walked him over to see the social worker, where he was supposed to "talk" about the fight.

For fuck's sake, he didn't know what was worse: being locked up or being forced to talk to a shrink.

Sure, he was glad to be out of solitary. He'd been dealing with heart palpitations, lying on the plastic-covered cot that crackled every time he moved when the lock to his cell disengaged. He swiped a few beads of perspiration along his hairline with the thumbs of his shackled hands as the CO knocked on the closed door. A muffled voice instructed them to come in. The officer pushed the door open for him, and he sauntered in, ready to get this bullshit over with, when his feet froze in their place.

His breath caught in his throat.

Ava.

Mother*fucker*.

Sitting behind the desk, one hand primly laying on top of the other, she raised her gaze to his. Her hazel eyes went round, mouth parting slightly. Dark mahogany hair cascaded down the sides of her face, much longer than when he'd last seen her.

Eight long years ago.

She wore a brown plaid suit jacket that engulfed her slim form, but she had the same build. Who could forget a tall, lithe body like hers? Or her high, round tits topped with delicious berry-tasting nipples?

His head cocked to the side as he observed her carefully. She'd always been the hippest person in a room, but her suit was...drab. Where was the party girl dressed in sexy little dresses, stripping nude any chance she got? Sassy, spirited, crazy. Here, she was dressed in an androgynous suit that didn't flatter of her slim figure, with subtle but definite curves. Her hair was the only sign of her femininity.

A frown creased his forehead. This woman had no laugh lines around her big eyes or her lush, sensual lips. The glint of mischievousness and humor was gone from her large doll-like eyes.

Instead, they stared out at him, serious and grave. It had been a long time, but he wasn't used to this look.

"Ava?" he asked with a rasp, his mouth suddenly dry.

She jerked slightly; calling her name had pulled her out of her own reverie. Instantly, her eyes shuttered, changing the color of her irises and sealing off the windows to her soul.

Officer Dipshit, as Puck had coined him, handed her his file, and said harshly, "You know this inmate? He just got into a fight." Concern laced his tone as he asked, "Want me to stay?"

Puck bristled at him.

"No, I'll be fine, Derick," she mumbled, her eyes fliting away from Puck's. "He's a kid from my old neighborhood."

Derick? His eyes swung to the CO and then back to her. *She's on a first-name basis with this jackass?* Guess it was to be expected since they worked in the same facility. Still, Puck didn't like it. He didn't like the man or his manner when it came to Ava. Ava was *his*, dammit. He recoiled slightly. No, she hadn't been his for a long time. He'd made sure of that, hadn't he?

Eyes roving over her, the CO asked, "You sure?"

Dipshit was checking her out. *Oh, hell no. Fucking NO.*

She tilted her chin toward Puck's hands in cuffs. "I'll be fine. Would you please uncuff him?"

Dipshit looked at her hesitantly.

"I know Mr. Rossi, Derick," she explained. Why did she have to explain herself? Dipshit didn't want to let this go.

Head down and sifting through the Puck's folder, she continued, "Come back in thirty minutes to take him back to his cell."

Damn, the husky tone of her voice had always turned him on. Apparently, today was no exception.

Dipshit seemed reluctant.

With a little huff, she glared up at him and clarified, "We don't have another social worker available. Until the county allocates enough funds to pay for a second social worker, we don't have a choice. God knows we need one."

Officer Derick Dipshit pressed his hand on Puck's shoulder. His muscles tensed with the urge to resist, but he wasn't going to fuck up his one chance at seeing Ava. Even though he'd recuperated fast, he was still reeling from the shock. Under Ava's watchful gaze, he consciously relaxed his body and allowed himself to be pressed down into the seat facing her.

"Behave yourself," the officer tossed out before leaving and softly shutting the door behind him.

Asshole.

He wasn't a fucking kid, and he sure as hell didn't hurt women.

Once Dipshit was gone, his gaze returned to Ava.

Damn, she was as stunning as ever. There was her long hair, which he knew glittered red in the sunlight, her multicolored eyes, and her lush, plump lips. He knew what it felt like to have those lips pressed against his. Or wrapped around his dick.

Fuck, he was getting hard, thinking about it. Sex with Ava had been spiritual, and it wasn't only because they'd been high. It was phenomenal no matter what they'd drank, smoked, or snorted. Hell, stone-cold sober and fucking her brought him to the highest of heights. Their bond just was, like the sun rising at dawn or setting at dusk. Like the turn of the seasons. Their lovemaking had been a phenomenon, like the Northern Lights. That's what fucking Ava was like.

Spectacular.

One of a kind.

It's the reason he didn't have an old lady, a baby mama, or even a steady fuck. After he broke up with her, he'd kept tabs on her for years. After he got his head on straight, he'd been tempted to show up on her doorstep. But in the end, he'd decided it was best to let sleeping dogs lie. Did he regret it? Fuck yeah, he did.

Seeing her in front of his, the regret seeped deeper into his bones.

That's why he decided that now—all bets were off.

Ava was back, and like catching sight of a deer in the crosshairs of his hunting rifle, she was his.

He eyed her carefully. Yeah, winning her back was going to be the fight of his life.

GET YOUR PUCK'S PROPERTY NOW>>

I APPRECIATE your help in spreading the word, including leaving a review. Reviews help readers find books! Please leave a review on your favorite book site.

Sign up to my newsletter to find out when I have new books!

MORE BY MONIQUE

Steamy Biker Romance Series

Kingdom's Reign (Book 1)
Cutter's Claim (Book 2)
Loki's Luck (Book 3)
Stanton's Sins (Book 4)
Puck's Property (Book 5)
Whistle's War (Book 6)
Her Hidden Valentine, A Squad Novella
(Book 7)

Lupu Family Mafia Romance Series

The lives of these powerful men revolves around three core elements: duty, sacrifice, and family. There's little time for women, and no time for love.
Each one of them will be cut off at the knees, humbled by a woman. Oh, how far these mighty men will fall before they learn the age-old lesson that the only way out is through...

The Chosen Heir (Alex's story)
The Recluse Heir (Luca's story)
The Savage Heir (Nicu's story)
The Perfect Heir (Tatum's story)
The Bastard Heir (Sebastian's story)
The Princess Heir (Emma's story)

Empire Academy Series
A High School Bully Mafia Romance Series

UNFORGIVABLE (Starlene's story)
UNREGRETTABLE (Crina's story)
UNFORGETTABLE (Gabriela's story)
UNDENIABLE (Zoe's story)